A Perfect Blend of Romance,
Suspense, and Police Procedural

OBSESSED

A POLICE ROMANCE

Laura Peterson

For Kelsey and Christopher

***

Obsessed: A Police Romance is the first title in the Obsessed Series.

This book can also be read as a stand-alone romance.

Author's Note: The book contains subject matter that may be sensitive to some readers. The book contains triggering content related to sex, abuse and violence. 18+ only. Please read responsibly.

Contents

Chapter 1

Friday Night, June 17

A darkness enveloped Dr. Peggy Scott. *This must be a nightmare*, she thought, as a sense of paralyzing fear gripped her. Struggling to wake up, she felt the bonds that held her immobile. It was as if the familiar softness of her bed sheets had transformed into gnarled serpents coiling tightly around her limbs.

The rays of sunlight that usually washed her bedroom in gold were conspicuously absent. Her heart sank as reality clawed its way through the fog of her confusion - she was trapped, bound with industrial zip ties in an alien bed, far removed from the warmth of her own.

Naked and vulnerable, except for her skimpy bra and panties, a biting cold gnawed at her exposed body, amplifying her feeling of helplessness. As the chill burrowed deeper into her skin, the tremors began, setting her teeth on edge. She could taste fear on her tongue combined with the bitter taste of a gag obstructing her desperate cries for help.

Wincing as the unforgiving plastic bit into her raw skin, she attempted to wrest herself from her physical bindings. Her mind, as restricted as her body, was clouded in a fog of confusion. She struggled to piece together the fragments of a frightening memory.

Her last clear memory was leaving the county morgue at Police Plaza, where she worked as a forensic pathologist. The cool night air had felt soothing against her skin as she waited for her ride home, idly scrolling through her cellphone. An unexpected arm had snaked around her neck, the sudden sharp stick of a needle piercing her skin, and then, nothing.

A sickening understanding washed over her. She had been drugged, likely ketamine. Her usual lifeline, the car service she had texted from her office, had failed to reach her in time. Careless with exhaustion, she forgot her laptop in her office and was reluctant to go back inside on such a beautiful summer night.

An ominous creak interrupted her thoughts. The sound of the door inching open, and footsteps drawing near sent waves of terror down her spine. The groan of the bed springs under the mysterious stranger's bulk sent her heart pounding against her chest. A rough, calloused hand touched her blonde hair, stroking it with an eerie gentleness that felt grotesquely out of place.

The gentle touch turned sinister as the hand traced a path down her bare back, grazing over her exposed thighs and buttocks. A sharp intake of breath broke the suffocating silence, soon replaced by uneven, heavy breathing, only interrupted by the occasional stifled moan. The stirring fear withing Dr. Peggy Scott was so profound, she couldn't move.

Hot tears streamed down Peggy's face as the stranger's hand ventured further, disappearing beneath her underwear. She cringed as she felt her panties being roughly yanked down exposing her naked buttocks to the faceless stranger. She felt the coarse touch of a mouth and the harsh stubble of a chin on her lower back. The brutal stranger was a man. A rush of agonizing pain surged through her as he bit into her buttocks, with an animalistic frenzy.

The sound of a zipper being undone filled her ears, followed by the man grunting and moaning. A shudder wracked her body as she felt him rubbing his naked erect penis against her, his guttural moans tainting the air. Hot, tears rolled down her face as she felt his sticky semen coat her naked back and buttocks. Disgust and shame welled up within her as she heard the sound of him zipping up after the crude violation she had just endured.

With a sharp tug, Peggy's panties were pulled back up, and the bed creaked once more as the monster rose and left the room. Peggy, now alone, attempted to scream, only to be muffled by the coarse fabric of the gag chafing her lips and the corners of her mouth.

Her stomach churned as she felt the drying evidence of the man's violation on her skin. The shivers running down her spine were no longer from the cold; they were the visceral reactions to her brutal assault. Darkness seemed to close in around her, her sobs swallowed up by the stifling gag.

Peggy desperately tried to retreat into her mind, seeking refuge in the sterile world of her profession. She was Dr. Peggy Scott, a pathologist, not just a helpless victim. However, focusing on her intellect did not erase the echoes of the man's heavy breathing, the musky smell of his sweat, or his invasive touch now tattooed on her skin.

A sense of hopelessness threatened to drown her, but Peggy was a fighter. She would not let this break her. With renewed determination, she began to work on the zip-ties that bound her, the sharp edges of the plastic biting into her skin. She welcomed the pain because it reminded her that she was alive and capable of fighting back.

The battle for her freedom had just begun.

Chapter 2

Monday, May 23 (One Month Ago)

T he county morgue, located inside Chicago Police Plaza, serves as a facility for the storage, identification, and autopsy of human corpses, as well as their burial, cremation, or other disposal methods. To delay decomposition, the corpses are refrigerated.

Inside the county morgue, a cold and sterile atmosphere prevailed. The spacious autopsy room featured green walls filled with stainless steel autopsy tables, while steel shelves and counters held an array of autopsy equipment. Along one wall stood stainless steel drawers, serving as the cool storage area for the bodies.

Forensic pathology is a branch of medicine that focuses on determining the cause of death through post-mortem examinations of corpses or partial remains. Autopsies, typically conducted by coroners or medical examiners, play a vital role in criminal investigations, and often involve confirming the identity of the deceased.

The purpose of an autopsy is to ascertain whether the death was natural or unnatural, identify the source of injury, determine the manner of death, establish the time of death, aid in the identification of the deceased, and examine and test relevant organs. It involves a surgical procedure, performed by specialized medical doctors known as pathologists, which meticulously dissects and examines the corpse to determine the cause, mode, and manner of death. Notably, the majority of deaths can be determined without the need for an autopsy.

On this particular day, Dr. Peggy Scott was conducting a forensic autopsy on an unidentified female murder victim known as Jane Doe. Such autopsies are performed when the cause of death is suspected to be a criminal act, such as murder. Dr. Scott, dressed in green scrubs, surgical gloves, safety glasses, and a surgical mask, spoke into a voice recorder throughout the procedure.

The official cause of Jane Doe's death was determined to be asphyxiation by strangulation. Rigor mortis had fully developed by the time her body was discovered, indicating a potential eight-hour interval since her death. Dr. Scott also observed that Jane Doe had recently been bathed, possibly postmortem, which may have hastened the loss of body temperature and accelerated the onset of rigor mortis.

During the autopsy, it became evident that Jane Doe had sustained over 100 distinct wounds across her body, including cuts, bites, and severe bruising. Her vaginal cavity exhibited significant swelling.

Dr. Scott collected specimens for toxicological testing, including Jane Doe's stomach contents, and swabbed her fingernails, genitals, and bite marks. She photographed the body, collecting any residue present on its external surfaces. Employing ultraviolet light, she meticulously searched the body's surface for evidence invisible to the naked eye, though no significant findings were found. Hair and nail samples were taken from Jane Doe, and her wounds were examined. Prior to the internal examination, Dr. Scott measured and weighed the body.

To facilitate the examination, Dr. Scott positioned a rubber block called a "head block" beneath Jane Doe's shoulders, hyperextending the neck and causing the spine to arch backward while elevating the chest. This position allowed for easier incisions and maximum exposure of the trunk. Dr. Scott proceeded to make a large, deep Y-shaped incision starting from each shoulder and running down the front of the chest, meeting at the lower point of the sternum (breastbone). She employed shears to open the chest cavity and cut through the ribs on the costal cartilage, allowing for the removal of the sternum. This careful approach ensured the heart, especially the pericardial sac, remained intact and undisturbed. Using a knife, Dr. Scott delicately detached the sternum from the soft tissue connecting it to the mediastinum and set it aside to be replaced at the end of the autopsy. With the sternum removed, the lungs and heart were fully exposed for examination.

Proceeding with her investigation, Dr. Scott carefully examined the internal organs. She skillfully removed all of Jane Doe's organs as a single unit, utilizing techniques such as dissection of the fascia, blunt dissection, and the use of fingers or hands with traction. This method allowed for a comprehensive inspection and sampling of the various organs. Each organ was meticulously examined, weighed, and tissue samples in the form of slices were collected. Even major blood vessels were carefully opened and inspected at this stage.

After examining the organs, Dr. Scott turned her attention to the examination and weighing of the stomach and intestinal contents. This analysis could provide valuable insights into the cause and time of death, as the natural progression of food digestion through the bowel plays a role. The extent of empty space within the gastrointestinal tract can indicate the duration since the deceased's last meal.

Dr. Scott re-positioned the body block to elevate the head, granting her access to the intricate web of the brain. With a steady hand, she traced the path of her incision, a delicate arc from one ear to the other, peeling back the scalp in two precise flaps. The front flap cascaded over the face, while the rear flap draped gently along the nape of the neck. Guided by the hum of the circular bladed reciprocating saw, she cut through the skull, creating a removable cap that revealed the hidden depths within. The brain, a fragile masterpiece of cognition and memory, lay exposed before her discerning gaze. With meticulous care, she severed the cranial nerves and spinal cord, cradling the brain in her hands for further examination.

In her search for evidence, Dr. Scott's thorough examination aimed to uncover any signs of trauma or other indicators that could shed light on the circumstances surrounding Jane Doe's murder.

Having meticulously dissected the body and conducted a thorough examination, Dr. Scott turned her attention to the task of suturing. With nimble fingers, she carefully sewed the body back together, a gentle act of reverence for the empty vessel that had once housed a vibrant life.

As Dr. Scott finished suturing Jane Doe, Dr. Janet McKenzie, the Chief Medical Examiner for the county, entered the morgue. Tall and slender, with vibrant red hair that seemed to mirror her fiery determination, she greeted Dr. Peggy Scott with a warm smile.

"Hi, Peggy. How did the autopsy of Jane Doe go?" Dr. McKenzie inquired.

"Fine. Death by strangulation, as you suspected," Peggy replied, a hint of weariness in her voice.

"Just a heads up, I have a meeting, so you will have to meet with Detective Vincente and Detective Keeley. They are on their way here," Dr. McKenzie informed her, with a touch of urgency.

Peggy's heart skipped a beat. Detective Anthony Vincente. The name had become synonymous with an array of negative traits in the halls of the morgue. Arrogant, abrasive, and socially inept, he had earned a reputation that preceded him. Stories of his explosive temper and relentless pursuit of perfection flooded Peggy's thoughts, making her uneasy. Whispers of a previous pathologist fleeing the morgue in tears only added to the mounting anxiety within Peggy.

"You'll be fine," Dr. McKenzie reassured her, her voice a lifeline of support. "Detective Vincente may be an asshole to work with, but he is undeniably brilliant. He used to be an FBI profiler, and his insights can be invaluable. Don't let him intimidate you. I think he may be on the autism spectrum, which can make him distant and unfriendly. Just remember, you are here to do your job, and you're more than capable."

With a hurried exit, Dr. McKenzie left Peggy to wrestle with her nervous anxiety. Alone in the quiet morgue, Peggy whispered to herself, "This is a great way to start my first day shift at the coroner's office."

At only 22 years old, Dr. Peggy Scott had started on her path as a pathologist just six months prior, joining the residency program on the graveyard shift. Fresh out of medical school, she carried both the excitement of new beginnings and the weight of uncertainty. Today marked her first encounter with the department's top special investigative team—Detective Vincente and Detective Keeley. Eager to make a lasting impression, Peggy prepared herself by repeatedly reviewing Jane Doe's autopsy in her mind.

***

Mac stood in the lime green corridor outside the morgue, a color she detested. As Detectives Keeley and Vincente from the Special Investigations Unit (SIU) approached, Mac knew they were anxious to hear about Jane Doe's autopsy.

"Detectives, the forensic autopsy of your Jane Doe is completed. Dr. Scott performed the autopsy; she is one of my most talented residents. She'll go over all the details with you. I have a meeting to attend," Mac informed them, eager to avoid being late and Detective Vincente.

"What? We had an agreement that you would handle all our cases," Detective Vincente complained, his anger evident as he threw his arms up in the air.

Detective Anthony Vincente, 31 years old, stood tall at 6'4" with a muscular build. His wavy medium brown hair and piercing brown eyes gave him a resemblance to a young Vincent D'Onofrio. Clad in a dark off-the-rack suit and tie, Vincente always wore his police badge on his lapel while inside the Police Plaza building. Known for his professionalism and no-nonsense approach, Vincente possessed an uncanny ability to read people. When questioning suspects, he invaded their personal space, using his hands and expressive gestures to make them uncomfortable and unsettled. Solving mysteries and puzzles was his forte, and he relished his role as a detective. A workaholic at heart, he dedicated himself fully to his job.

But behind Vincente's formidable exterior lay a complex persona. Highly intelligent and perceptive, he had a deep appreciation for classical music, art, theatre, literature, and poetry. Yet, he also indulged in a less conventional interest—classic pornography. His extensive collection of DVDs spoke to his hidden pastime. When off duty, Vincente spent most of his free time immersed in online video games, bonding with the friends he had known since childhood, and watching porn.

Detective Samantha Keeley chuckled, anticipating the drama would unfold. In her early forties, Keeley exuded both attractiveness and toughness, traits shaped by her upbringing in an Irish cop family. Wearing her signature ensemble of dark jeans, a short leather jacket, and sturdy leather boots, she radiated an air of confidence. Having previously worked in vice, Keeley had developed a reputation for not tolerating any nonsense. Known for her unabashed honesty and sharp wit, she often spoke her mind without a filter. While some colleagues considered her sarcastic, Detective Vincente respected and genuinely liked her.

Keeley's partnership with Vincente in the SIU had been a condition of her promotion from vice. Vincente had gone through three previous partners before her. The captain had made it clear to Keeley that she needed to find a way to make it work with Vincente, or she would be sent back to vice.

Initially, Keeley had reservations about working with Vincente. He proved to be very annoying, with his constant fidgeting and irksome habits. Having trained as an FBI profiler at Quantico after college, Vincente had returned to the city to care for his ailing aunt. He was immediately hired as a detective by the Special Investigations Unit.

Vincente had an uncanny ability to extract confessions from suspects, making him an exceptional interrogator. Despite his brilliance, however, he was not known for his social skills. Vincente's brooding, introverted nature often left his colleagues perplexed, struggling to comprehend his unusual thought processes. He seldom smiled and carried an air of seriousness that seemed unyielding. At times, his unconventional theories about cases raised eyebrows, but more often than not, he proved to be right.

Keeley had learned to accept Vincente's idiosyncrasies. While he may not have been the most fun person to be around, she valued his professionalism and the results he delivered. Their partnership thrived because Keeley overlooked his peculiarities and acted as a buffer between him and other departments. They made an effective team, working tirelessly and supporting each other unconditionally. Keeley genuinely liked Vincente, appreciating his dedication to the job.

Mac, the department head, had a no-nonsense approach when dealing with Vincente's demands. "Well, Vincente, I am a busy person and not at your beck and call. You need to learn to share your toys in the sandbox!" she retorted, emphasizing the need for cooperation.

Keeley couldn't help but notice the vibrant shade of red in Mac's hair that day, adding a touch of fire to their conversation.

"Dr. Scott is our finest pathologist. She's currently in the residency program and has been working the graveyard shift for the past six months. This is her first day shift, so be gentle with her and do not repeat the incident with the previous pathologist," Mac advised, hoping to avoid any further discussion.

Vincente, surprised to learn that Dr. Scott was just a resident, looked slightly taken aback. Meanwhile, Keeley couldn't resist asking, "Is she the hot, new girl everyone's been talking about?"

Vincente massaged his forehead, anticipating a headache, while Mac rolled her eyes and walked away in frustration. "This is going to be interesting," Keeley mused as they approached the sliding glass doors of the morgue.

As Detectives Vincente and Keeley entered the morgue, Dr. Peggy Scott turned around too quickly and accidentally knocked over a tray of instruments, causing a loud crash. In her attempt to prevent the tray from falling, she lost her balance and ended up sprawled on the floor, legs splayed in front of her. The detectives exchanged a glance and hurried over to Dr. Scott.

Peggy's safety glasses were fogged up, obstructing her vision. Frustrated, she removed them and ran her hands through her blonde hair, hoping to give it some volume after being flattened by her surgical cap.

Sitting on the floor and struggling to regain her composure, Peggy noticed a pair of black, size 13 police shoes standing next to her. She looked up and saw Detective Anthony Vincente, his brow furrowed in an annoyed expression. Vincente's strong presence loomed over her, his hands in his pockets and feet planted firmly apart. The sight surprised her. With his athletic build, towering height, and thick, wavy brown hair that complemented his brown eyes, Vincente resembled a football player. Peggy hadn't expected Detective Anthony Vincente to be so good-looking and hot.

Vincente's voice, laced with a hint of rasp, broke the silence. "Are you alright?" he inquired, raising an eyebrow and tilting his head to the side, his gaze fixed on Dr. Peggy Scott.

Detective Vincente couldn't help but notice the youthful appearance and striking beauty of the petite pathologist – too young to be a doctor. Her thick blonde hair cascaded down to her shoulders, framing a face with high cheekbones, mesmerizing royal blue eyes adorned with long, dark lashes, and pale pink, full lips. Her flawless complexion resembled a work of art, and the fragrance she wore evoked the scent of freshly picked lilacs. Vincente tried not to be mesmerized by Dr. Scott.

"I'm fine. Thanks," Peggy replied, slightly embarrassed by falling on her behind. She couldn't help but observe Vincente's rugged charm, noticing his unshaven face and disheveled dark, curly hair that gave him an effortlessly appealing look. His thoughtful, dark eyes held a depth that intrigued her, igniting a magnetic attraction she had never experienced before.

Detective Sam Keeley introduced herself and Vincente. Peggy smiled and nodded in acknowledgment as she stood up from the floor.

Vincente wasted no time engaging in small talk. He approached a steel counter, donned a pair of surgical gloves, and made his way to the autopsy table, focusing his attention on the unidentified victim before him. Peggy noticed his deliberate and purposeful demeanor, appreciating his dedication to the task at hand.

As Vincente closely examined the naked body of Jane Doe, he couldn't help but compare Jane Doe's and Dr. Scott's striking similarities— young, beautiful, and petite blondes. Peggy watched as Vincente meticulously examined every inch of the victim, his fists clenched with determination. Bending down, he concentrated on the victim, gently touching her mouth before leaning closer and sniffing her closed lips.

Peggy admired Vincente's professionalism and the absence of lewd comments about the victim's nudity, a stark contrast to the behavior she had encountered from other male detectives in the past.

Stammering slightly, Peggy began sharing her findings. "The victim is female, approximately 18 to 25 years old. The cause of death was asphyxiation due to strangulation, estimated to have occurred within the past 24-48 hours. She stands about 5'4" tall and weighs 115 pounds. She was discovered naked, having endured over 100 distinct wounds that vary in location, nature, and severity. Her injuries include cuts, bite marks, and severe bruising. Her vaginal cavity shows significant swelling."

Peggy couldn't help but feel intimidated by Vincente's intense presence and silence. She noticed his unwavering focus, setting him apart from other male detectives she had encountered. He did not leer at her body or flirt with her like the other male detectives did.

"Sick bastard," Keeley remarked, her disgust evident.

Vincente, his voice filled with a mix of anger and analysis, declared, "She was murdered in a frenzy—a sexual frenzy. There is a lot of rage in her injuries."

Peggy continued, her voice tinged with anxiety, "There is no semen present, but I did find a small particle of a condom. Despite her hair being blonde, it's not her natural color, as evidenced by her pubic area. Her fingernails and toenails have been recently trimmed, and she appears very clean. There's a faint scent of bleach on her body. It's possible the killer cleaned her inside and out after the rape. I've taken swabs of her genitals, but I'm doubtful we'll find the killer's DNA. Her breasts and buttocks have bruises and faint bite marks. She seems to have taken care of herself, with well-maintained teeth—likely visited the dentist."

Vincente's mind raced as he paced around the victim as Peggy spoke. He could tell that Dr. Scott was intelligent, and very well educated. She obviously knew a lot about pathology and forensics – he was duly impressed. Noticing her figure beneath the scrubs, he couldn't help but appreciate her shapely body— curvy in all the right places - narrow waist, round bottom. Vincente could tell from the way she stood, that she was self-conscious of her large breasts. Vincente thought that she had a naivete and innocence about her that would captivate most men.

Peggy directed their attention to the victim's stomach. "A small amount of a granola bar was found in her digestive system," she revealed. Pointing at the victim's neck, she continued, "And here, you can see a puncture wound. It suggests that she may have been drugged. The tox screen will likely reveal the presence of ketamine."

"Ketamine," Vincente interjected, "a medication primarily used for anesthesia induction and maintenance. It induces dissociative anesthesia, providing pain relief, sedation, and amnesia."

"The distinguishing features of ketamine anesthesia are preserved breathing and airway reflexes, stimulated heart function with increased blood pressure, and moderate bronchodilation." replied Peggy.

Detective Keeley rolled her eyes.

"She was a beautiful woman. 'Death lies on her like an untimely frost upon the sweetest flower of all the field'", quoted Vincente.

Recognizing the quote, Peggy asked, "Shakespeare?"

Vincente ignored Dr. Scott's question.

Vincente chose to ignore her question, his mind already drifting back to the case. He and Peggy engaged in a lengthy conversation about forensics, which annoyed Keeley.

"Get a room," Keeley muttered.

Vincente thought that the young pathologist and victim could have been sisters, because they looked so much alike. They were both petite, young, and beautiful blue-eyed blondes. Vincente was disturbed by the brutal homicide of this beautiful, young woman.

"Thank you, Doctor," Vincente stated curtly as he made his way toward the morgue's sliding glass doors, his face etched with a scowl and the weight of his thoughts. Detective Keeley followed closely behind.

Just as Vincente was about to exit, Peggy raised her voice and said, "oh, Detectives there is one more thing," prompting him to turn around.

Vincente looked at Peggy. He raised his eyebrows and cocked his head, conveying a mix of curiosity and skepticism. He was frowning.

There is Tony's trademark condescending move, thought Keeley, *Dr. Scott is going to run out of the morgue crying like the last one.*

Peggy's voice quivered as she made her bold statement, "Um, I think she was killed by a serial killer. A very organized serial killer. He has obviously killed before."

"Uh oh." Keeley whispered.

"Are you a detective, Doctor?" Vincente asked – his displeasure evident.

Peggy shook her head, "Um no."

Interrupting, Vincente asked about her experience, "How long have you been a coroner in the residency program?"

"Almost seven months," she replied.

Vincente's condescension became apparent as he responded, "A serial killer? Serial murders typically take place over more than a month with a threshold of two or more murders by the same individual as the baseline. I see only one victim here. This woman was killed in a rage, probably by somebody she knew. I think you have been watching too many television shows."

Undeterred, Peggy pointed at the body, "If you look at her pubic region, there is something odd."

Reluctantly, Vincente approached the body, his gaze fixed on the victim's pubic area. He found himself asking, "Well? What? I don't see anything!"

Peggy continued, "The pubic hair has been groomed—brushed or styled. It feels somewhat stiff, possibly indicating the use of hair gel or mousse. Furthermore, if you look here," she gently parted the victim's thighs, "there is a clump of pubic hair missing, right next to the vestibule—opening. It appears to me that it was deliberately pulled out. Maybe the killer wanted a trophy."

Vincente and Keeley's eyes fixated on the tiny bald patch on Jane Doe's vagina, absorbing the disturbing observation.

"Serial killers may be more likely to engage in fetishism, partialism or necrophilia, which are paraphilias that involve a strong tendency to experience the object of erotic interest almost as if it were a physical representation of the symbolized body. Individuals engage in paraphilias which are organized along a continuum; participating in varying levels of fantasy perhaps by focusing on body parts - partialism, symbolic objects which serve as physical extensions of the body - fetishism, or the anatomical physicality of the human body; specifically, regarding its inner parts and sexual organs." Peggy lectured.

Vincente, growing increasingly frustrated, crossed his arms and raised his eyebrows, clearly annoyed by Peggy's lecture.

"Or, it could have been pulled out during a rape or rough sex." Muttered Vincente as he focused on the victim's pubic area.

"I don't think so. Hair fetishism, also known as hair partialism and trichophilia, is a partialism where a person finds hair—most commonly head hair—particularly erotic and sexually arousing. Arousal can stem from seeing or touching hair, whether it's head hair, armpit hair, chest hair, or fur. Manifesting in various behaviors, a hair fetishist may enjoy seeing or touching hair, pulling or cutting another person's hair. These activities can elicit sexual arousal. It can also be described as an obsession, as in the case of hair washing or fear of hair loss. Arousal from head hair can be triggered by its length, wetness, color, or specific hairstyles. Some may even fantasize about engaging in sexual activities involving hair. Pubephilia, on the other hand, refers to sexual arousal at the sight or feel of pubic hair." Peggy explained.

Vincente considered the merit of Dr. Scott's theory, recognizing that it might warrant further investigation.

"Trichophilia, derived from the Greek word 'trica-' meaning hair, and the suffix '-philia' denoting love, encompasses various sources of excitation, with human head hair being the most common but not exclusive. This paraphilia extends to facial hair, chest hair, pubic hair, armpit hair, and animal fur. Excitation can arise from factors such as texture, color, hairstyle, and length. Variants of this paraphilia include arousal from long or short hair, blonde fetishism, redhead fetishism, and appreciation for different hair textures. Trichophilia may also involve the excitement derived from plucking or pulling hair or body hair." Vincente's gaze fixed on Dr. Scott as he delivered his analysis.

Keeley couldn't help but feel a chill run down her spine and announced, "Well, that is a whole new level of twisted sick!"

Vincente's annoyance began to subside as the weight of the Dr. Scott's revelation settled upon him. He realized that their investigation had taken a darker turn, they were dealing with a killer whose motivations extended beyond the typical homicide. The revelation of the victim's meticulously groomed pubic hair and the deliberate removal of a clump was leading them into the realm of fetishism and the deviant behavior of the killer.

As Detectives Vincente and Keeley exited the morgue through the sliding glass doors, a sense of relief washed over Peggy. She was pleased that the esteemed investigative team had taken her insights into consideration. Though unsure if Detective Vincente truly took her seriously, she was proud of herself for mentioning her serial killer theory.

"Detective Vincente, you certainly are arrogant and condescending," Peggy muttered to herself as a smile crept across her face as she reminisced about their interaction. She found Vincente's good looks and raspy voice appealing and had enjoyed their intellectual conversation.

In the confines of the elevator, going up to the Special Investigations Unit, Detectives Vincente and Keeley engaged in a conversation about the pubic hair revelation.

"So, what are your thoughts on the whole pubic hair thing?" Keeley inquired.

Vincente, contemplating the matter, replied, "I'm not entirely sure... perhaps... I don't know. I might reach out to a friend at the FBI and discuss Dr. Scott's theory with him."

Keeley couldn't resist teasing, "Shakespeare, Tony! Quoting Shakespeare to her? Why don't you just ask her out?"

Vincente raised an eyebrow, his face furrowed with uncertainty.

As they walked into the SIU, Vincente's mind wandered to Dr. Peggy Scott. Communicating with women, especially attractive ones, had always been difficult for him. Yet, his interaction with Dr. Scott felt different. Her profound knowledge of forensics and pathology sparked an intellectual connection that he rarely experienced with other women. Still, she was too young and beautiful for him, preferring to pursue relationships with women closer to his age or older.

Chapter 3

January 2 (Five Months Earlier)

The watcher observed her, captivated by her presence. She stood out from the rest, radiating a beauty that stirred desires deep within. Thoughts of her consumed his mind, causing the blood to rush in his veins and his palms to sweat. Unlike his usual prey, she was different, special.

Every day, he followed her, studying her routine. He recalled the first encounter, the scent of her perfume lingering in his memory. She was a vision of perfection in his eyes. The women he typically pursued, violated, and discarded were mere objects, devoid of humanity. But she, she was a goddess, a living embodiment of his every fantasy. Her long blonde hair, piercing blue eyes, and the body of a centerfold fueled his obsession.

Determined to uncover more about her, the watcher searched for information. His efforts on Google proved futile; she had no trace on social media. He scoured the internet, hoping to unearth anything about her. Then, he stumbled upon the Police Plaza website, where her name appeared—an aspiring pathologist working in the Medical Examiner's office.

The internet made stalking so effortless, he mused, enjoying the access it granted him.

The killer unearthed details of her education, identifying the medical school and college she had attended. Dr. Peggy Scott became his newfound fixation. Cautious not to attract attention, he planned meticulously, evading surveillance cameras. There was no need for haste; he knew where she worked, where she lived, and even where she bought her coffee. He discreetly took pictures of her with his cell phone. He watched her movements, careful to remain unnoticed.

Dr. Scott led an unremarkable life, seldom venturing beyond her work and occasional walks.

"You are so dull, my exquisite muse," he whispered.

In the depths of his mind, the killer indulged in fantasies—images of possessing her, violating her. His thoughts twisted into vivid scenarios of primal desire, envisioning her naked, frightened, and tied up. Day and night, she consumed his every thought, denying him sleep as he obsessed over her. The intensity of his yearning grew insatiable, an ache that wouldn't subside. He could barely eat; his sole focus was possessing her, claiming her for himself. No one else could have her. He longed to inhabit her very skin, to scrutinize her every move. Yet, she remained elusive, surrounded by countless witnesses and unyielding surveillance.

Even when he slept, he dreamed of her, his desires intertwined with restless nights. The hunger within intensified, a painful craving that consumed him entirely. He had to have her, to possess her, no matter the cost.

Chapter 4

Saturday, May 14 (Two Weeks Ago)

The watcher, driven by his insatiable craving, attempted to satiate his growing need with a woman who looked like Dr. Peggy Scott. He knew that targeting the real Dr. Scott would be far too risky. One fateful night, he spotted a woman resembling her leaving a college bar late at night. It felt like destiny. Returning the following night, he observed her once again. Waiting until the parking lot was empty, he cut the wires to the security camera facing the area. Returning the next night, he seized the opportunity and abducted her just as she was about to enter her car. No witnesses. The killer found satisfaction violating and killing the young woman, but deep down, he knew it wasn't enough. He craved the real Dr. Peggy Scott.

Chapter 5

Wednesday, May 23

Detective Keeley found Detective Vincente at the Police Firing Range. Always struck by his imposing height, Vincente stood with his legs apart, shooting with impeccable accuracy at a target using his Glock 22. Wearing shooting glasses and protective headphones, he demonstrated his unparalleled marksmanship. Keeley knew this was his sanctuary for contemplation and approached him as he reloaded.

Vincente's thoughts lingered on Dr. Scott's theory about the pubic hair and the unsettling nature of the Jane Doe case. Something about the brutal homicide unsettled him deeply. Having already reached out to his former FBI profiler colleague, he eagerly awaited a call back regarding any potential signatures involving pubic hair. The missing pubic hair was a remarkable discovery from the young pathologist, leaving Vincente genuinely impressed. Dr. Scott intrigued him, standing out from the beautiful women he had encountered in the past. She puzzled him—a rarity for someone as perceptive as Vincente.

Interrupting his train of thought, Keeley tapped Vincente on the shoulder, prompting him to remove his headphones.

He looked at Keeley as he spoke, "The Glock is a brand of polymer-framed, short recoil-operated, locked-breech semi-automatic pistol designed and produced by Austrian manufacturer Glock. Glock pistols have become the company's most profitable line of products, and have been supplied to national armed forces, security agencies, and police forces in at least 48 countries. The Glock 22 is a .40 S&W version of the full-sized Glock 17 introduced in 1990. The pistol uses a modified slide, frame, and barrel to account for the differences in size and power of the .40 S&W cartridge. The standard magazine capacity is 15 rounds. The Glock Model 22 is favored and used by multiple law enforcement agencies around the world—"

"I don't care," Keeley interrupted, pulling out her cellphone. "We received the lab report on Jane Doe."

"Anything?" Vincente inquired.

"Nothing surprising. As we suspected from the puncture mark on her neck, the tox screen revealed ketamine. You should read the email from Dr. Scott." Keeley smirked.

Vincente began disassembling his gun as Keeley shook her head, reading aloud, "Dear Detectives, attached you will find the lab report, blah blah blah. Have you given any more thought to the serial killer theory?"

Keeley glanced at Vincente, who responded by raising an eyebrow and rolling his eyes in typical fashion.

Keeley continued to read Dr. Scott's email, laughing, and shaking her head. "I would be happy to make myself available," Keeley said, in a low and sexy voice. "And help you review any open murder cases with that particular signature. In fact, I could write a small computer program to look for the signature faster, if needed. Please do not hesitate to contact me."

Vincente rolled his eyes.

"Wow, Tony, she's offering to write you a computer program! She's kind of annoying," Keeley remarked playfully.

Vincente responded dismissively, "She's green. She's just trying to impress us."

"She's trying to impress you, Tony!"

Chapter 6

Friday, May 27

Peggy stepped out of the door to Police Plaza's cafeteria and spotted Detective Vincente heading in the same direction. Lost in thought, Vincente walked down the hall with clenched fists. Peggy observed his distinct gait—a long stride with swinging arms. Unaware of Dr. Scott's presence, Vincente didn't notice her standing in the doorway. Peggy wanted to talk to him about the case and had found herself thinking about him in the past few days.

Positioned sideways in the partially open doorway of the cafeteria, Peggy was about to call out to Detective Vincente when another patron forcefully pushed open one of the heavy cafeteria doors, causing it to slam into her left breast.

"Ah!" Peggy cried out, hunching over in pain. She discreetly cradled her injured breast.

Detective Vincente witnessed the incident, immediately reaching out to grab Dr. Scott's arm and pull her out of harm's way.

"Are you alright?" he asked, his hands gently holding her upper arms.

Peggy was too embarrassed to speak, her face and neck turning red.

"Do you need to go to the ER?" Vincente inquired, his gaze shifting to her injured breast, genuine concern etched on his face.

"I'm fine. I just need to sit down," Peggy managed to respond, her voice slightly shaky.

"Wait here. I'll go grab some ice from the cafeteria, then I'll help you back to your office."

Vincente guided Dr. Scott by the arm, escorting her to her small office. She settled onto the worn-out brown fake leather couch across from her desk, and Vincente joined her, sitting with his legs spread out. He sat next to her, eyeing her injured breast before handing her the bag of ice. Peggy held the ice pack against her left breast, discreetly hidden beneath her white lab coat.

"Are you sure you don't want to go to the ER?" Vincente inquired, sounding concerned.

"Yes, thanks. I'm sure it's just bruised," Peggy reassured him, offering a small smile.

"Well, as long as you're alright, I need to head back," Vincente stated, standing up from the couch.

As Vincente prepared to leave her office, Peggy seized the opportunity to inquire about the Jane Doe case. Hoping to engage the detective in conversation, she asked, "What's going on with the Jane Doe case? Have you given any more thought to the missing pubic hair?"

Peggy secretly wished to suggest meeting across the street for coffee and discussing the case further. But before she could ask him, Vincente interrupted, glancing at her chest, and remarking, "Take care of yourself."

With that, Vincente departed, leaving Peggy to ponder his response. She couldn't help but wonder if he had dismissed her question. Yet, she found herself appreciating his concern about her embarrassing injury.

Vincente hurried to the elevator. The lingering image of Dr. Scott's full breasts in his mind made him uncomfortable. He wondered what her heavy breasts would feel like in his calloused hands. Quickly pushing those thoughts aside, Vincente refocused on his work.

Chapter 7

Wednesday, June 1

The Special Investigations Unit squad room was a busy place. Several grey metal desks were scattered around the large room with detectives busy at work. The SIU was always loud - detectives talking on phones, apprehensive victims and witnesses being escorted to and from the small interrogation rooms, perps loudly being led out of the squad room for processing, and the captain constantly yelling orders through the open door of his corner office. Sitting at their desks, Detectives Vincente and Keeley were immersed in their investigation, poring over missing person reports, desperate to unveil the identity of Jane Doe.

Suddenly, Vincente's cellphone pierced through the air, its screen flashing "Unknown Caller." With a swift motion, he answered the call, immediately recognizing the voice on the other end. It was Agent Jeffrey Battistoni, Vincente's former partner when he briefly worked for the FBI.

"How are you, Tony?" Battistoni's voice rang through the phone, carrying an air of seasoned experience.

"Doing fine. What do you have for me, Jeff?"

Battistoni wasted no time. "I delved into a multitude of unsolved homicides of women across the country in recent years. I specifically searched for any distinctive signatures, such as trichophilia or missing pubic hair. Surprisingly, I've discovered three cases fitting those criteria, scattered throughout the Midwest. No clear pattern emerges, except that they were all sex workers. Some were blonde, but not exclusively. It seems your pathologist is onto something here. I'll email you the files."

"That's great news, Jeff. I appreciate it."

Battistoni continued, "I also consulted with the profilers, and their findings align with the usual profile: a white male, aged between 30 and 50, likely single or divorced, harboring a deep-seated hatred for women. He's organized, probably holding a steady job, not a transient, and possesses an above-average IQ. Should he strike again and this evolves into a serial murder investigation, we'll need to bring in the FBI Rapid Response Team. They'll assemble a task force. You know the protocol, Tony. Keep me informed if you require any further assistance."

Vincente acknowledged the gravity of the situation, aware that the pursuit of this killer could escalate to a larger scale. "Thanks, Jeff. I will keep you posted," Vincente ended the call, his voice filled with determination. The weight of their investigation hung heavy in the air as Keeley eagerly asked about the FBI contact's findings.

"Well, Tony, what did he say?"

"He discovered at least three similar murders in the Midwest, all involving female sex workers. It seems we may be dealing with a serial killer, one driven by a specific hair fetish," Vincente relayed, his voice filled with a mix of concern and professional analysis.

Vincente opened his laptop and accessed the FBI website, sharing his findings outloud, "Psychopathic behavior commonly exhibited by serial killers includes sensation seeking, a lack of remorse or guilt, impulsivity, the need for control, and predatory tendencies. It's worth noting that psychopaths can often appear 'normal' and even charming."

"Serial killing is often driven by psychological gratification, with many cases involving some form of sexual contact with the victims. Motives can range from anger and thrill-seeking to financial gain or attention seeking. The murders tend to follow a consistent pattern, with victims sharing certain commonalities such as demographic profile, appearance, gender, or race. Of course, there is possibility that Jane Doe may have been murdered by someone she knew, indicating a different motive." Vincente stated.

Vincente ran a hand through his thick brown hair, as he continued reading. "Serial killers may also exhibit tendencies toward fetishism, partialism, or even necrophilia, which are paraphilias involving intense fascination with specific body parts or symbolic objects that represent the body. These behaviors can exist along a continuum, where individuals engage in varying levels of fantasy related to body parts or anatomical aspects. For example, necrophilia involves a sexual attraction to the deceased."

Vincente continued, "The FBI's Crime Classification Manual, a roadmap to the minds of these murderers, classifies them into three categories: organized, disorganized, and mixed. Organized killers meticulously plan their crimes, abducting victims, and disposing of them in separate locations. Their ability to lure victims by appealing to sympathy or targeting vulnerable individuals, such as prostitutes, demonstrates a chilling level of control.."

"Organized serial killers demonstrate a methodical approach to their crimes, carefully planning each step. They often abduct victims, killing them in one location and disposing of the bodies elsewhere. Their tactics may involve manipulating victims with appeals to sympathy or specifically targeting vulnerable individuals such as prostitutes who may willingly go with a stranger. These killers maintain a high level of control over the crime scene and possess a solid understanding of forensic science, allowing them to cover their tracks effectively, whether by burying the body or submerging it in water after weighing it down."

"Well, Tony, Dr. Scott believes the killer is organized."

Vincente rolled his eyes and continued reading. "Children, lacking control over their own suffering, often retreat into a self-constructed reality—a fantasy world where they hold absolute power and where the concepts of right and wrong and empathy towards others become distorted. In this distorted realm, the boundaries between fantasy and reality blur, and dark desires of dominance, control, sexual conquest, and violence take hold. The detachment from empathy and the dehumanization of others become hallmarks of the twisted psychology of serial killers." Vincente read.

"Serial killers", he explained, "are often motivated by psychological gratification and exhibit traits such as psychopathy, lacking remorse or guilt while seeking control and indulging in predatory behavior. These individuals may appear charming, might maintain a facade of normalcy, blending into society with families and steady jobs, making their true nature all the more elusive."

Keeley sighed in frustration as she stated, "So, our potential perpetrator could be charming, seemingly normal, have a stable job, and a family. More good news! Let's hope Jane Doe's murder was committed by someone she knew rather than a serial killer."

Keeley's sarcastic remark hung in the air, a grim reflection of the daunting task ahead. The possibility that their perpetrator could be charming, seemingly normal, with a steady job and a family added another layer of complexity to their investigation. To Vincente's dismay, Keeley added, "Tony, if this is indeed a serial murder case, it's possible that this individual has been killing for quite some time."

Vincente could only hope that Jane Doe's murder had been a result of a personal connection rather than the chilling work of a serial killer.

Chapter 8

Monday, June 6

A week had passed since Dr. Peggy Scott had sent the lab results to Detectives Vincente and Keeley, offering her assistance in the Jane Doe case. Yet, she hadn't heard a word from them. Undeterred, she carried a stack of old autopsy files to the file room, dressed in scrubs and a lab coat. As she walked through the main hallways of the Police Plaza Building, she saw Detective Vincente walk out of the elevator, determination flickered in her eyes. This was her chance to ask Vincente about the case, to offer her insights and expertise.

Watching Vincente approaching, his face etched with a deep frown, Peggy steadied her nerves as she shouted, "Hi, Detective Vincente..." him, only to stumble over her own feet, sending the stack of files sprawling across the floor. The sudden commotion drew the attention of everyone in the hallway, their gazes fixed on the fallen pathologist.

In an unfortunate turn of events, Peggy tripped over her own feet and fell to the ground, scattering the files in every direction. All eyes in the hallway turned toward her as she lay sprawled on the floor, face down.

Without hesitation, Vincente rushed to her side, stooping down to assess the situation. Politely, Vincente grasped Peggy's arm, offering her support as he helped her to her feet. Peggy felt a rush of nerves and intense attraction, unsure of what to say in the moment.

Vincente raised an eyebrow and cocked his head as he asked, "Are you alright?"

"I'm fine, thanks..."

Peggy quickly got on her hands and knees, quickly gathering the papers and stuffing them into random file folders. Vincente remained close by, maintaining eye contact as he observed, "Doctor, I can't help but notice that you're quite clumsy."

Vincente couldn't fathom why such a beautiful woman seemed to have a tendency for clumsiness.

Admitting her nervousness, Dr. Scott blushed and confessed, "Yes, I tend to get clumsy when I'm feeling nervous."

"What are you nervous about?" Vincente asked.

Vincente's gaze never wavered from Peggy's eyes, captivated by the vulnerability and genuine awkwardness that seemed to emanate from her.

"I'm not great at this, umm... I just wanted to express my appreciation for your professionalism as a detective. Your knowledge of forensics and pathology is truly impressive and refreshing." She smiled. Peggy was too nervous to ask him out for coffee.

Vincente furrowed his brows, his gaze piercing into Peggy's captivating blue eyes. Peggy felt he could see right through her. Breaking the silence, he asked, "Are you flirting with me, Doctor?"

Dr. Scott's response was quick and defensive. "No, no."

Vincente's furrowed brow betrayed his intrigue as he peered into her eyes, seemingly seeing through her façade. The truth hung heavy in the air. Sensing her unease, Peggy averted her gaze, a telltale sign of her struggle to conceal her feelings. The vulnerability between them lingered, unspoken but palpable.

Summoning her courage, Peggy stuttered through an invitation, "Well, um, I was wondering if you'd like to, maybe, get together for coffee sometime? Just to discuss the case, of course. There's a café across the street. No pressure." Vincente's smile revealed his own flattery, realizing that this beautiful, intelligent woman had just asked him out. *If I don't have coffee with her, she might end up falling and breaking her neck!* He thought as he took a moment to consider her proposal.

Noticing the brilliant smile and amazing dimples on the always stern detective's face, Peggy felt a tingling igniting her core. She thought, *I want to kiss him – feel his large hands roam all over my body...*

"How about tonight after work, say 6:00 p.m.?" Vincente suggested interrupting Peggy's almost sexual fantasy.

Vincente's suggestion was met with a joyous reaction from Peggy. In her excitement, she dropped the recovered files, oblivious to her mishap. With anticipation, she replied, "Great, it's a date. I mean, it's coffee. I mean... I will see you there."

Before Vincente walked away, he noticed a stray lock of Dr. Scott's blonde hair had loosened from her ponytail and he was surprised by his desire to touch her hair. *What the fuck?* He thought as he walked away. Planning to meet her a quick cup of coffee, he would briefly inform her about the case, and then politely take his leave.

Meanwhile, Peggy couldn't shake her thoughts about Detective Anthony Vincente. She felt apprehensive, unable to fathom how someone like him could ever be interested in someone like her.

Vincente must have been a football player or a popular jock in high school, she speculated.

Dr. Scott had always been a geek throughout school, too intelligent for her own good. She had skipped multiple grades due to her gifted intellect and attended an all-girls' private math and science academy. She started college at the young age of 15, never experiencing a typical teenage life.

Detective Vincente probably dates more experienced women, Dr. Scott assumed, feeling frustrated by her young age and lack of sexual encounters.

Her mind wandered back to her past, remembering her unpleasant loss of innocence during her freshman year with a college professor—a painful, unexpected "me too" moment in his office. Her only other relationship had been similarly awful, leaving her with a sour taste in her mouth.

Chapter 9

6:00 p.m

D etective Anthony Vincente sat patiently at a table with two cups of hot coffee, in the coffee shop across the street from Police Plaza. The fatigue weighed heavily on him as he removed his suit coat and loosened his tie. The chair beneath him offered little comfort, its hardness a reminder of the long hours he had been putting into the Jane Doe case. Vincente absentmindedly rubbed his stubbled jaw and blood shot eyes, evidence of his sleepless nights since the investigation began.

Vincente was in a hurry to get home. He was anxious to get home, fall into bed and sleep. The summer sun was still out as he waited. He went over the lack of evidence from the Jane Doe case in his mind. He took out his notebook and started reviewing his notes. Maybe something new would occur to him. He was old school - he took notes by hand instead of relying on his cellphone.

As he waited, Vincente's mind wandered, and he found himself thinking about his ex-girlfriend, Vanessa. The memory of their tumultuous relationship contrasted sharply with his present situation. Dr. Scott was nothing like Vanessa, he concluded. He and Vanessa had occasionally crossed paths in their Chicago neighborhood, attending the same high school but never really getting to know each other until later in life. After returning to care for his ailing aunt, Vincente had encountered her at a friend's party and subsequently they began dating.

During his college years, Vincente had a few casual relationships, always preferring women slightly older than himself. But it was Vanessa who captured his attention, their on-again, off-again dating evolving into a more serious commitment. They would often break up and then get back together, the cycle repeating itself over the course of several years. Their most recent breakup had occurred six months ago.

Vanessa's reasons for ending their relationship echoed in Vincente's mind. She accused him of being too focused on work, lacking time for her and the relationship. Vincente saw her once or twice a week, which he considered sufficient, but it fell short of her expectations. She complained about his lack of romance, the absence of passion, and his not wanting to have sex often enough. She claimed he was too intense, lacked ambition, prioritized his cases over their relationship, played video games excessively, watched porn too often, and wasn't ready for marriage or children.

Vincente's reluctance toward commitment became apparent during their discussions about the future. While Vanessa envisioned buying a house the suburbs, getting married, and starting a family, Vincente preferred to live near his job in Chicago. He didn't like change and feared taking the next step. Although he cared about Vanessa and could imagine a life together, he couldn't meet her expectations.

Vincente felt comfortable with Vanessa, but she wanted him to be passionately in love with her. Vincente struggled to understand her need for an all-consuming love, believing their intimacy and shared commitment should be enough. Maybe he wasn't' in love with her but he cared about her – he could see spending the rest of his life with her. Vincente knew that they didn't get along as well as they could. The sex was okay, but not often enough for her – "I can work on that", he thought.

He had attempted to make up with Vanessa on his last visit to her apartment, but their conversation spiraled into an argument.

"Tony, I don't think you even love me!"

"What is love anyway? It is an emotional state that keeps human beings together to facilitate the continuation of the species. It is Intimacy, passion and commitment! Which we have!"

"I want a man who is passionately in love with me."

"We have passion – we have sex."

"That is not the same thing!"

Vincente had pleaded, "C'mon Vanessa, don't be like that!"

He had tried to kiss her. She had pulled away, leaving Vincente to exit her apartment feeling rejected. That was over six months ago, he had thought they would get back together by now.

Since then, Vincente occasionally missed the companionship of a girlfriend, but quick hook-ups were not his style. Instead, he found solace in watching vintage porn DVDs, providing temporary relief from his loneliness. He remained focused on his work, not succumbing to the pressure of seeking superficial hook-ups to fill the void.

Vincente heard the door to the almost empty coffee shop open and looked up. There was Dr. Peggy Scott smiling at him.

As Dr. Scott walked in the young male barista yelled, "Hey Dr. Peggy Scott! How are you? You look nice tonight! The usual?" The barista couldn't contain his excitement upon seeing her, showering her with compliments and eager attention. Vincente couldn't help but notice the stark difference in treatment compared to when he had entered moments earlier.

Vincente noticed that the barista was practically drooling over her. It seemed every guy wanted to be with her, a realization that left him feeling a tinge of jealousy.

What the Hell, thought Vincente, *did every guy want to sleep with her?*

He had heard the other cops in the SIU talking about Dr. Scott. They either wanted to date her, sleep with her, or both. Dr. Peggy Scott possessed an irresistible sexual allure that drew men to her like moths to a flame.

"Hi, Danny, Great thanks, and you? I don't need anything."

Dr. Scott headed right to Vincente's table. The Barista scowled at him.

As Peggy approached Vincente's table, ignoring the barista's flirting, Vincente couldn't help but appreciate her professional outfit. Her dark fitted pants and loose white blouse exuded a sense of confidence and elegance. Her thick blonde hair cascaded over her shoulders, framing her face in a soft, radiant glow. Vincente's gaze was captivated by her pale pink lipstick, accentuating her full lips, and the subtle touch of makeup that highlighted her mesmerizing blue eyes and high cheekbones. She was a vision of beauty that took his breath away.

Peggy saw Vincente already seated with two coffees. He was too big for the small table and towered over it. She noticed he was engrossed in deep thought, intently studying his leather notebook. His scruffy appearance only added to his rugged charm, his unkempt brown curly hair looked like a lover had just run her hands through it. When their eyes met, the intensity of his gaze prompted a smile from her, she longed to have a connection with the attractive and enigmatic detective.

As Peggy settled into her seat, she hung her shoulder bag on the back of the chair opposite Vincente. However, before she could fully sit down, her bag slipped off and fell to the floor. She swiftly bent over to pick it up, unwittingly granting Vincente an intimate view of her shapely bottom. A raise of his eyebrows and a shift of his gaze helped him regain his composure.

"Detective, hi! How are you?" Peggy greeted her heart fluttering with a blend of nerves and excitement.

"Thank you for the coffee." She remarked as she took a sip, a perfect mark of her pink lipstick adorned the cup's edge.

Vincente nodded, offering a slight smile in return. He couldn't help but notice the genuine joy that radiated from Dr. Scott whenever their paths crossed. No woman had ever shown such genuine happiness upon seeing him, and the attention she showed him was undeniably flattering. In her presence, he felt lighthearted as if he were a carefree teenage boy again.

Though Vincente felt a slight attraction towards Dr. Scott, he couldn't ignore the age difference. At 31 years old, he considered her 22 years to be too young for him. He had heard stories of the problems that often accompanied relationships with very young, beautiful women, and he preferred to avoid any drama.

"Please, my friends call me Tony," Vincente replied.

"Okay Tony, my friends call me Peggy. How is the Jane Doe case coming?" Peggy asked, her curiosity evident.

"Slowly. We're still waiting for an ID," Vincente responded, a tinge of frustration in his voice.

"What about the missing pubic hair? Do you think it was a serial killer?" Dr. Scott asked, her mind focused on what she believed was the serial killer's signature.

"I contacted one of my contacts at the FBI. He is looking into open murders involving missing pubic hair. He has found three in the Midwest, so far. I still don't think Jane Doe was murdered by a serial killer."

Vincente sighed, weary of Peggy asking about the Jane Doe case, wanted to steer the conversation away from it. Sensing his reluctance, Peggy swiftly changed the subject, eager to connect with him.

"I heard you used to be an FBI profiler," she remarked, trying to uncover more about his past.

"Yes, about ten years ago, after college, I joined the FBI and trained as a profiler in Virginia. However, I had to leave when my aunt, who raised me, became terminally ill. I returned home to care for her and eventually found my way into the Special Investigations Unit as a detective," Vincente shared, his hands gesturing animatedly. Peggy was impressed at how demonstrative and confident Tony was.

"What about you, Doc? Why did you become a pathologist?" he inquired, genuinely intrigued by her chosen profession.

"I was always fascinated by true crime and forensic science, so I pursued a career as a pathologist. Gifted in math and science, I skipped several grades and attended an all-girls Math and Science Academy. By the time I was fifteen, I was already in college, and I completed med school at the age of twenty-one," Peggy recounted.

Vincente had thought Dr. Scott had been a popular girl or cheerleader in high school, but now he realized she was gifted, perhaps a child prodigy. She was not at all what he expected. Intrigued, his interest in her deepened.

She went to college when she was only 15, still a child, that would explain why she seemed so naïve and insecure. Vincente thought.

"Wow! An all-girls math and science academy. What was that like?" Vincente asked.

"It was rather dull, to be honest. No proms or homecomings, just endless studying and the occasional weekend indulgence in 'The Sims.' I was a geek," she admitted, her words painting a picture of a committed and focused young woman. "What about you? What were you like in high school? I bet you were a football player."

"No, I wasn't into sports at all. I was tall, broody, and introverted. My friends and I were clueless when it came to girls. We spent our free time playing video games, getting drunk, and smoking hash. I took all AP classes and dabbled in theater tech for a couple of years. Crime and forensics always fascinated me, which led me to major in criminology and English in college, with the goal of becoming an FBI agent. So, after I graduated, I applied to the FBI and got hired. I trained as a profiler. " Vincente revealed.

Peggy was genuinely interested in learning more about Vincente's family. She asked, "What about your family?"

Vincente's voice softened as he shared his story, "My parents died in a car accident when I was two years old. I have no memories of them. My aunt, my mother's sister, raised my older brother and me. We grew up in the city, and despite losing our parents, we had a wonderful childhood. What about your family?"

Dr. Scott replied, her voice tinged with a hint of sorrow, "My mother passed away a few weeks after I was born, due to complications from childbirth. So, my father raised me as an only child. He never remarried; I don't think he has ever gotten over my mother's death. He was a loving father, always trying to make up for the absence of my mother."

Vincente and Peggy spent the next few hours talking about their shared passion for crime and forensics, losing track of time in each other's company. Vincente marveled at how easy it was to converse with Dr. Peggy Scott, feeling a sense of comfort and connection that he rarely experienced with beautiful women. Her intelligence and charm left a lasting impression on him, and he found himself genuinely enjoying spending time with her. However, he couldn't see a romantic relationship between them— he was willing to be friends with her, but nothing more.

Peggy, on the other hand, was captivated by Vincente's unwavering self-confidence and admired his ability not to care about what other people think. She found herself increasingly drawn to him.

All of a sudden, Vincente's cell phone buzzed. He pulled it out of his pocket and read the text message. He frowned. It was his best friend's wedding this weekend, and Vanessa, his ex-girlfriend, would be attending with her new boyfriend. Vincente had hoped to reconnect with Vanessa at the wedding, but now his plans were ruined. He needed a date to accompany him to the wedding.

Without overthinking, Vincente turned to Dr. Scott and impulsively asked, "Hey, I'm the Best Man at my best friend's wedding this weekend. I usually don't bring a date to these events... Would you like to go with me, as a friend?"

As soon as the words left his mouth, Vincente regretted his decision. He didn't want Dr. Scott to misunderstand his intentions. However, the thought of Vanessa attending with a new boyfriend pushed him to bring a date himself, someone gorgeous like Dr. Scott. Vincente would show Vanessa that he had moved on too.

Peggy's eyes sparkled with delight, her face radiating joy as she accepted Vincente's invitation. "Sure," she replied, her voice filled with enthusiasm.

Chapter 10

2:00 a.m.

Peggy had trouble falling asleep due to replaying the promising conversation she had with Tony at the coffee shop. When she finally fell asleep, she dreamed...

Peggy was sitting up in bed in a sleazy motel room. Tony was standing towering over her. He gently sat on the bed, leaned down and kissed her mouth, her neck, her ears, her nose.

Peggy's fingertips traced a delicate path along Tony's scruffy jawline, sending shivers down his spine.

As they embraced, their hands roamed freely, eagerly exploring each other's bodies. Tony's fingers traced a path down Peggy's spine, causing her to arch her back in response, a soft gasp escaping her lips. Every touch was an electric jolt, igniting a desire within Peggy that could no longer be contained.

Tony's manhood was straining against the crotch of his pants. With trembling hands, Peggy began to unbutton Tony's shirt, revealing a chiseled chest that made her pulse quicken. Her fingers trailed across his defined muscles, leaving a trail of goosebumps in their wake. Tony's breath hitched as Peggy's hand moved lower, teasingly tracing the outline of his growing desire.

Suddenly, Tony and Peggy were naked. His body, muscled and broad, glistening with sweat. Her breasts exposed, her hair fanned out over the pillow, and her legs spread open like butterfly wings.

She was a mess of golden blonde hair and creamy pale skin. Her lips were pink, the nipples of her large breasts were erect, and her blue eyes were brimming with desire. Tony's body was chiseled and muscular with 6-pack abs. Dark brown curly hair lightly covered his large chest. His buttocks were firm and well-muscled, the veins of his large and impressive manhood stood out in anticipation of release.

Tony kissed her with a sweet, slow urgency. His tongue moved in circles around hers, exploring every inch of her mouth. Peggy's breathing quickened beneath him. His hands moved over her breasts, tracing her nipples with his thumbs until she moaned. He took each of them into his mouth and teased them with his tongue until Peggy was writhing beneath him.

He moved down her body then, licking and sucking every inch of it as he went. His lips and tongue caressed her flat stomach and she shuddered beneath him as his tongue darted inside her navel. He explored further south then, tasting the sweet wetness between her legs until she was trembling against him in pleasure.

Peggy's breathing quickened as Tony rose up above her again and pressed his erection against the wetness of her slit. He found her entrance and slowly pressed into her warm, eager opening. She wrapped her legs around his hips as he slowly penetrated her - pushing further and further into her depths as she pulled until it seemed as if they'd become one.

Skin against skin, they relished the intimate connection that bound them together.

The bed frame squeaked as the bed moved beneath them. Their movements were a symphony of wet slapping sounds, and the low grunts and moans of pleasure.

Peggy felt her climax approach like an unstoppable force, building and intensifying with every heartbeat.

Finally, she came while Tony thrusted harder and faster before finally letting himself go. With one final shudder he emptied his hot semen into Peggy.

The steamy smell of sex and sweat was pungent in the room.

When Tony pulled Peggy into his arms she looked up at him with wonder in her eyes and spoke for the first time since they'd arrived at the motel: "I love you."

Peggy woke up from her erotic dream with a start.

"Oh my God, what?" Peggy said out loud as she sat up.

She was shaking and aroused. *Did I have my first orgasm in a dream?* She asked herself.

Chapter 11

Saturday, June 11

Detective Anthony Vincente stood in the opulent white marble lobby of the Downtown Plaza Hotel, awaiting Dr. Peggy Scott's arrival. Vincente's mind wandered to Vanessa, his ex-girlfriend, who had already made her entrance with her new boyfriend. Jealousy gnawed at him as he observed Vanessa's striking new look—a sleek chin-length bob, accentuating her exotic Italian features. Her tight black dress showcased her toned runner's physique, evoking memories, and desires within Vincente.

Vincente thought about asking Vanessa to dance at the wedding reception. Despite their past troubles, he couldn't deny his lingering affection. A smirk played on his lips as he thought of the possibility of a sexual encounter between them if she were to show up in his hotel room. He was uncertain whether he wanted Vanessa back, but if she wanted to see him again, he would not say no.

***

Meanwhile, Peggy's car service dropped her off in front of the grand entrance of the Downtown Plaza Hotel. The evening sunbathed the exterior of the upscale hotel in a warm, golden hue. Stepping out of the luxury car, she commanded attention in her high heels, wearing a designer strapless dress. The tight bodice accentuated a hint of cleavage, while the dress cascaded in thin, silky layers, hugging her every curve. It was a custom-made, exquisite designer creation, adorned with shimmering Swarovski crystals that caught the light with every step. Her hair was artfully styled in a loose, seductive chignon, courtesy of her personal hairdresser.

Peggy's heart fluttered with nerves, determined to make a lasting impression on Detective Anthony Vincente. She longed for him to notice her, to find her irresistible.

As Peggy made her entrance through the revolving doors, her eyes locked with Tony Vincente's gaze. He was wearing a jet-black tuxedo and looked very elegant and handsome. She was excited to spend the evening with him and hoped this was the beginning of a connection between them, something other than friendship. As for Detective Anthony Vincente, time seemed to stand still as he beheld her beauty. The sight of her took his breath away.

Astonished by Peggy's appearance, Vincente couldn't help but think, *she is absolutely stunning!* The nude-colored dress, fitting her like a second skin, reminded him of bare flesh. Its strapless design revealed her graceful shoulders and generous breast, while her messy blonde chignon added a touch of disheveled sensuality. Vincente found himself captivated by her high cheekbones, piercing royal blue eyes, and luscious pink lips. It was the first time he had laid eyes on her long, sleek legs, accentuated by seductive nude high heels.

With each step Peggy took toward Vincente, an aura of intoxicating sex appeal enveloped her. She radiated a rare sexual power, unaware of the magnetic effect she had on those around her. Every onlooker, both men and women, turned their heads to catch a glimpse of her enchanting presence. Peggy exuded poise, grace, and an underlying confidence that was unlike her professional persona. As she approached Vincente, waves of attraction washed over him, amplified by the intoxicating smell of perfume.

Vincente did not want to acknowledge his growing attraction to Dr. Scott. To get his mind off his feelings, he clinically thought about sexual attraction, *Sexual attraction is attraction on the basis of sexual desire or the quality of arousing such interest. Sex appeal is an individual's ability to attract other people sexually and is a factor in sexual selection or mate choice. The attraction can be to the physical or other qualities or traits of a person. The attraction may be to a person's aesthetics or movements or to their voice or smell, among other things. The attraction may be enhanced by a person's adornments, clothing, perfume, or style.*

Vincente did not appreciate the admiring gazes at Dr. Scott from the men in the lobby. Even though being by the side of such a stunning woman boosted his ego. He eagerly anticipated the moment Vanessa would see him with the gorgeous doctor.

The confidence Peggy had felt when she put on the dress faded instantly as she saw Vincente's expression—a raised eyebrow and a near-scowl. Self-consciousness washed over instantly.

Peggy chastised herself, *this dress reveals too much, making my breasts look too big. The color makes me look naked. I should have worn my plain black dress, that hides my curves.*

As Peggy walked up to Vincente, the shiny marble floor beneath her caused her to slip and stumble forward. Acting swiftly, Vincente caught her in his strong arms, feeling a strong chemistry between them. However, he immediately dismissed such thoughts from his mind.

Vincente silently reminded himself, *I won't pursue a romantic relationship with Dr. Scott. She is too young.*

Concern etched on his face, Vincente asked her, "Are you alright, Doc? You look perfect." He smiled as he carefully released her, hoping she wouldn't stumble again.

"Just nervous," Peggy confessed, trying not to blush in embarrassment.

"No need to be nervous," Vincente reassured her. "We're here to have fun—dancing, drinks, and food. No pressure. Then I'll take you home. Remember, you're doing me a favor. My friends aren't used to me bringing a date to these events."

Peggy smiled, trying to conceal her disappointment. She felt foolish for going to great lengths to impress Tony, investing effort into her dress, hair, and shoes, only to learn that he wanted nothing beyond a friend for the evening. Tony's lack of romantic interest was evident to her, shattering her hopes for a relationship with the elusive detective.

Unbeknownst to Peggy, the only reason Vincente had invited her to the wedding reception was to provoke a reaction from his ex-girlfriend, Vanessa.

The grand ballroom exuded an atmosphere of celebration, accommodating around 200 guests. Smiling faces and lively conversations filled the space. The decorations were almost too much - extravagant floral arrangements, adorned with balloons, chairs elegantly dressed in white bows, mirrored walls, and a colossal wedding cake serving as a centerpiece. Two open bars were busy with wedding guests, while a small stage was being set up for a DJ and his equipment.

As Vincente escorted Peggy into the ballroom, all eyes fixed upon her. Even the groom, Vincente's best friend, couldn't help but stare. Every man in the room was secretly envious of Vincente's beautiful and sexy guest, giving him high fives behind Peggy's back. Vincente, on the other hand, felt a mix of embarrassment and discomfort from the attention he was getting.

Vincente took the opportunity to introduce Peggy to the bride and groom. Having grown up with them, he introduced Peggy as his friend, though he could sense that no one believed their relationship was purely platonic. The stares from everyone in the room made it clear that they were impressed by Dr. Peggy Scott. Yet, she remained blissfully unaware of the effect she had on men.

Throughout the reception, Vincente couldn't help but notice Vanessa's piercing glares from across the room. Jealousy radiated from her, as she paid no attention to her new boyfriend. In that moment, Vincente felt a deep gratitude for Dr. Scott's agreement to accompany him to the event.

Meanwhile, Peggy caught Vincente repeatedly stealing glances at a tall, dark-haired woman on the opposite side of the ballroom.

As the DJ instructed everyone to take their seats for dinner, Vincente promptly brought Peggy a glass of white wine from the open bar. He escorted her to a table far away from the head table, where he would be seated with the bridal party. Peggy found herself surrounded by unfamiliar faces, couples who introduced themselves one by one. However, the man seated next to her couldn't seem to tear his eyes away from her breasts. He introduced himself as Phil, the groom's cousin, and proceeded to boast about his countertop business, lecturing Peggy on the various types available. Phil even went so far as to offer an estimate at a discounted price, suggesting he visit her home. Peggy promptly informed him that she was Vincente's date and not attending the reception alone.

Observing from the head table, Vincente's displeasure grew as he noticed Phil's persistent gaze fixated on Peggy's breasts.

Sipping her wine, Peggy found it impossible to take her eyes off Vincente. His relaxed smile, charming demeanor, and friendly personality amazed her. He was a stark contrast to the Vincente she knew at work—fidgety and scowling. Though she was undeniably attracted to him, Peggy knew he didn't have the same feelings for her, after introducing her to several guests as his friend.

Thank God for wine. She thought as she drained her glass.

Deciding to calm her nerves with alcohol, Peggy poured herself a glass of champagne from the bottle on the table, determined to make it through the evening with a touch of intoxication. A waiter, resembling a male model, approached her with an offer to bring anything she desired. She smiled politely, declining his offer.

Peggy listened to Phil's incessant chatter, opting to drown out his words with more champagne. From the corner of her eye, she caught sight of a tall, dark-haired woman approaching Vincente at the head table. The same woman that Tony had been secretly watching all evening. The woman leaned in close to him, whispering in his ear with an air of intimacy.

Phil, noticing Peggy watching Vincente's and the woman's intimate interaction, exclaimed, "Uh, oh! Don't look now, but Tony's ex, Vanessa, is making a move! They were hot and heavy for a while, quite the couple, you know. Everyone thought they'd tie the knot before they called it quits a few months back. Looks like you've got some competition!"

With a mix of disappointment and hurt, Peggy clarified, "Tony and I work together. We're just friends."

It suddenly became clear to Peggy why Vincente had asked her to accompany him to the wedding reception—to make his ex-girlfriend jealous. The realization left her feeling deeply hurt, almost on the verge of tears. If she hadn't worked with Vincente, Peggy would have gotten up and left.

Peggy's anxiety grew, threatening to escalate into a panic attack. Searching through her evening bag, she retrieved an anti-anxiety pill, swiftly swallowing it with a full glass of wine. The combination of lorazepam and alcohol left her feeling lightheaded. Deciding to ignore Tony Vincente, she aimed to spend the remainder of the evening in relative silence.

As the speeches concluded and the DJ started playing music, the newlywed couple took the dance floor for their first dance. The wedding party joined in, including Vincente, who found himself dancing with one of the bridesmaids.

Turning her attention back to Phil, Peggy declined his invitation to dance, politely saying, "No, thank you."

The young waiter, Nate, approached Peggy, flashing a charming smile. "Can I get you anything?"

"A glass of white wine, please," she requested, discreetly slipping him a $50 bill from her evening bag.

"Thanks! I'll make sure your glass is always full. By the way, I'm not really a waiter. I'm a third-year law student, and I happen to be single," Nate revealed, winking at Peggy.

Graciously, she responded, "Thanks." Her coy smile encouraged him.

"I'm Nate. Maybe we can exchange phone numbers later?" he suggested.

"Sure, I'm Peggy." She handed Nate her cellphone, allowing him to enter his number before returning it to her. As their hands briefly touched, Peggy felt flattered but not truly interested in Nate.

As Vincente swayed with the bridesmaid, his attention was drawn to a young, attractive waiter who was flirting with Peggy. The waiter's infatuation was obvious, and Peggy appeared to enjoy the attention.

After the wedding party dance ended, the DJ changed the tempo to a slow song. Vanessa approached Vincente, wrapping her arms around his waist, and they started dancing intimately. Vincente had wanted to ask Peggy to dance, but now she was talking to the waiter. Vincente saw them exchange phone numbers. *What the fuck!* He thought.

Watching Vincente and Vanessa on the dance floor, Peggy averted her gaze. She chugged another glass of wine, attempting to drown the emotions that stirred within her.

"How have you been, Tony?" Vanessa asked, her hand caressing his back.

Struggling to focus on Vanessa, Vincente's mind kept wandering back to Peggy and the waiter. It was obvious they had developed a connection.

"I'm good. And you?" Vincente replied, his thoughts still consumed by Peggy and the waiter.

"Great! So, who's the young blonde you brought? She looks barely 18!" Vanessa asked sarcastically.

"She's one of the pathologists I work with, Dr. Peggy Scott. She's in her twenties."

Vanessa, relieved by the response, commented, "She doesn't seem like your type."

Once again, Vincente glanced over at Peggy's table, where the waiter had delivered yet another glass of wine to her.

"And what exactly is my type?" Vincente asked, his eyes lingering on Peggy.

Vanessa's attention shifted to Vincente's gaze; her words almost pleading. "Me. Tony, I miss you. I was hoping we could give it another try."

Vincente's gaze flickered back to Vanessa. In that moment, he realized he had no desire to rekindle things with Vanessa. While he wasn't certain about pursuing a romantic relationship with Dr. Peggy Scott, he felt a growing attraction towards her.

"Sorry, Vanessa, but it's over, at least for now," Vincente stated as the dance ended.

Vanessa let go of Vincente, walking away with a mix of disappointment and jealousy.

Vincente made his way over to Peggy's table; he held out his hand. With a final gulp of wine, she reluctantly took his hand, and he led her to the dance floor.

The DJ's played a slow and sensual song. As Vincente's hand lightly rested on Peggy's slender waist, an electric current surged through his body. She moved with such grace, effortlessly following his lead. They flowed together, their bodies harmonizing with the music. Vincente couldn't tear his eyes away from her, captivated by her beauty, leaving him yearning for a connection with the alluring doctor. He wished the music would never end.

Breaking the silence, Vincente asked, "Are you enjoying yourself?"

Peggy hadn't spoken much to him, she seemed distant. Vincente sensed that something was wrong.

"Sure," she replied with a slight slur, her voice lacking enthusiasm.

"You are a great dancer." Vincente commented trying to bridge the gap between them.

"Thanks, years of ballet and jazz lessons," Peggy responded, avoiding his gaze.

"That waiter seems to really like you."

Vincente realized he was jealous.

"Oh really, I hadn't noticed." Peggy looked down as she replied.

Vincente did not understand why Peggy was lying. The waiter was obviously hitting on her. He was confused.

Is she intentionally trying to make me jealous? Vincente wondered.

Suddenly, the DJ dimmed the lights, setting the mood for a fast-paced, provocative song. The lyrics were sexually explicit. The combination of the wine and the drug Peggy had consumed took hold, freeing her inhibitions. She danced with abandon, the music guiding her movements. She didn't care what Vincente thought about her. Her body swayed, hips gyrating in sync with the rhythm, arms raised above her head. Her eyes closed, biting her lower lip, Peggy surrendered herself to the music. Every curve of her full breasts and shapely bottom bounced to the beats. Her confidence, sexiness, and innate talent as a dancer had everyone in the room watching her. Vincente, feeling a mix of discomfort and possessiveness, couldn't deny her innate allure. Peggy's sensual display held the wedding male guests captive. It almost seemed like she was giving every man in the room a private lap dance. Vincente, like the others, knew she most gorgeous and sexy woman on the dance floor. He felt an intense sexual chemistry with her that he had never felt with any other woman.

Vincente's desires grew more primal. He yearned to taste Peggy's lips, to slide his tongue in her mouth. He fantasized about picking her up and carrying her to his hotel room. He wanted to do naughty and delicious things to her naked body. He wanted Dr. Peggy Scott.

The song came to an end, and the DJ announced that the bride would toss the bouquet, beckoning all the single ladies forward.

Vincente grinned mischievously and tugged Peggy along to join the group of single women. Reluctant to participate, Peggy stood at the back, off to the side, feeling out of place. She longed for another glass of wine and the comfort of home. The DJ's music filled the air as the single women grew increasingly excited, anticipating the toss of the bouquet. And just like that, the bride's flowers landed in Peggy's hands, a direct throw. The crowd erupted in applause, Vincente among them.

"Hey, congratulations," Vincente said, beaming with delight.

Peggy looked at bouquet and rolled her eyes. Meanwhile, the DJ called for the single men to gather as the groom prepared to toss the garter. Confused, Peggy had never seen this wedding ritual before. Vincente approached the groom and whispered something in his ear before joining the rowdy crowd of single men.

Suddenly, the DJ played loud stripper music. The bride sat in a chair placed in front of the crowd of jeering men. The groom knelt before her, lifting her wedding gown to reveal the garter on her upper thigh. The men cheered and applauded as the groom slowly removed it. Then, with a triumphant toss, the garter landed directly in Vincente's awaiting hands, eliciting cheers from the crowd.

Vincente grabbed Peggy's hand, with a big smile on his face.

"I'm sorry, but tradition dictates that I put the garter on your leg since you caught the bouquet," he whispered.

Peggy's mortification was evident as she questioned, "What?"

"Don't worry, it won't be weird," Vincente assured her.

Seating Peggy in the chair previously occupied by the bride, in front of the boisterous crowd of single men, Vincente playfully got down on his knees. Peggy tightly closed her legs, feeling utterly embarrassed. Her skimpy panties and bare legs heightened her self-consciousness. The music blared louder, the cheers, wolf whistles, and catcalls growing more intense.

"Go Tony! Show us some leg!" the crowd shouted.

"Tony! Show us her panties!" Phil yelled, standing right at the front.

Peggy froze as Vincente, clutching the garter in one hand gently took hold of her right foot with the other.

Looking up at Peggy, Vincente reassured, "It's okay."

Seeing Peggy's embarrassment and nervousness, her slight trembling and flushed cheeks, Vincente couldn't help but find her innocence and vulnerability incredibly sexy. He longed to see her blushing while completely naked, a thought that aroused him.

Carefully, Vincente removed Peggy's right high heel, cradling her bare foot in his large hand. With a soft smile, he slowly and modestly slipped the garter over her foot, barely grazing her exposed skin as he guided it up her calf.

Amidst the whistles and screams, the men yelled for more. Vincente gradually raised Peggy's dress, exposing the tops of her knees. The crowd erupted with excitement as Peggy's blush deepened. Vincente, ignoring the screaming men, positioned the garter just above her right knee, refusing to go any higher. With care, he gently pulled down her dress, and helped her out of the chair.

Sincerely, he asked, "That wasn't too bad, was it, Doc?" His eyes locked with hers, searching for a response.

Overwhelmed by the sensuality of feeling Vincente's hands on her, Peggy found herself speechless. Vincente's touch had ignited a fire within her, leaving her wanting more.

The DJ changed the boisterous mood with an explicit, slow song about oral sex. Vincente led Peggy to the dance floor, his hands resting on her waist, and hers resting on his shoulders. They embraced each other closely, moving in perfect synchrony. Peggy rested her head on Vincente's chest, her body tingling from the wine coursing through her veins. She felt a connection with Tony, that left her filled with emotions she had never experienced before.

When the song ended, the groom tapped Vincente on the shoulder, directing his attention towards the stage. Reluctantly, Vincente released Peggy from his arms, promising to return shortly.

As Vincente and the groom made their way to the small stage, the DJ announced the start of karaoke. Vincente and the groom joined forces, harmonizing their voices in a rendition of the timeless ballad, "Endless Love."

My love, there's only you in my life

The only thing that's right

My first love

You're every breath that I take

You're every step I make

And I, I want to share

All my love with you

No one else will do

And your eyes, your eyes, your eyes

They tell me how much you care

Ooh, yes

You will always be

My endless love

Two hearts

Two hearts that beat as one

Our lives have just begun

Forever (oh)

I'll hold you close in my arms

I can't resist your charms

And love, oh love

I'll be a fool for you I'm sure

You know I don't mind (oh)

You know I don't mind

'Cause you

You mean the world to me (oh)

I know, I know

I've found, I've found in you

My endless love

Ohh

Boom, boom

Boom, boom, boom boom, boom, boom

Boom, boom, boom boom, boom

Oh, and love oh, love

I'll be that fool for you I'm sure

You know I don't mind

Oh, you know I don't mind

And, yes

You'll be the only one

'Cause no one can deny

This love I have inside

And I'll give it all to you

My love, my love, my love

My endless love

Source: LyricFind

Songwriters: Lionel B. Richie / Jr.

Endless Love lyrics © Warner Chappell Music, Inc

Laughter filled the room as Vincente and the groom serenaded each other, their voices harmonizing in perfect unison. Their unexpected musical talents captivated the crowd, everyone laughed and applauded.

With his gaze fixed on Peggy, Vincente sang the lyrics, "This love I have inside, and I'll give it all to you, my love, my love, my love, my endless love." Peggy couldn't believe her ears, momentarily glancing behind her to see if he was singing to his ex-girlfriend. Relieved not to find Vanessa, Peggy turned back to Vincente, who winked at her and smiled. The intoxicating mix of emotions and alcohol left Peggy confused. She wanted to go home.

After the song ended and Vincente worked his way through the crowd to Peggy, she remarked, "I didn't know you could sing."

Vincente chuckled, shaking his head in disbelief. "I can't!"

"I wish I had recorded that on my phone for Keeley and Mac." Peggy teased.

"I would have never heard the end of it!"

"It's late. I should be getting home." Peggy announced.

Vincente pleaded, "Just one more dance," leading her back to the dance floor.

The DJ selected another slow, seductive song, with provocative lyrics. Vincente held Peggy tightly against him, pressing the front of his body against hers. Peggy wrapped her arms around his back, burying her head on his chest, while Vincente rested his chin atop her head. Peggy pressed her body against his. Vincente felt the curve of her full breasts against his chest. She was intoxicating - he was fighting not to get hard. He liked having her in his arms. Holding her. They swayed with the music, and Vincente lightly caressed her delicate bare back with his fingers. The sensation sent tingles to her core, igniting a desire to remain locked in his embrace.

As the song ended, Vincente promised, "I'll be back in a minute. Wait here, and then I'll take you home."

Peggy watched as Tony approached Vanessa. He stood very close to her while they spoke. He hugged her. Anger flared within Peggy, and she walked away, determined to find her own way home.

Unbeknownst to Vincente, Peggy was aware of his past relationship with Vanessa. His hand grasped her arm as she was walking toward the lobby of the hotel, "I want to take you home," he pleaded.

Peggy politely responded, "That's okay. I can take a taxi. You have a room here, so there's no need for you to leave. Thank you for a lovely evening." She began to walk away again.

Determined to walk Peggy home, Vincente insisted, "Wait, wait, I insist. I want to take you home. It's a beautiful night, and your place isn't far. Let me walk you home."

After a brief pause, Peggy relented. "Okay."

Peggy, lost in a haze of wine and lorazepam, felt a strong desire to avoid any confrontation or conversation with Vincente. Meanwhile, Vincente couldn't understand Dr. Peggy Scott's abrupt changes in behavior. One moment she was pressed against him on the dance floor, and the next she was walking away. Vincente prided himself on being able to read people easily, but Peggy remained a mystery to him.

Night wrapped around them, while a gentle summer breeze caressed them. It was well past midnight, and the full moon and the lights of the city illuminated their path as Vincente escorted Peggy home. They strolled through the busy streets of her touristy upscale neighborhood, the city still alive with activity. Despite his confusion, Vincente couldn't help but feel happy as they walked side by side. He wanted to see Peggy again, to explore the chemistry between them. He wanted to get to know her

Funny how fate can change things, Vincente mused. Earlier in the evening, he had hoped for a reunion with Vanessa, yet now he found himself drawn to the captivating allure of Peggy. She was a remarkable woman—beautiful, intelligent, and effortlessly sexy. Their conversations flowed effortlessly, and dancing with her had been delightful. The way she blushed when he placed the garter on her leg had stirred something within him.

Vincente wanted to hold Peggy's hand, to wrap his arm around her as they walked. He intended to ask her out to dinner. He wanted to ask her the cause of her aloofness this evening. Peggy, however, was preoccupied with her own thoughts. Her tipsiness threatened her balance, and she stumbled, nearly falling. Vincente swiftly caught her arm.

"I think you've had a little too much wine," Vincente observed.

"I'm fine," Peggy curtly replied, her words laced with irritation. In truth, Peggy's mind was clouded by her jealous thoughts of Vincente and Vanessa together. She felt a mix of emotions—jealousy, hurt, and anger—all of which she tried to suppress. Peggy didn't want Vincente to know she had feelings for him.

Attempting to maintain her composure, Peggy focused on placing one foot in front of the other as they continued walking. She couldn't wait to escape from Vincente's presence, her mind consumed by her feelings for him. The last thing she wanted was to have a conversation with him.

Vincente, sensing Peggy's emotional distance, felt apprehensive about asking her out again. Her hot-and-cold behavior confused him. Determined to be genuine, he decided to share some vulnerable things about himself. Nervously, he began, "I normally don't tell women this, but I'm a rather complex guy. My work is of utmost importance to me, and I often find myself working long hours. Women I have been in relationships with have complained about me not spending enough time with them. I am introverted and can be moody at times. I am a loner. Although, I do enjoy playing online video games with my friends. I have diverse interests, such as reading poetry, appreciating art, watching movies and theater, and exploring literature. And, umm, I watch pornography too—not anything kinky or strange, just ordinary stuff. Now, it's your turn to share something you don't usually reveal."

Vincente hoped his confessing his vulnerabilities would bridge the growing gap between them.

Peggy couldn't understand why Vincente was sharing personal details about himself when he was still involved with his ex-girlfriend. In her state of inebriation and frustration, she no longer cared about Vincente's opinion of her. With a mix of anger and resignation, she responded, "I have never had an orgasm."

Vincente halted in his tracks, taken aback by Peggy's confession. They both stopped walking and faced each other. Trying to understand, he asked, "You mean you haven't experienced sexual pleasure? How about when you touch yourself."

Peggy sighed and truthfully responded, "I lack sexual experience. I've tried touching myself, but it feels awkward and uncomfortable."

Vincente reassured her, "There's nothing to feel awkward about. Self-pleasure is a natural part of sexual discovery."

Peggy rolled her eyes, unconvinced by his words.

Vincente pressed further and asked, "What about foreplay?"

She replied with a hint of bitterness, "In the few instances I've had sex, it was rushed and lacked intimacy. Clothes off, and that's it. I don't even enjoy it. It's uncomfortable, messy, and sometimes painful."

Vincente and Peggy resumed their walk, their conversation veering into uncomfortable territory. Vincente decided to provide some guidance, saying, "Men may be ready for sex quickly, but women need foreplay. It's essential for arousal—romance, touch, kisses, embraces. A man must exercise patience when making love to a woman."

Peggy struggled to hide her shock, not expecting such a candid discussion.

Vincente continued, "Foreplay is a set of intimate acts between two people meant to create sexual arousal and desire for sex. Time spent on foreplay is an important part of becoming sexually aroused. It can consist of various sexual practices such as kissing, sexual touching, removing clothing, and oral sex. Women need stimulation in order to have an orgasm. Sexual organs need to receive more blood flow for arousal. Females require longer acts of foreplay to become sufficiently stimulated and pleasured."

Feeling uneasy, Peggy suggested, "Maybe I have a sexual dysfunction." She had no interest in discussing her sexual problems with Detective Vincente.

As they arrived outside Peggy's expensive and exclusive apartment building, Vincente thought, *I didn't know resident pathologists earned so much money.*

He turned to Peggy as he said, "I doubt you have anorgasmia. Women require more time for sexual arousal and orgasm compared to men. Direct sexual stimulation is the most common way for women to achieve orgasm." Vincente deliberately and slowly looked over Peggy's body, his gaze lingering. "Orgasms can vary in intensity, and the frequency and level of stimulation needed differ among women."

Vincente's unwavering gaze and the conversation left Peggy feeling embarrassed and a little aroused. She was desperate to go home, go to sleep, and pretend this evening had never happened.

"Umm, thank you for a nice evening, Detective, um I mean Tony."

Peggy turned to leave, but Tony gripped her upper arms. The summer breeze was rippling her dress and tousling her hair – it looked tousled and sexy. Her dress floated above her knees almost to the tops of her thighs. Vincente thought she looked damn sexy. He could barely resist the urge to kiss the Hell out of her.

"Wait a moment, Doc," Vincente pleaded, his smile radiant. He had never asked out a woman as beautiful as her. "I'm trying to ask you out."

Peggy frowned, her confusion deepening. "What do you mean?" she asked, unsure of Vincente's intentions.

"I mean, if you're not planning to go out with that waiter. Are you?"

Meeting his gaze directly, Peggy replied, "No. Are you going to get back together with Vanessa?"

Vincente was taken aback. *How did Peggy know about Vanessa when they had only danced once?* "How do you know about Vanessa?" he asked.

Peggy explained, "The groom's cousin, Phil, told me. He mentioned you and Vanessa being 'hot and heavy'."

Vincente felt relieved because he realized that Peggy's recent aloofness, drinking, and flirting happened because she was upset with him because of what Phil told her.

"No. I am not going to get back together with Vanessa. She asked me to call her, but I told her that it was over. It was over a long time ago."

A smile spread across Peggy's face as she moved closer to him, and Vincente sensed her relief.

Curious about his initial question, Peggy asked, "So, what were you asking me?"

Vincente gently held her upper arms, his voice filled with sincerity. "I'd like to see you again. Would you go to dinner with me next Saturday night?"

Peggy's reply was immediate. "Yes, I would love to."

Vincente released his grasp on her arms as Peggy turned towards her building. The doorman held the door open for her, and Vincente bid her farewell, saying, "Great, see you at work."

As Peggy turned around, she smiled, and Vincente smiled back at her. He continued walking down the street but couldn't resist calling out to her, "Hey Doc, I love foreplay."

Peggy laughed, her blush spreading across her cheeks. She really liked Detective Anthony Vincente.

Vincente was consumed by his attraction to Peggy. The desire he felt for her surpassed anything he had experienced before. Thoughts of her lips, mouth, breasts, legs, hair, and those captivating blue eyes kept him awake at night. Knowing she was young, inexperienced, and somewhat naive, he decided to take things slowly and see where their relationship would lead.

Unbeknownst to Detective Anthony Vincente, by the following Saturday, Dr. Peggy Scott would be gone.

Chapter 12

Monday, June 13

The watcher fantasized about killing Dr. Peggy Scott. He fantasized about torturing her. He fantasized about violating her in every possible way while listening to her whimpers and screams.

He could usually control his urges. But he couldn't when he thought about his beautiful muse, Dr. Scott.

He believed he was an apex predator. Once a year he would hunt – and travel to the other side of the country to stalk and grab a prostitute. He had been hunting and killing one girl every year for about 17 years. He was good at it. Masterful. He was sure he would never be caught. He was too smart and too careful.

The watcher enjoyed the look in their eyes when he was strangling them. The fear. He fed on it. He felt powerful, almost godlike.

Since he never hunted this close to his residence, abducting the beautiful unaware doctor was going to be a problem. He had tried to resist this young woman but had failed. So, he watched her. He learned her schedule. He learned her habits. He took his time.

Taking her will not be as difficult as I thought. The watcher smiled.

Chapter 13

Monday Night, June 13

D etective Anthony Vincente could not stop thinking about Dr. Peggy Scott. She consumed his thoughts with such an intensity that he even dreamed about her while he slept. He found himself yearning to reach out to her, to hear the sound of her voice and see the sparkle in her eyes. The mere thought of her seeing her enticed him to consider visiting the morgue, where he could steal a glimpse of her at work. He recalled dancing with her, their bodies swaying in perfect harmony, and the feeling of her warmth as he held her close. He imagined holding her hand. He wanted to run his fingers through her hair. The memory of those instances when she stumbled and he caught her, flooded his consciousness. He thought about exploring every inch of her with his tongue, and all the sensual things he wanted to do to her body to make her come. He thought about how her body would feel underneath him during lovemaking while his swollen cock was deep inside of her. The anticipation of their upcoming dinner date on Saturday ignited a fire within Vincente that burned with an unquenchable passion.

Chapter 14

Tuesday, June 14

S eated at their desks, Detectives Vincente and Keeley sat almost next to each other in the bustling squad room, focusing on the frustrating Jane Doe case. Vincente meticulously sifted through a stack of missing person reports, determined to uncover the identity of Jane Doe. Keeley, on the other hand, focused her attention on writing a report for a recently closed case. Their concentration was interrupted by the shrill ring of Keeley's cell phone laying on her desk. She immediately answered the call.

As Keeley ended the call, she triumphally announced, "We've made progress on iden-tifying our Jane Doe. Her name is Cassie Greaves, a 21-year-old woman who matches a missing person report filed by her boyfriend. She worked as a full-time waitress at a college bar near the University. Cassie never returned home after her shift a few weeks ago, and her car remains parked in the lot."

Vincente nodded solemnly, his mind already piecing together the puzzle. "It's likely she was abducted from the parking lot after her shift," he deduced.

Keeley called a forensics team and told them to examine the lot and Cassie's vehicle. Keeley then called the Greaves's boyfriend and scheduled an interview for the following day. Determined to gather more information, Vincente proposed they pay a visit to the bar to question the bartender and Cassie's co-workers.

Later that day, Vincente and Keeley climbed into an unmarked police car, with Keeley taking the wheel as usual. Their destination: Harry's, the college bar where Cassie Greaves had worked. The bar stood approximately three miles away from the University, and was currently closed until 11:00 a.m. Upon arrival, Vincente noticed a security camera positioned to capture the view of the parking lot, a potential source of valuable evidence.

Vincente and Keeley entered the run-down establishment and were greeted by the typical sights of a college bar—a ping pong table, pool table, dart boards, and video games. Flashing their detective badges, they introduced themselves to the man tending the bar, Harry Buckley. Harry was a very average looking man in his thirties.

"We want to ask you about Cassie Greaves." Keeley stated.

"Of course. Poor Cassie! What a terrible thing. I can't believe she was murdered!" The bartender looked shaken as he answered, making a feeble attempt to wipe down the wooden bar.

Detective Vincente paced in front of the bar, while opening and closing his fists. He stopped pacing every so often to look at the pictures behind the bar or to pick up and closely examine a dirty glass. Keeley smirked as she observed the tall and powerful detective's nervous and fidgety behavior that always seemed to intimidate people. She wanted to believe that Vincente acted this way deliberately to rattle people, but she suspected that Vincente wasn't cognizant of his sometime erratic and intimidating behavior.

"We noticed a security camera facing the parking lot. We need to look at video from the last night she worked." Vincente said as he slammed his leather notebook on the bar.

The bartender flinched before he said, "I'm sorry, but that camera has been out for over a week. The wires were cut."

Vincente and Keeley looked at each other.

"We need to take any videos that you may have saved," Vincente ordered.

"Sure. I will get them," Harry replied, looking somber and impatient.

"First, we need to ask you some questions, "Keeley interjected, placing her cell phone on the bar and opening a recording app.

"Tell us about Cassie," she prompted.

With tears glistening in his eyes, the bartender began to share his memories of Cassie. "Cassie was a great waitress. She worked here for a couple of years, and everyone knew and adored her. She worked hard, often pulling 8 to 10-hour shifts, juggling her classes at the University. Her dream was to become a nurse."

Vincente's probing instincts kicked in as he remarked, "Maintaining an apartment, a car, and covering college expenses is quite a financial burden for a 21-year-old."

Harry nodded; his voice tinged with sorrow. "Cassie was very independent. She wanted to prove herself, to do everything on her own."

At that moment, Gina, Harry's girlfriend, and a close friend of Cassie, joined the conversation, her eyes red from crying. With her dark hair pulled back in a ponytail, dressed in jeans and a t-shirt, she resembled a college co-ed.

Keeley probed further. "Did Cassie have a boyfriend? Derek Jasper reported her missing, claiming to be her boyfriend," she asked while dramatically placing the missing person's report on the bar.

Gina's voice trembled slightly as she responded, "Yes, she was dating Jasper."

"Tell us about Jasper," Keeley pressed.

"Derek owns a tattoo parlor on May Street. He's a tattoo artist, single, probably in his early 40s," Gina explained.

Intrigued by the age difference between Cassie and Jasper, Vincente interjected, "How did they meet?"

Harry answered Gina, his voice tinged with concern. "They met here at the bar. They dated for about six months or so. Derek used to visit after work."

Vincente probed further, a sense of unease creeping in. "Used to? What changed?"

"Yeah, well, Derek has some control issues. He didn't like it when Cassie talked to other guys. He would sit and watch her, getting angrier whenever she waited on male customers. I had to ask him to leave a few times. He would glare at anyone who approached her. Eventually, I had to ban him from the bar whenever Cassie was working. I will go get the computer with the security videos for you."

Abruptly shifting her attention to Harry, Keeley questioned, "Where were you on the night Cassie disappeared, Thursday, May 12th?"

Harry's reply was quick. "Cassie closed that night, and I left early around one in the morning. I went home. Gina came over to my place after her shift at around 2:00 a.m."

Taking a mental note of the details, Keeley turned to Gina, her eyes searching for answers. "Why did Cassie continue seeing Derek despite the red flags?"

Gina sighed, a mix of emotions flickering across her face. "Well, Derek is attractive. At first, Cassie was drawn to him. He was charming. He paid a lot of attention to her—bringing her flowers, taking her out for dinner, stuff like that. But then he became possessive and needy. He called and texted her constantly. Derek's behavior got even more strange and controlling. He didn't want Cassie working here or even talking to other men. He started stalking her -- showing up at her university classes and waiting for her in the parking lot after work. He was obsessed with her. He even asked her to marry him, but Cassie turned him down. So, then he started pressuring her to move in with him." Gina explained.

The detectives exchanged glances, the pieces of the puzzle gradually falling into place.

Vincente leaned forward; his voice filled with curiosity. "How did Cassie react?" he inquired, eager to unravel the events leading up to her disappearance.

Gina paused for a moment, "She reached her breaking point. Just a couple of days before she vanished, she told me that she was planning to end things with him," she revealed, her voice laced with a mix of concern and sadness.

Keeley, sensing an opportunity for more information, probed further. "Was she afraid of him?" she asked.

Gina shook her head and replied, "No, not really. If anything, she felt sorry for him."

Keeley pressed on. "Was he at the bar around the time of her disappearance?" she asked, her eyes focused intently on Gina.

"No, he wasn't. But he did come to the bar the next day, looking for her. He was worried since she hadn't been answering his calls or texts. Derek went to her place, but she didn't open the door." Gina recounted.

Intrigued by what Gina had revealed, Vincente asked, "What else can you tell us about their relationship?"

Gina sighed she chose her words carefully. "Cassie didn't complain about him much, at least not until he started stalking her."

Vincente pressed further; his voice filled with concern. "What did she say about his behavior?"

Gina visibly shivered as she recounted the troubling details. "She said he was controlling, always demanding to know her where she was. He had an insatiable sex drive -- he wanted to have sex all the time. He wouldn't leave her alone. He even demanded that Cassie pierce her pussy or tattoo his name on her body. They argued about it all the time."

Detective Keeley exchanged a glance with Vincente. Vincente raised an eyebrow, his expression reflecting a mixture of disdain and determination.

"Were there any unfamiliar men lurking around the bar, bothering or observing Cassie before she disappeared?" Keeley inquired.

Gina furrowed her brow, wracking her brain for any recollections. "No, not that I can recall. Most of the guys who frequent this place are university students," she replied.

Vincente shifted the focus towards the parking lot, a critical piece of the puzzle. "Did you notice anyone loitering around the parking lot on the night she disappeared?" he asked, hoping for a lead.

Shaking her head, Gina answered. "No, I left around 1:45 a.m., about 15 minutes before Cassie. The parking lot was empty, and I didn't see anyone around. Cassie had to close the bar that night and was supposed to leave at 2:00 a.m.

As the pieces began to fit together, Keeley looked at Vincente. "So, it's highly likely that Cassie was abducted around 2:00 a.m. while she was closing up the bar and making her way to her car in the empty parking lot," Keeley concluded.

The bartender, Harry, returned, holding a laptop computer in his hands. He handed it to Keeley, his eyes reflecting a glimmer of hope. "The security videos from the past six months are stored here. I hope you find something useful," he offered.

Keeley accepted the laptop gratefully, her grip firm as she reassured him. "Thank you, Harry. We'll make sure to return it once we're done. And if you or Gina remember anything else, please don't hesitate to reach out," she said, handing them her business card.

The two detectives made their way toward the parking lot. Vincente spoke, his voice filled with a sense of purpose. "I believe it's crucial that we speak to the tattoo artist, Derek, when he comes in for questioning tomorrow morning."

Keeley nodded in agreement; her gaze fixed on the path ahead. "Before that, let's conduct a search of Greaves' apartment. It might provide us with some clues," she proposed.

They noticed the forensic team had finished their search of the parking lot and Cassie Greaves' car.

Keeley eagerly asked, "Did you find anything?"

Their response was frustrating. "No, nothing."

Keeley, Vincente, and the forensic team redirected their search to Greaves' residence, a modest studio apartment located a mile away from Harry's bar. Hours were spent combing through the space, and dusting for fingerprints. They found several sets of prints but nothing else.

Chapter 15

Wednesday June 15 (Early in the Morning)

As the early morning of Wednesday, June 15 approached, Detective Vincente found himself preoccupied with thoughts of Dr. Peggy Scott. Her image lingered in his mind; her sexy nude-colored dress etched permanently in his memory. A surge of desire coursed through him as he imagined making love to her. He was anticipating their dinner date on Saturday and the passionate goodnight kiss that would follow.

Vincente's feelings for Dr. Scott went beyond infatuation; they had developed into intensity he had never felt before. Each thought of her rekindled the excitement of a teenage crush, an eagerness to be near her and seek her out at work. It was a magnetic attraction, fueled by desire, that he felt deep in his soul.

Intrigued that Peggy had never come or experienced sexual pleasure, Vincente became determined to change that. He wanted to fulfill her desires, igniting pleasure within every inch of her body. He craved to explore her body. He wanted to trace his finger through the silky strands of her long hair. He was driven by an unselfish desire to pleasure and sexually satisfy Dr. Peggy Scott.

Today, Vincente had planned to make a stop at the morgue to see Peggy, he hadn't seen her since the wedding. The urge to see her, to remind her of their date on Saturday, was strong. Phone calls or text messages couldn't compare to seeing the beautiful doctor in person. The Greaves case consumed his attention, leaving little time for anything else, but Vincente was determined to stop by the morgue today.

Later that day, Derek Jasper, the tattoo artist, voluntarily came in the SIU for questioning. As Keeley and Vincente returned from a meeting with the captain, they found Jasper already seated at the table in an interrogation room. Keeley took a seat across from him, while Vincente remained standing, gripping the case file on Cassie Greaves tightly in his hand. A subtle nod from Keeley signaled the technician behind the two-way mirror to start recording the interview.

Introducing themselves as detectives from the Special Investigations Unit, Keeley began the interview. "I am Detective Keeley, and this is Detective Vincente. We're investigating the murder of Cassie Greaves. Are you Derek Jasper?"

"Call me Derek," he responded casually.

Derek's body was a canvas of tattoos, covering his exposed arms, neck, and chest. He had multiple piercings in his ears, nose, and eyebrows. His jet-black hair fell to his chin, and despite his skinny frame, he was muscular. Clad in tight black jeans and boots, he looked like an aging rock star.

"Nice tattoos," Keeley remarked, acknowledging the artwork on Derek's skin.

"Thanks. I did most of them myself," Derek replied proudly.

Vincente's attention was drawn to a particular tattoo—a knife dripping with blood—on Derek's arm. He was curious so he asked, "Is that a knife dripping with blood?"

Derek looked delighted as he responded, "Yeah, cool, isn't it?"

Shifting their focus to the investigation, Keeley asked, "Where were you on Thursday, May 12th, around 2:00 a.m.?"

Vincente leaned casually against the wall, glaring at Derek.

"I was home, watching TV," Derek replied, his voice steady.

Keeley probed further. "Alone?"

Derek nodded. "Yeah, all night."

Continuing their line of questioning, Keeley reviewed the events following Cassie's disappearance. "You reported Cassie as missing on Friday morning, May 13th. How did you know she was missing?"

"Well, like I said, I was alone that night, but after her shift ended around 2:00 in the morning, I started calling and texting her. She didn't answer. My calls went straight to voicemail. I fell asleep around 3:00 a.m. When I woke up at 6:00 a.m., I tried contacting her again, but she still didn't answer. So, I went to her apartment. She didn't answer the door when I knocked. Her car wasn't there either. I headed to the bar, and it was closed but her car was still in the parking lot. I called Harry and asked if he had seen her or if she had left with anyone. He said no. Worried; I reported her missing. The dumb cops didn't file the report until a couple weeks later! They thought she had probably run off with some guy!"

Vincente was angry as he walked over to Derek purposefully and dropped the Cassie Greaves file on the table, causing her autopsy pictures to scatter face up. Each gruesome image revealed her naked body -- violated, mutilated, stabbed, marked with bite wounds, and strangled.

Vincente shouted. "That is how we found Cassie—naked, raped, mutilated, stabbed, covered in bite marks, and strangled. She was dumped like garbage in a ditch!"

Jasper put his head in his hands and started crying.

"What the Fuck! Man, Oh my God. Cassie! Oh my God. Why are you fucking showing me this? Why are you doing this? I wouldn't do this! I would never hurt Cassie! I loved her!"

Vincente leaned in closer, his face inches away from Jasper's and said, "Take a good look at Cassie's wounds. It's obvious that her killer was consumed by rage as he tortured and killed her. He was furious with her!"

Keeley interjected, "We've heard Cassie was going to break up with you, Derek."

Keeley adjusted the photos, allowing Jasper a clearer view. His immediate denial followed. "No! That's a lie. She loved me!"

"That's not what we've heard. We received reports of you stalking her—showing up at the bar, lurking around the university, bombarding her with texts and calls. The bartender even banned you for glaring at any man who spoke to her," Keeley stated firmly.

Detectives Keeley and Vincente shared an unspoken understanding. They knew Jasper was lying.

"Cassie was a beautiful, young woman. 21 years old - a juicy, college coed. And you, Jasper, you're a middle-aged man. Aren't you in your forties?" Vincente probed.

"I'm thirty-nine!" Jasper yelled defensively.

Vincente held up a headshot of Cassie Greaves, an 8x10 print of her university ID photo. He let out a low whistle. "She was a babe. I bet she got a lot of male attention. Look at her, Derek—she was gorgeous, and that body, wow! I bed that smokin hot body made heads turn. She could have had any man she wanted. I can understand why you might have been jealous – all that sexual attention —so many men wanting to get into her pants. There was Cassie strutting her hot little body at the bar teasing all the young college guys. Did she like to party, Derek? I bet she liked to party. College girls like to party – I know I went to college. I know how they are! What did she go to a frat party – did she find some young, rich, frat boy? Is that why she dumped you? Did she tell you that she wanted to date other guys? Did she tell you she just wanted to be friends? C'mon Derek, we know you were obsessed with her. You were calling and texting her all the time. You wanted her to quit that job -- you wanted to marry her –– you wanted her to move in. You wanted her all to yourself! I understand how you wanted to control her –"

"We never broke up!" Jasper's voice cracked.

Vincente kept goading Jasper, "C'mon Derek. You just couldn't keep your hands off her! You wanted to have sex all the time – I can't blame you – just look at her – she was so sexy! How many guys do you think she has been with? I wouldn't have minded – "

"Shut up! Just shut the fuck up! It wasn't like that. We were in love. I never stalked her. I never tried to control her!" Jasper shouted, his composure slipping.

"Is that right? You wanted to tattoo your name on her body! Pierce her labia! Do you have some kind of fetish, Derek?" Keeley confronted him, her tone laced with disbelief.

"No! Labia piercing is for sexual enhancement. Women love it. You would love it," Jasper retorted.

Keeley replied. "I could just slap you."

Vincente's voice boomed, inches away from Jasper's face. "I understand, Derek. I get it. You couldn't handle her. You just lost it. She drove you crazy. You didn't mean to kill her. You lost your temper. You accidently killed her in a jealous rage! She just wouldn't listen, would she? She didn't want you anymore—those young, horny college guys were always sniffing around her. Maybe she craved variety in bed. Or perhaps you simply couldn't satisfy her in bed anymore. What happened, Derek? Weren't you enough for her? Is that why you had the sick idea of piercing her labia? Did she need sexual enhancement because she wasn't getting it from you? You weren't young or man enough for her anymore!"

"No. She loved me." Jasper screamed as he pounded the table with his fist.

"Why did you kill her, Derek?" Vincente screamed, his face contorted with anger.

"I didn't kill her! I swear I didn't! I would never harm her. I want a lawyer!" Jasper exclaimed and started sobbing.

Detectives Keeley and Vincente left the interview room. They knew they did not have enough to arrest Jasper.

"Well, I like him for it. Tony, what do you think?"

"I will talk to a judge and get a search warrant for his home and the tattoo parlor." Tony replied, determined to find the proof they needed.

Chapter 16

Thursday, June 15

L ate in the afternoon, the search warrant was finally approved. Detectives Vincente and Keeley met the forensic team at Jasper's residence. They knew they needed evidence linking Jasper to Cassie Greaves' murder before they could arrest him. Their hopes rested on finding that evidence either at Jasper's apartment or his tattoo parlor.

Jasper lived in a one-bedroom apartment within a posh building near the university Cassie had attended. The apartment was impeccably organized, each surface spotless. The furniture was modern, chrome accents and black leather. Framed pictures covered the walls, showcasing nude women adorned with tattoos and piercings. In the living room, a state-of-the-art flat screen TV loomed large, surrounded by video game consoles, virtual reality headsets, and a top-of-line laptop.

"No surprises here. Just a typical man cave," Keeley remarked with a touch of cynicism.

Detectives Keeley and Vincente slipped on surgical gloves, ready to start searching.

"Bag the laptop. The techs can analyze it," Vincente instructed one of the crime scene technicians.

"Let's start in the bedroom," Keeley suggested.

Entering Jasper's bedroom, they were greeted by a king-sized platform bed – the sheets and comforter made of black satin. The walls and ceiling were covered with mirrors.

"Really?" Keeley exclaimed; her disgust palpable. "I'm surprised he doesn't have a waterbed! What a creep."

"He likes to watch. We should check for hidden cameras," Vincente suggested, his voice filled with a mix of revulsion and determination.

As he opened the top drawer of one of the nightstands, Vincente's eyebrows shot up in surprise. "Got something," he announced. Carefully, he picked up a box of condoms and put it in a clear evidence bag. "I'll ask Dr. Scott to determine if these match the condom piece found with Cassie Greaves," Vincente proposed, hoping for a solid lead.

Keeley approached the open drawer and looked inside. "Handcuffs, whips, and sex toys—maybe he likes it rough," she remarked with distaste.

"Greaves was bound with zip ties," Vincente stated.

Keeley discovered a plastic tube in the drawer. Her expression twisted with disgust. "Anal lube. Eww! What a pig!"

"That doesn't make him a murderer."

Interrupting their search, a forensic technician stuck his head into the bedroom. "We found a half-empty bottle of bleach in the laundry room," he reported.

"Bag it," Vincente commanded.

"Tony, Jasper doesn't have an alibi. He was stalking Greaves. I bet she tried to break it off with him, and he killed her. We found bleach and condoms in his apartment. That's all the evidence I need. We should go to the District Attorney," Keeley urged, convinced of Jasper's guilt.

"I don't think a bottle of bleach and a box of condoms will be enough for the DA. Let's search the tattoo parlor," he suggested, opting to continue their investigation.

After an exhaustive search, Detective Keeley, Detective Vincente, and the forensics team came up empty-handed at Derek Jasper's tattoo parlor. It was nearing 11:00 p.m., and the detectives were exhausted. Deciding to call it a day, Vincente and Keeley decided not to return to the station. They needed rest and to recharge. Keeley drove the unmarked police car, dropping off Vincente at his apartment before heading home herself.

Vincente had intended to stop by the morgue earlier in the week to see Peggy and remind her about their dinner date on Saturday. However, Greaves's case kept him busy. Now, it was too late. Determined, he made a mental note to visit Peggy tomorrow, on Friday, and talk to her.

Chapter 17

Thursday, 11:10 p.m.

In the dimly lit back entrance of the morgue, Dr. Peggy Scott stood dressed in scrubs, waiting for her driver. The street was empty, illuminated only by the light from the doorway where she stood beneath a security camera. Holding her cellphone, she scrolled through her messages, hoping to hear from Detective Vincente before their upcoming dinner date on Saturday night. Disappointed from not hearing from him, she assumed Tony was occupied with the Jane Doe case, now that the victim had been identified. Nevertheless, she was excited about their dinner date and was hoping to run into him at work tomorrow.

Just as Peggy was about to put away her phone, she felt someone behind her. Before she could react, a gloved hand covered her mouth, and a sharp pain pierced her neck like a bee sting. Within moments, Dr. Peggy Scott was unconscious as the masked assailant carried her away, leaving the empty street to its silence.

Chapter 18

Friday Morning, June 17

C aptain Delacroix of the Special Investigations Unit sat wearily behind his
desk, gazing out the window. He was an African American man in his late
fifties looking forward to early retirement. Balding and overweight, he looked disheveled in his wrinkled navy-blue suit and crumpled tie.

In the midst of his contemplation, Captain Delacroix received a call that the Police Commissioner's billionaire friend's daughter, had gone missing. The Commissioner requested the presence of the Captain, Detective Vincente, Detective Keeley,
for a meeting with the billionaire in just twenty minutes. Apparently, the billionaire
specifically requested that Vincente and Keeley be in charge of the investigation. As
the weight of the situation settled upon him, Delacroix couldn't help but mutter to
himself about Vincente.

"Great, a billionaire with a missing daughter is going to be here in a few minutes
and wants to meet with me, Vincente, and Keeley." Captain Delacroix said to
himself, "I almost got through a whole week without a problem with Detective
Vincente. He is going to be the death of me!"

Detective Anthony Vicente was a perpetual and annoying presence in the captain's life. The thought of a billionaire with a missing daughter and the subsequent meeting only increased his anxiety.

Fuck, thought the captain, Vincente *is going to be the lead detective on a high-profile case. A case that the FBI should probably be handling!*

The commissioner had reminded Delacroix that this tech billionaire always donated generously to the City's Police fund. The captain popped a Tums in his mouth. His heartburn was acting up just thinking about the new circle of hell this case would bring.

While the captain recognized Vincente's exceptional detective skills, high proficiency in interrogation and case-solving, there was a definite problem with his demeanor. Rumblings within the department depicted Vincente as arrogant, condescending, and socially inept. His blatant disregard for politics and his tendency to clash with authority figures only exacerbated the situation. Delacroix was thankful for Detective Keeley, knowing she was a positive influence on Vincente, and kept a watchful eye on him.

Thank God for Keeley, thought Delacroix, as he braced himself for the upcoming meeting, *she keeps him in line.*

Most of the time, Keeley managed to rein in Vincente's wild theories about cases, although he often proved himself right. The captain knew Vincente's perceptiveness was exceptional, almost bordering on the eerie. He had an innate ability to read people, delving into their thoughts and emotions with an uncanny accuracy.

"Too bad Vincente is such a fucking asshole!" The captain muttered.

***

Half an hour later...

Detectives Vincente and Keeley sensed something was up as they made their way to the captain's office. Delacroix was busy, locked in a closed-door meeting with a renowned computer tech billionaire. As the detectives entered the office, they noticed the captain's troubled expression as he popped a Tums into his mouth. Keeley and Vincente sat in chairs next to the billionaire, Delacroix neglected to make any introductions.

Vincente recognized the wealthy man from magazine covers but couldn't remember his name. The billionaire seemed visibly upset. He was an attractive man in his fifties.

Vincente estimated that the man was approximately 5'8". With a lean frame, he had blonde hair tinged with strands of gray and piercing blue eyes. He wore an exquisite bespoke suit with custom-made leather shoes. He clutched the latest iPhone model, his gaze frequently darting towards the phone as if expecting an important call.

Without wasting any time, Vincente asked, "What's going on, Captain?" The detectives felt the pressing need to work on the Cassie Greaves homicide case, believing they were running out of time.

"My daughter is missing, Detective," the billionaire responded, directing his gaze squarely at Vincente.

Curious about the details, Vincente probed, "Alright, how long has she been missing?"

"It's been around nine hours now. When her driver arrived to pick her up from work last night around 11:00, she was nowhere to be found. She's also not at home. I've been calling her repeatedly, but all I get is her voicemail," the billionaire's voice quivered.

Keeley, seeking further clarification, asked, "How old is she?"

"She's only 22 years old—a mere child," he replied, tears welling in his eyes.

Vincente rolled his eyes, his frustration showing. He looked at Keeley and voiced his skepticism, "Nine hours? You know the protocol, right? A person isn't considered missing until 48 hours have passed! She probably went out partying last night, either crashing at someone's place or sleeping off a wild night with some guy she picked up."

Vincente was unwilling to indulge a billionaire's concerns over his missing, young, and privileged daughter.

Vincente rose from his seat, preparing to leave. "And besides, if it is a kidnapping, which I highly doubt, you need to call the FBI."

"Detective Vincente!" the captain's voice thundered, halting Vincente in his tracks. "She is one of our own!"

"Detective Vincente, my daughter is Dr. Peggy Scott."

Silence and fear swallowed Vincente as thought about Peggy's disappearance. He sank back into his chair, his hands instinctively reaching up to rub his face, a gesture of distress.

"Oh my God," Keeley whispered, her voice laced with shock and concern.

"I'm sorry you had to find out this way, Detective Vincente," Mr. Scott apologized, his voice heavy with sorrow. "Peggy speaks very highly of you. She told me you and Detective Keeley are the best detectives on the force."

"My apologies, sir," Vincente apologized, his voice laced with humility.

The captain was astounded, he had never seen Vincente apologize to anyone before.

"Mr. Scott, did Dr. Scott have any enemies?" Keeley inquired gently.

Mr. Scott's tears flowed freely as he spoke, his grief palpable. "No. Peggy is such a sweet girl. Everybody likes her. She is so young. She graduated from high school when she was only 15. She was gifted in math and science. I have always protected her. She is naive, inexperienced, and immature. She doesn't know how hard life can be. Her mother died when she was just a baby. I have sheltered her her whole life. It's my fault. I've spent my life overprotecting her. I should have gotten her a security guard, but I thought she would be safe working in the Police Plaza building!"

With trembling hands, Mr. Scott handed Keeley a folder filled with information. "I have compiled some information you might need on my daughter. I've included copies of her most recent credit card and bank statements, a list of phone records and recent texts spanning a year, as well as the names and addresses of her friends. There's also a list of schools she attended, her email accounts and passwords. I've informed her doorman to grant you access to search her penthouse. If you need anything else, please let me know, and I will provide it."

Keeley asked, "Does she have any social media accounts?"

"Peggy doesn't have any social media accounts," Mr. Scott replied. "I've asked her to keep a low profile online. It's safer for her if no one knows she's my daughter. It may be overkill, but I know a lot about the internet and how information can be used." He handed Vincente and Keeley his business cards. "Please call me day or night if you find out anything."

Vincente remained unusually quiet, his mind swirling with a mix of shock and disbelief, struggling to process Peggy going missing.

"Thank you, Mr. Scott. This will save us some time," Keeley expressed gratitude. "If you don't mind my asking, where were you last night when she went missing?"

"Not at all, Detective. I was on my private jet, flying home. I had business in London," Mr. Scott replied. "The driver who was on duty last night is waiting in the lobby to talk to you."

Keeley's questioning continued. "Was Dr. Scott dating anyone?"

Mr. Benjamin Scott's gaze met Vincente's, as he answered, "No, not really. She doesn't date much. She is inexperienced when it comes to men. She's only had one significant relationship that I know of. She dated Montgomery Clearmont for a few months—a lawyer from the District Attorney's office."

"We've heard of him," Keeley interjected, acknowledging the familiarity.

"I should mention that he wasn't pleased when she ended things a few months ago," Mr. Scott continued, his tone somber. "She told me she felt like he was following her after the breakup."

Keeley inquired further. "Why did they break up? Do you know?"

"Peggy told me he asked her to move in with him, but she declined because she wasn't that serious about him," Mr. Scott explained. "He became furious. He claimed he planned on marrying her, wanting her as his wife. He thought she was making a big mistake because he planned to become the governor someday." Mr. Scott rolled his eyes, a hint of disdain coloring his voice. "Peggy had heard rumors about his involvement with other women, so she couldn't understand his reaction. I met him once, and I didn't like him. I thought he was after her money, probably seeking a wealthy wife to further his political ambitions. I expressed my concerns, but she assured me they were just casually dating. So, I didn't worry until she ended it and he became angry."

Vincente leaned forward, and asked, "Why did she suspect he was stalking her?"

"Peggy spotted him multiple times lurking near her block. I think it frightened her. She mentioned he was too controlling. She was relieved when she ended the relationship."

"Well, we'll certainly have a conversation with Mr. Clearmont," Keeley declared with resolve.

The captain interrupted and announced, "I had the surveillance footage pulled from the camera outside the rear entrance of the morgue—the door where she waits for her driver. Just received it."

The captain swiveled his laptop to face them, and Vincente instinctively rose from his seat, drawn closer to the screen. The black and white video flickered to life; its grainy quality was eerie. The timestamp read 11:10 p.m., capturing Dr. Scott standing outside the back entrance of the morgue on Second Street. They watched as Dr. Scott, engrossed in her cellphone, was oblivious to any danger. Suddenly, a figure emerged—a man covered in dark clothing, wearing a hoodie and ski mask. He appeared behind her, his hand swiftly encircling her neck. A syringe-like object pierced her skin, rendering her unconscious. Her phone and bag tumbled to the ground. The masked assailant swiftly picked them up, effortlessly lifted Dr. Scott's limp body and vanished from the camera's sight. In a matter of seconds, Dr. Peggy Scott was gone.

Everyone was shocked. Mr. Scott's gasped is disbelief. Vincente's mind raced, recognizing the significance of the video. Peggy's abductor had intimate knowledge of her life.

"I'm calling in the crime scene techs to secure the area," the captain announced decisively. "I'm also contacting the FBI in case this is a kidnapping for ransom. Mr. Scott, the FBI will set up wiretaps on your cellphones, work and home phones, in case the kidnapper tries to contact you."

Mr. Scott's voice trembled as he responded, "Of course, I will do anything to bring my daughter back."

"We will need to call a press conference," the captain declared. "Maybe somebody saw something. You may want to say a few words."

Mr. Scott nodded in agreement; his face etched with grief.

Vincente turned to Keeley, "Keeley, let's gather some uniformed officers and head downstairs. We need to canvass the area, see if anyone saw anything. Then we'll interview her driver."

As Mr. Scott prepared to leave, Vincente extended his hand, offering reassurance. "We will do everything we can to find your daughter, Sir."

"Thank you, Detective Vincente. I know you will."

Vincente and Keeley handed Mr. Scott their business cards.

Once Mr. Scott had left the captain's office, Vincente voiced his thoughts. "I believe Dr. Scott was abducted by someone familiar with her routine. This wasn't a random act. The abductor planned it, knew exactly where she would be last night."

Keeley furrowed her brow, contemplating Vincente's words. "So, she might have known her abductor?"

"Maybe, but one thing is certain—he knows her."

Keeley pointed out the obvious. "She works in the morgue. It wouldn't be difficult for someone to find out who went in and out while she was at work."

Vincente nodded, his mind already racing with the possibilities. "Every person entering the morgue has to scan their ID or sign in. I'll reach out to Mac and obtain Dr. Scott's work schedule. I'll also contact the techs—they should be able to provide us with a list of everyone she came into contact with during her shifts."

The captain added, "Tony, you and Keeley should conduct background checks and interviews with each individual on that list. Let's see if anything stands out."

Vincente hesitated; his voice tinged with guilt. "Captain, I have something to confess. I may have a conflict of interest in this case."

Perplexed, the captain inquired, "What are you talking about?"

Vincente took a deep breath and confessed, "Dr. Scott and I were seeing each other. We went out a couple of times."

The captain and Keeley looked at each other.

"Were you intimate with her?" The captain asked.

"No, not at all. It was just a few casual dates," Vincente clarified.

The captain dismissed any notion of a conflict of interest. "Then I don't see a problem. Keeley, can I speak with you?"

Vincente left the captain's office, his mind consumed with Peggy's abduction. Seeing Mr. Scott's distress and the haunting image captured by the surveillance camera, Vincente's felt a mix of emotions—anger at the perpetrator, a fierce protectiveness towards Dr. Scott, and a gnawing sense of responsibility to find her. He knew that time was of the essence, that every passing moment the trail to find Peggy would become colder.

"Keeley, do you think this is going to be a problem?" The captain asked after Vincente left.

"No, Tony will focus on the case."

The captain couldn't hide his surprise. "They were dating? I always thought he was gay!"

Keeley shrugged her shoulders and left.

Keeley joined Vincente in the squad room. She wondered if his personal connection to Dr. Scott would hinder their investigation.

"Do you think this will be an issue, Tony?"

"No."

***

While Vincente took the elevator to the morgue, he ruminated on the timeline of Peggy's abduction. He chastised himself for going home last night and not returning to work at the SIU.

Fuck! Why didn't I stop by the morgue last night and make sure she got home safely? He asked himself. Thoughts of Dr. Scott consumed him, regrets simmering beneath the surface. He was consumed with worry about her. He needed to control his emotions and focus on the investigation. He silently promised Peggy and himself that he would leave no stone unturned to find her.

Outside the back entrance to the morgue, Detective Sam Keeley found Vincente crouched down, his gloved hands carefully inspecting the ground beneath the view of the security camera. The area had already been cordoned off with crime scene tape by the forensic crime scene techs, who were meticulously securing the surroundings.

Vincente rose to his feet, with his game face on and his mind consumed by the investigation.

***

Keeley thought about the demands of being a detective in the SIU. The job was far from easy—it involved countless hours of tireless work: interviewing witnesses, canvassing neighborhoods, scrutinizing crime scenes, analyzing forensic evidence, poring over video footage in the hopes of finding a lead, sifting through phone records, social media accounts, and financial transactions. She hoped that with hard work and their many years of experience with criminal investigations, they would be able to find Dr. Scott and bring her home safely.

Keeley was curious about Vincente's relationship with Dr. Scott. She couldn't help but ask, "Did you know who Dr. Scott was?"

Vincente frowned. "No, I had no idea."

"What do you think of Benjamin Scott? I had no clue he even had a daughter! Every time I see him in the news, he's accompanied by a different young model. Do you think he could be involved in her abduction?"

Vincente dismissed the notion with the shake of his head. He reasoned, "No, he has an alibi. Besides, he may be controlling, but I think he's just overprotective. Remember, she was practically a child when she started college."

Unconvinced, Keeley argued, "Did you look inside that folder? He knows everything about his daughter. With his money, he could have easily hired someone to abduct her."

Vincente maintained his focus. "I believe Dr. Scott was being stalked. The perpetrator knew her. We need to get the footage from all the surveillance cameras around the Police Plaza building and the entire block. We should search the videos for any suspicious individuals hanging around. We also need to get the video recordings from the vicinity of her penthouse and check any red-light cameras along this street right before, and during the time of the abduction. We'll run the license plates."

Keeley questioned his theory. "You think it was someone she knew and not a stranger?"

"Yes, but we can't afford to make assumptions. We still need to interview everyone and verify their alibis," Vincente emphasized.

With long strides, Vincente led the way down the street, closely followed by Detective Keeley. He scanned their surroundings, mentally reconstructing the events leading to Dr. Scott's abduction.

He loosened his tie and ran a hand through his hair. "It appears the abductor must have waited for her to leave work, right here," Vincente surmised, pointing toward the spot near the alley adjacent to the morgue's back entrance.

"He knew there was a camera here," he theorized, pointing at the surveillance camera, "because he had on a ski mask." Vincente grabbed Keeley's arm, positioning her in the same spot where Dr. Scott had stood.

Using Keeley as a stand-in for Dr. Scott, Vincente carefully reenacted the scene. "The video shows Dr. Scott coming out of the sliding doors and waiting right here for her ride," he explained. Moving from the entrance to the alley, Vincente approached Keeley, demonstrating how the abductor had approached their victim from behind.

Placing his arm around Keeley's throat, Vincente continued, "He came up behind her like this, then injected her with something to knock her out. He carried her back here to the alley. I suspect his car was parked right here." Pointing to the entrance of the alley, he noticed a fresh oil stain. "See that? I bet it was from his car."

Frustration gnawed at Vincente. He was angry, upset, and deeply concerned for Dr. Scott. Yet, he knew he had to keep his focus on the case. He needed to find her.

"Fuck!" Vincente exclaimed; his voice filled with exasperation. "She was abducted right here, outside the morgue behind Police Plaza! She vanished into thin air!"

He took a deep breath, trying to regain composure. *If only*, he kept thinking over and over again, *I had paid her a visit last night instead of going home. Maybe this nightmare wouldn't have happened.*

"Tony, look at me," Keeley stared into Vincente's bloodshot eyes. "We need to stay on task," she grasped his forearm. "We have to work the case, follow the evidence, and find her. Let's go interview the driver. He's waiting."

***

In the interrogation room, Detectives Vincente and Keeley confronted Dr. Peggy Scott's driver. Sitting across from him, Keeley took a seat while Vincente dragged a chair right next to the driver, the loud scraping sound of the legs on the hard floor was meant to grate on the driver's nerves. The driver appeared frightened, his gaze fixed ahead, avoiding eye contact with the detectives. Vincente excelled at finding ways to rattle witnesses and perpetrators.

Closing the scant distance between them, Vincente deliberately dropped his heavy leather notebook onto the metal table, with a deliberate loud slap to provoke the driver. The small grey room crackled with tension.

"Hello, I'm Detective Keeley, and this is Detective Vincente."

As Keeley introduced themselves, she placed her cellphone on the table touched the record icon. "You are Bradley Simon, employed by Dr. Scott's car service. Can you tell us details of what happened last night when Dr. Scott was abducted?"

The driver's gaze remained fixed on Keeley, deliberately avoiding Vincente's piercing stare. An uncomfortable silence settled in the room as they awaited his response.

The driver shifted uneasily in his seat, as he spoke. "Umm, well Peggy texted me at about 11:00 p.m. She told me she was ready to be picked up," Vincente opened his heavy notebook with such force that it slapped against the metal table. The driver continued, his voice laced with fear, "Umm, I replied that I would be right there."

"Where were you at that time?" Keeley inquired.

"I was at a coffee shop a few blocks away. I knew she was getting off at eleven, so I left the office and waited close to the morgue."

Eager for any leads, Keeley probed, "Did you notice anything unusual before you arrived?"

"No. The coffee shop was empty."

Keeley pressed on, "And then what happened?"

"I got in the car and drove to the back entrance of the morgue. But she wasn't there. It was around 11:15 p.m. I assumed she might be running late, so I waited."

Vincente turned his head to the side and leaned forward, his eyes focused intently on the driver. "Did you see anything out of the ordinary while you waited?"

Shaking his head, the driver responded, "No, I didn't see anything. The street was deserted, no traffic. I waited for 45 minutes. I texted her, but she didn't reply, which was unusual. So, I called her, but it went straight to voicemail. I contacted my boss and asked what I should do. He said to wait a little longer and he called Mr. Scott, Peggy's father. So, I stayed there, waiting for almost two hours before I went back to the office."

Vincente's pen scribbled hastily across the pages of his notebook as thought about the driver's statement. After a long pause, he asked, "During those two hours, did you just remain in the car?"

The driver shook his head adamantly. "No, I couldn't just sit there. I walked around the entire block, desperately searching for her. But she wasn't anywhere! I didn't see anybody!"

Observing the driver's nervous reactions, Keeley interjected, "Tell us about your relationship with Dr. Scott." As Vincente continued to jot down notes, the driver opened up, "Well, I'm her regular driver. I've been driving her for about a year now. Peggy has always been kind to me. She always takes an interest in my life, asking about my career. You see, I'm an actor."

Keeley couldn't help but inquire with a hint of sarcasm, "Oh, really? An actor! Have been in anything?"

"Not really. I go for auditions all the time, but I'm mostly an out-of-work actor. I did a commercial and a play in the suburbs, I haven't had much luck," he admitted sounding disappointed.

Keeley pretended to look impressed.

Vincente redirected the conversation. "Tell us, do you drive Dr. Scott anywhere besides work?"

"Well, Peggy leads a rather quiet life for a 22-year-old. I usually drive her to and from the morgue. Once a week, I take her to her father's house for dinner. Occasionally, she meets her father at a restaurant, and I drive her there. Oh, and a few months ago, I drove her and a female friend to the movies."

"Have you ever noticed any suspicious individuals hanging around while you were with Dr. Scott?"

The driver shook his head emphatically. "No, I've never seen anything like that. I haven't noticed anyone lurking around."

Vincente closed his notebook with a resolute thud. The detectives exchanged a glance, a shared understanding passing between them. They were no closer to finding Dr. Scott. Her abduction remained a mystery.

"What about boyfriends? Does she date much?" Keeley asked, hoping the driver would shed some light on Dr. Scott's personal life.

"No, not in a while. She had been seeing this lawyer from the DA's office for a couple of months. I drove them once to a fundraiser," he revealed, with a disapproving tone to his voice.

Keeley quickly picked up her phone and found a picture of Clearmont. "Was this the guy?" she asked, holding it up for the driver to see.

Recognition flashed across the driver's face. "Yeah, that's the guy. I'll never forget him. He was a creep. On the way back from the fundraiser, he was all over her. He was drunk, and I swear he wanted to have sex with her in the backseat, with me watching. He kept eyeing me."

Anxious for more details, Vincente inquired, "How did Dr. Scott react to his advances?"

"Peggy was not happy. She kept telling him no, pushing his hands away when he tried to touch her breasts. But he wouldn't take no for an answer. He kept taunting her, saying things like, 'C'mon, don't be a prude.'"

Vincente arched an eyebrow and exchanged glances with Keeley. He probed further. "What did you do?"

Sounding angry, the driver replied, "I got pissed off when he wouldn't stop. I asked Peggy if she wanted me to pull over."

Keeley asked, "And how did she respond?"

The driver chuckled. "She slapped him hard across the face. Then she told me to take him home."

Vincente couldn't help but feel proud of Peggy. "What was Clearmont's reaction to her response?"

"He fucking lost it! He called her a bitch and threatened to have her arrested for assault. At the next stoplight, he jumped out of the car, slamming the door behind him. I asked Peggy if she was okay, and she told me she was fine. She actually apologized for his behavior and for making me uncomfortable. But I told her she deserved someone better. That guy was a complete asshole. I think she broke up with him the next day because her father contacted the office, warning us to be on the lookout for him."

"Did you ever see Clearmont again? Mr. Scott believes he may have been stalking Dr. Scott." Keeley probed.

"No, I never saw him again," the driver confirmed.

Keeley couldn't help but observe, "You seem to really like Dr. Scott."

"Sure, who wouldn't? She's gorgeous!"

Vincente immediately asked, "Did you ever consider asking her out?"

A self-deprecating chuckle escaped the driver. "Nah, man. She's way out of my league."

"We appreciate your cooperation, Mr. Simon," Keeley handed the driver her card. "If you think of anything else that could be helpful, please don't hesitate to contact us."

"My boss will email you the names and addresses of all the service's drivers," the driver added. "I just hope you find her soon. Peggy doesn't deserve this."

Escorting the driver out of the interrogation room, Vincente promised, his voice filled with determination, "We'll do everything we can to bring her back safely."

Vincente mind raced with new leads and unanswered questions, as he and Keeley walked back to their desks in the busy squad room.

"Well, Tony, what do you think?"

Vincente leaned back in his chair, deep in thought. "I don't believe he had anything to do with it, but let's dig a little deeper into his background, just to be thorough."

Nodding in agreement, Keeley reached for her computer, ready to start a background check on the driver.

Chapter 19

Saturday, June 18

E arly on Saturday morning, Keeley arrived in an unmarked police car to pick up Vincente. Their mission: to search Dr. Peggy Scott's penthouse, hoping to uncover some clue to her abduction.

"Maybe we will find something in her penthouse." Keeley expressed.

Vincente simply nodded, his weariness evident. The sleepless night weighed heavily on his mind; worry for Peggy consumed him.

The doorman granted them access to her luxurious penthouse. The sight that greeted them could have been straight out of the pages of "Architectural Digest." The open-concept design exuded elegance, with four bedrooms, three bathrooms, and an outdoor patio. Wide plank hardwood floors were in every room, while gas fireplaces added warmth to the living room, kitchen, and master bedroom. The expansive kitchen, painted in pristine white, had top-of-the-line black stainless-steel appliances and gleaming white quartz countertops.

Vincente directed Keeley's attention to an oversized painting in the living room. "That's a Jackson Pollock. He was a renowned American painter and a prominent figure in the abstract expressionist movement. His 'drip technique,' where he poured or splashed household paint onto a horizontal surface, allowed him to view and paint his canvases from every angle. One of his paintings sold for nearly $200 million a few years ago."

Keeley couldn't help but marvel, "Wow! Must be nice to be rich! Did you see her trust fund?"

"Let's focus on searching her penthouse. I don't feel comfortable invading her privacy."

The detectives began their search in Dr. Scott's bedroom. The bedroom had a king-sized bed, a fireplace, dressers, and a vast walk-in closet brimming with designer dresses, shoes, and handbags. Keeley meticulously combed through the dressers and closet, while Vincente examined the nightstands and looked beneath the bed. They found nothing.

Keeley declared, "The bedroom is clean. No porn, no sex toys, no sexy lingerie, no drugs—Dr. Scott must be a nun!"

Moving on to another room, they discovered an office. Expensive bookcases covered the walls, showcasing an extensive collection of books on pathology, forensics, crime, and serial killers.

Keeley couldn't resist teasing, "Wow, Tony, this room must be your wet dream!"

"I've read most of these books." He said as he walked around and perused the shelves.

Eager to explore further, Keeley checked Dr. Scott's desktop computer. "The laptop we found in her office was clean according to the computer geeks," she explained. Turning on the desktop, she discovered that it was not password-protected. "No password to get in... and once again, nothing here. Her browser history is boring—no porn, nothing."

Despite their thorough search of Dr. Scott's entire penthouse, they found nothing. They were no closer to finding Dr. Scott after over 24 hours of investigating.

As they took the elevator down to the lobby, Keeley offered her theory, "She could have been grabbed by a stranger."

Vincente, considering their next move, suggested, "We need to pay a visit to that attorney in the DA's office she used to date. Maybe he knows something."

Keeley agreed, "We can go to the DA's office first thing Monday morning and talk to Clearmont."

As they climbed into the unmarked car, Vincente received a text from the captain. "The captain just texted me. He got all the videos from all of the cameras we requested. We can spend the rest of the weekend watching the videos."

Chapter 20

Sunday, June 19

S unday arrived, and while the two detectives reviewed the countless hours of videos to find a clue to Peggy's abduction, they took a short break and focused their attention on the flat-screen TV in the squad room. Captain Delacroix and Benjamin Scott were conducting a press conference addressing the abduction of Dr. Peggy Scott. The TV displayed a blown-up image of her employee ID badge, showing her face. Delacroix played the video of Dr. Scott being forcefully taken outside the morgue.

The captain shared the details of the abduction—time, date, and place—and asked anyone with information to call the provided phone number. He also implored the public to come forward if they recognized the masked abductor.

Introducing Benjamin Scott, the captain gave him the opportunity to plea for his daughter's safe return. In addition, Mr. Scott announced a reward of a million dollars for any information that would help find his daughter.

Keeley couldn't help but exclaim, "Oh my God! A reward of a million dollars? Do you know how many calls we are going to get? It is going to be a fucking nightmare!"

Vincente sighed, "Yes, Mr. Scott just made things worse. The captain is having uniforms screen the calls, so we can keep working the case."

Keeley hopefully offered, "Well, Tony, maybe somebody saw something."

Vincente, however, remained skeptical. "I doubt it. This guy is too smart."

Chapter 21

Monday, June 20

O n a gloomy Monday morning, rain fell from the sky and wind whipped through the streets, Detectives Vincente and Keeley drove to the county courthouse in an unmarked police car. Keeley took the wheel, her focus unwavering. Their destination: the DA's office. As they drove, Keeley couldn't help but share some background on Montgomery Clearmont. " Montgomery Clearmont -- old money, big society name. He has a reputation as being a player – he likes the ladies." Keeley smirked. "He was voted one of the city's most eligible bachelors. He is in his thirties. He graduated from Harvard Law School and works in the DA's office."

"Yes, and his family fortune is dwindling – the money is almost gone." Vincente added.

Upon arrival at their destination, Keeley parked the car in front of the courthouse building. The relentless rain pelted them as they dashed from their vehicle to the revolving door in front of the old building. Once inside, they displayed their badges and asked about Clearmont's whereabouts. A secretary pointed them to his office—a tiny space with a nice view of downtown Chicago. Behind the desk sat Clearmont, engrossed in his laptop. He looked up, his annoyance evident as the two detectives dripped rainwater on his carpet.

Vincente thought Clearmont looked like the quintessential all-American boy next door. With his blond hair, piercing blue eyes, and movie star good looks, he exuded an air of sophistication. His fingernails looked freshly manicured, and he wore an expensive designer suit. His diplomas from Ivy League institutions were proudly displayed on the wall behind him, along with pictures of himself shaking hands with influential people that were strategically placed on his desk and bookshelves.

Keeley began the interview, stating, "Mr. Clearmont, we are Detectives—"

"I know who you are," Clearmont interjected, his annoyance obvious. "What can I do for you?"

Taking a seat in one of the chairs opposite Clearmont's desk, Keeley politely smiled. Meanwhile, Vincente wandered around the office, studying the displayed diplomas and pictures, and perusing the books on the bookshelf. He dramatically reached out to touch one of the volumes, drawing a reproachful scoff from Clearmont.

"Oh, sorry," Vincente muttered, retracting his hand and joining Keeley in the other chair across from Clearmont's desk.

Keeley continued, "I'm not sure if you've heard, but Dr. Peggy Scott, your ex-girlfriend, was abducted last Thursday night." She paused, observing Clearmont's reaction, but there was none. "We need to ask you some questions."

Keeley activated the recording app on her cellphone and placed it on Clearmont's desk, to capture every word. Clearmont sighed and rolled his eyes.

Vincente deliberately slapped his heavy leather notebook down on Clearmont's desk. A few framed photographs fell over. Not bothering to hide his anger, Clearmont frowned and righted the pictures.

"I heard—such a shame. I hope she is okay," Clearmont replied, his tone carefully composed.

"How long were the two of you dating?" Keeley asked.

"Hmm." Clearmont threaded his hands together on the desk. "We dated for a couple of months, then we broke up. That was over six months ago."

Keeley pressed further, "When was the last time you saw her?"

Clearmont hesitated for a moment before responding, "I don't know. A couple of months ago? I saw her in the courthouse. She was testifying for a case."

"We've heard that you were not happy with the breakup." Keeley stated.

Clearmont retorted, a hint of defensiveness creeping into his voice. "I don't know who you've been talking to, but the breakup was mutual."

"We heard she dumped your ass!" Keeley exclaimed hoping to provide the condescending Assistant District Attorney.

Clearmont snapped, "That is really none of your business."

Vincente, unable to contain his frustration and anger any longer, rose from his seat. His imposing 6'4" figure loomed over Clearmont as he shouted at him, "Listen. A woman is missing! You need to cooperate with us now! We can either do this here in your office, or we can haul your arrogant ass down to the station to answer our questions!"

Clearmont let out an exasperated sigh, he relented, "Fine. I asked her to move in with me. She said no. We broke up. Her loss, not mine."

"It sounds like you were pretty serious about her." Keeley knew Clearmont was gaslighting them about his relationship with Dr. Scott.

Clearmont's voice swelled with frustration. "I could have given her the world! I am going to be Governor someday. She could have been my first lady. But she wasn't interested—she would rather carve up dead bodies all day!"

Keeley pressed on. "You sound pretty angry. Where were you last Thursday night?"

"What? You think I had anything to do with it? That's crazy!" He threw his hands up in the air, attempting to dismiss the question.

"We heard you were obsessed with her. You were stalking her after the 'breakup.'" Keeley lied to provoke a reaction from Clearmont.

"I never stalked Peggy. That is a lie! I don't know who you've been talking to, but let me tell you, detectives, I was not obsessed with her!" Frustrated, Clearmont retrieved a sheet of paper from his desk and began writing. "I was with this woman all night—you can call and ask her."

Keeley snatched the paper after Clearmont was finished writing and responded, "Oh, we will."

Vincente remarked dryly, "You sound pretty obsessed to me."

Leaning forward with both hands planted firmly on the desk, Vincente leaned into Clearmont's personal space. But Clearmont ignored him, refusing to acknowledge the detective's dominance.

Clearmont smirked as he remarked, "Well, she is a beautiful woman. A babe. You know, big tits, smokin' hot bod, great ass—but she's frigid. She doesn't perform in the bedroom. A prude. No blow jobs, no anal. She doesn't know anything about sex or pleasing a man!"

"You know, I have never seen a man with such small hands before!" Keeley said as she looked at Clearmont's hands. "You know what they say, small hands small di.."

Interrupting, Vincente shouted, "Do you know what I think? You wanted a trophy wife! Someone to finance your political career! How did it feel for a successful Ivy League graduate, from a high society family, being dumped by the daughter of a newly rich tech billionaire? You dated her for the money! Your family fortune has dried up, and all you have left is the family name! Did you promise her the world in exchange for her marrying you? She has the trust fund, and you have the family name. You never cared about her! That's why you couldn't please her in bed!"

Clearmont abruptly stood up, his voice seething with rage. "Thank God for lubricated condoms because she was a dry, dead cunt!"

The tension in the attorney's office was palpable.

Keeley couldn't contain her sarcasm, blurting out, "You were voted one of the City's most eligible bachelors? I bet that election was rigged!"

Vincente's voice boomed with indignation, "Pawing at her, trying to impress her driver with your sexual prowess! Or did you just want him to watch? Maybe that's a turn-on for you, having a man watch you fuck!"

"She loved it! She came on to me!" Clearmont shot back.

"That's not what I heard! I heard the driver offered to pull over just to pull you off of her!" Vincente exclaimed!

"I was glad to be rid of that cold bitch," Clearmont spat.

Keeley interjected sarcastically, "I bet she was sorry to see you go!"

Vincente had reached his breaking point. He lunged across the desk, seizing Clearmont by the lapels of his expensive three-piece suit. "Listen, asshole, a woman is missing! You need to show some respect!"

Clearmont's eyes widened with fear.

Needing to diffuse the escalating situation, Keeley grabbed Vincente by the arm, pulling him away from Clearmont.

"We'll be in touch. Don't leave town." Keeley warned.

The rain had finally stopped as Vincente and Keeley returned to their unmarked police car, the anger still raging within Vincente. As Keeley started the engine, she voiced her thoughts, "I think Mr. Scott may have a point. I suspect Clearmont in the kidnapping. He's still angry over her dumping him."

Vincente shook his head, disagreeing. "No, he may be a misogynist asshole, but he's not involved. We need to verify his alibi for last Thursday night, call the person he claims to have been with."

"Yeah, I'll call his alibi. What a jerk!"

Sadness tugged at Vincente's heart. It bothered him that Peggy had been involved with someone like Clearmont.

Having texted Mac earlier, Keeley stated, "Tony, I texted Mac, and she can meet with us in half an hour. Let's head back to Police Plaza."

***

The detectives entered Mac's office, finding the Chief Medical Examiner seated behind her desk. Keeley settled into one of the chairs, facing Mac, while Vincente remained standing.

"Human Resources has compiled a list of names and addresses of current and former employees who worked in the morgue. This is truly awful. Poor Peggy. I hope she is alright." Mac said with tears in her eyes.

"Can you think of anything, no matter how insignificant, that happened before she was abducted?" Keeley asked.

"No, I've wracked my brains, but nothing comes to mind."

Vincente probed further, remembering Peggy's previous shift. "What about when she worked the graveyard shift? She did overnights for about six months when she was newly hired, right?"

Mac sighed, "Yes, but I wasn't there during those hours. Most of the time, she was alone or with a couple of autopsy techs."

"Mac, tell us about the techs she worked with." Vincente instructed.

"Well, there was an older man named Ray, but he retired five months ago and moved to Florida. I highly doubt he had anything to do with her abduction. The other tech was Eric Troy. He's currently on family medical leave, taking care of his mother who has Alzheimer's. He went on leave over a month ago. He and Peggy were friends; he was one of my best techs. Always on time, never called in sick, helpful, friendly, and extremely professional. A great guy. He used to bring coffee for everyone."

Keeley interjected, "Ted Bundy was a 'nice' guy too."

Mac was quick to defend her employees. "Come on, detectives. None of my people were involved!"

Vincente paced around the office, his mind racing. "Well, it had to be someone Dr. Scott knew. The perpetrator was aware of her schedule, knew when she would leave last Thursday night and which door she would exit."

"Maybe it was one of your people. A cop." Mac stated.

"Why do you think that?" Vincente asked.

"Well, we've always had issues with a pair of homicide detectives from the 3rd precinct – Reyes and Walters. They like sexually harassing the women here."

Keeley chimed in, "Yeah, I've heard Reyes is a pig. Did they bother Dr. Scott?"

"Well, Reyes slapped Peggy on the behind during an autopsy."

Vincente's anger flared, his voice seething with indignation. "What! Did she report it?"

"No. Peggy was new, and she was afraid to cause trouble. Instead, she avoided Reyes and Walters. I urged her to fill out an incident report, but she refused, insisting that she could handle them. In fact, she didn't even inform me about the incident – Eric did."

Vincente became suspicious about the tech and inquired, "That's interesting. When Eric mentioned it, did he sound jealous or angry?"

"No, he simply mentioned it casually when I saw him one morning in the hallway. He said something along the lines of 'Reyes and Walters are at it again, slapping Dr. Scott on the behind.' Reyes and Walters are known for hitting on and sexually harassing women. All the women in my department steer clear of them. Sexual harassment from macho male cops is an unfortunate part of the job if you're a woman."

Expressing their gratitude, the detectives thanked Mac for her assistance. In parting, Mac said, "Let me know if there's anything else I can do to help. I pray to God that you find her."

As the Detectives walked into the hallway outside Mac's office, Vincente stated, "We need to find out everything we can on Walters, Reyes, and that very helpful lab tech before we pay them a visit.

Chapter 22

Tuesday, June 21

On an early Tuesday morning, the sun cast a harsh glow on Detective Vincente as he stepped into the coffee shop, the same place where he and Peggy had shared a cup of coffee just a couple of weeks ago. Determined to gather more information, he wanted to interview the young barista who had shown a keen interest in Peggy when she walked into the coffee shop.

Spotting the barista behind the counter, Vincente flashed his detective's badge, catching the young man's attention. The barista responded politely, "Yes, officer, may I help you?"

Vincente got straight to the point, his tone serious, "Did you hear about the abduction of Dr. Peggy Scott?"

"Yes, I did. It's absolutely horrifying. The women who work here are scared to walk the streets at night."

"Can you recall your whereabouts last Thursday at 11:00 p.m.?"

"Well, the coffee shop closes at 9:00 p.m. on weekdays. After closing, I went straight home. I spent the entire night there with my girlfriend. I can give you her name and phone number."

Vincente nodded appreciatively. "Thank you for your cooperation. Have you ever noticed anyone lurking around, perhaps observing Dr. Scott?"

"No, most of our customers are police officers. To be honest, we're usually quite busy when she comes in. I've never seen anyone watching her."

"Alright, could you please provide me with a list of the current employees and their contact information? We need to speak with anyone who might have had contact with her before the abduction."

"Of course. There are only a few of us working here. I'm the only male employee, and the rest are women. I'll provide you with a complete list."

Vincente expressed his gratitude as the barista handed him the employee list, along with the name and number of his girlfriend. Exiting the coffee shop, Vincente couldn't help but feel disappointed. Another dead end, leaving him with more questions than answers.

***

Later That Day...

Detectives Vincente and Keeley found themselves seated at their desks, immersed in not only Dr. Peggy Scott's abduction, but the murder of Cassie Greaves as well. Vincente's mind was consumed with thoughts as he carefully reviewed the notes he had taken on both cases. Meanwhile, Keeley focused her attention on her laptop, reading the recently received employee file of Eric Troy, the autopsy technician who had worked closely with Dr. Scott.

"Eric Troy was an exemplary employee!" Keeley smirked. "Almost too good to be true."

"Let's pay him a visit."

Quickly jotting down Troy's address, the detectives took the Eisenhower expressway to the suburban home of Eric Troy, who was currently on medical leave, caring for his ailing mother. Traffic was so congested it took them over an hour to reach Troy's house.

Vincente's impatience grew with each passing minute. The absence of any ransom demands or substantial leads following the press conference and offering of a reward deepened his concern for Peggy's life. Fears of her being held captive by a sociopath or, worse yet, already dead, her body tossed in a ditch, gnawed at his mind. He started to think about the haunting similarities between Cassie Greaves' homicide and Dr. Scott's abduction, Vincente started to think that the two cases were somehow related.

Vincente was worried that Peggy was being held captive by some sociopath, or worse, dead. Then Vincente started to think about the Cassie Greaves homicide. Greaves's abduction and Dr. Scott's abduction were eerily similar.

Finally arriving at Troy's mother's house using the unmarked car's, the detectives stood before a tiny, old-fashioned brick bungalow. The house, built in the 1950s, was almost identical to the surrounding houses. As Vincente and Keeley walked up the front steps, they couldn't help but notice an elderly neighbor peering curiously from her window, watching their every move. Keeley pressed Troy's doorbell twice.

The door swung open, revealing Eric Troy, dressed in green scrubs, wearing a warm smile. The morgue attendant was pleased that the police had finally come to question him about Dr. Peggy Scott.

Eric thought, this is going to be fun!

He was impressed that the two best detectives, Vincente and Keeley, were assigned to the case, even though Eric thought Keeley was a snarky bitch, and Vincente was a big arrogant asshole.

"I am Detective Keeley, and this is my partner, Detective Vincente. We would like to speak with you regarding Dr. Peggy Scott," Keeley introduced herself as she entered Eric Troy's residence.

"I know who you are. Please come in." Troy, a tall and thin man, welcomed them inside. Despite being single, in his forties, and needing to live with his ailing mother, he seemed happy with his life.

As they stepped into the living room, an elderly woman sat in a lift chair, snoring while the television blared loudly. She was covered in a homemade, crocheted afghan. The house reeked of urine.

"Do you mind if I talk this in the kitchen? My Mom isn't well – Alzheimer's – and she likes to watch TV in the living room." Eric said as he escorted them to a small kitchen. "May I get you some coffee? Poor Peggy, I heard about it on the news. What a shame, such a nice young woman."

The kitchen, much like the rest of the house, reflected a bygone era with its outdated decor. Yellowed pink floral wallpaper covered the walls, and a vintage 1960s kitchen table stood in the center of the small kitchen. The white appliances were ancient and dirty.

Seated around the Formica kitchen table, the detectives prepared for the interview. Keeley placed her cellphone on the table, ready to record their discussion. After Vincente sat in the chair next to Troy, he abruptly scooted his chair right next to him.

"You went on family medical leave six months ago?" Keeley asked.

"Yes, my mother can't be left alone. She is in the final stage of Alzheimer's. I can't afford a full-time caretaker, so I took leave of absence."

"That's very nice of you. So, what was your relationship with Dr. Scott?" Keeley asked as she smiled at Troy.

Troy hesitated briefly, then responded, a smile on his face, "We were friends, or still are, I suppose. She's one of the nicest pathology residents in the department. I assisted her during autopsies, and she always treated me as an equal. We used to buy each other coffee. Sometimes we took breaks together. I really don't know that much about her."

Vincente leaned in closer, his voice taking on a more probing tone, "She's a beautiful woman. Did you ever have romantic feelings for her?"

"No." But I fantasized about having sex with her all the time, thought Troy. "If I recall, she was dating an attorney in the DA's office."

Keeley asked, "Where were you on Thursday night, June 16th?"

Vincente, restless and fidgety stood up and wandered around the kitchen. Troy looked nervous as Vincente started opening cabinets and looking in drawers.

"Don't mind him. He can't sit still. He was diagnosed with ADHD as a child." Explained Keeley.

"I was here all night, taking care of my mother. I distinctly remember the TV remote stopped working around 9:30 or 10. I went next door to our neighbor, Mrs. Krantz, an elderly lady, and borrowed batteries from her. I am sure she will corroborate my story if you ask her."

Cops are such idiots, she could be bound and naked in my basement right now and you wouldn't even know it, thought Troy.

"Thank you. We will definitely reach out to Mrs. Krantz," Keeley replied. "Mr. Troy is there anything else you can tell us about Dr. Scott that might help us find her? We are kind of at a loss as to what happened to her. Did she ever talk about having any enemies? Maybe someone stalking her?"

"Well," Troy sighed, "there were a couple of cops who liked to hit on her. In fact, sometimes I would hang around when they came into the morgue, so they wouldn't harass her."

"What happened?" Vincente walked over to Troy.

"Detective Reyes and Detective Walters from the 3rd precinct came in to look at a body – a homicide victim. While Dr. Scott was showing them the body, Reyes slapped her on the behind."

"How did Dr. Scott react?" Vincente asked, settling back into the chair next to Troy.

"She ignored him. I came over and asked if she needed any help and they left. I told her to report them, but she didn't want to. She was new and didn't want to cause any problems."

"So, you saw yourself as her protector?" asked Vincente.

"No, but you know how cops can be. They think they can get away with anything. They were jerks, and I felt sorry for her having to deal with them," Troy replied, his disdain evident.

"You know what is interesting Eric? We pulled video from cameras from stores and streets surrounding the morgue. Guess what? You are in several of the videos." Keeley explained.

"Well, I did work there. So, I would probably show up on video."

"No, this was after you went on medical leave. In fact, you were recorded several times in the area, including recently. There is video of you on walking down the street a week before Dr. Scott was abducted." Keeley revealed as crossed her arms over her chest.

Troy offered an explanation, "I still visit the area occasionally. I refill my mother's prescriptions at the pharmacy on the corner, a block away from the morgue."

Vincente leaned in closer to Troy.

Troy continued, "I used to have the prescriptions filled while I worked there, and I haven't transferred them to this location. I enjoy driving to the city, especially when the hospice aide comes twice a week to bathe my mother. It gives me a change of scenery and helps me relax. So, I'm sure if you check the pharmacy, they'll have video footage of me picking up her prescriptions."

Cops are such fools - did they really think I wouldn't have an explanation for being filmed by those video cameras, thought Troy.

Vincente's gut gave him a bad feeling about Troy. He had an answer for everything. He even had an alibi for the night Peggy was abducted.

Keeley thanked Troy for his cooperation. "We appreciate your assistance, Mr. Troy. If there's anything else you remember, please don't hesitate to reach out to us." Keeley handed Troy one of her business cards. "Thank you for your time. We'll be in touch."

"No problem. I'm willing to do whatever it takes to help find Dr. Scott," Troy assured the detectives.

After leaving Troy's residence, the detectives made a detour to speak with the nosy elderly neighbor, Mrs. Krantz. She corroborated Troy's alibi.

Back inside their unmarked police car, Keeley took the driver's seat, turning to face Vincente.

"Well, it looks like we can cross him off our list. He has a solid alibi," Keeley concluded.

"Maybe. But there's just something about him that doesn't sit right with me," Vincente voiced his unease.

"Yeah, he's a loser, but that doesn't make him a kidnapper. I'm starting to think we may be looking in the wrong direction, that it might be a stranger."

As drove back to the SIU in the unmarked police car, the detectives contemplated everything they had learned so far about Dr. Peggy Scott's life.

"Keeley, we need to talk to those detectives from the 3rd precinct." Vincente couldn't shake off the feeling that they were missing something crucial. The case continued to elude him, and the urgency to locate Peggy intensified.

Chapter 23

Tuesday, June 21 (Late at Night)

B eing held captive, Dr. Peggy Scott lost all sense of time and reality. She didn't know
if it was day or night. Her body ached, her wrists and ankles sore from the restraints
that bound her. Every movement was a struggle against the stiffness that had settled into
her limbs. Disoriented and weak, she existed in a perpetual fog, wearing only her skimpy
bra and panties.

Always silent, her captive continued his haunting routine of watching her. He never
spoke, never turned on a light. He was always in the shadows, concealed from her view.
Sometimes he would free her ankles and lead her to the small bathroom in the corner so
she could relieve herself.

The water he gave her to drink always tasted bitter. Peggy suspected he laced it with
drugs, further clouding her mind. Occasionally, he would hold a granola bar to her mouth
so she could eat because he would not remove the zip-ties that bound her wrists. Isolated
and vulnerable, she felt the weight of despair settle upon her. Gagged and unable to speak,
communication with her captor was impossible. He only removed the gag when she ate
or drank. Dirty, cold, and hopeless Peggy believed she was going to die.

Often the man would sit on the bed next to Peggy. He would lean over and stroke her
hair. His fingers would graze her face, leaving behind a trail of discomfort and revulsion.

When she felt his hot, heavy breath on her face, she would try and pull away from him, but she couldn't move. At times, he would lay down behind her, gripping a handful of her hair and roughly pulling it, making her whimper in pain. She hated the feeling of his grotesque presence as he leaned in close and moaned in her ear. He would laugh when she cried, enjoying her anguish. Then, with a sudden surge of aggression, he would sit up and slap her face and breasts over and over again, the sound of each strike an echo of his sadistic pleasure. And then, in the depths of his depravity, he would sink his teeth into her breasts and buttocks, biting her savagely but not breaking her skin.

Tonight, the sound of the man unzipping his pants pierced the air, causing Peggy to wince in fear. The room filled with the obscene sounds of the man masturbating, his panting and moaning growing louder and louder. Then she felt his ejaculation splatter across her chest. Peggy trembled uncontrollably as she had a full-blown panic-attack. She was so distraught she didn't even hear the door close as he left the room.

Chapter 24

Wednesday, June 22

A t almost 8:00 p.m., Vincente and Keeley were sitting in the captain's office. Delacroix couldn't hide his displeasure as he looked at the detectives. He popped a Tums in his mouth.

"Any developments with the Scott case? The police commissioner and Mr. Scott call me every fucking day!" The captain yelled.

Vincente spoke up, "I think Dr. Scott was abducted by somebody that knew her – somebody that came into contact with her here at work."

The captain scoffed at Vincente's theory, and asked, "Didn't Mac give you Dr. Scott's work schedule a week ago?"

"The computer techs are still working on a list of everyone she came in contact with during her shifts, since she started working for the coroner's office." Keeley answered.

"Well then find out what is taking them so God damn long! The police commissioner and Mr. Scott call me every fucking day! C'mon detectives, we need to make some progress. She has been missing for a week now!"

Keeley offered, "I'll head over there and pressure the techs. Once we have the list, we can conduct background checks and interviews, see if anything pops."

"I will assign other officers to conduct those background checks. You two focus on the obvious suspects—the driver, the lab technician, the ex-boyfriend-"

Vincente interrupted, "I have a gut feeling about Eric Troy, the morgue technician."

"Tony, he has an alibi." Keeley reminded him.

"Keeley and I are still looking at the video feeds from all the cameras. First thing tomorrow morning we are going to talk to two homicide detectives over at the 3rd precinct. Mac said they were sexually harassing Dr. Scott and other female employees."

"I don't believe a cop abducted her!" Delacroix exclaimed.

Keeley interjected, "Well she was abducted right outside the Police Plaza building."

"We're running out of time. Find something!" Delacroix demanded.

Chapter 25

Thursday, June 23

On Thursday morning, Detective Vincente and Detective Keeley drove over to the 3rd precinct in their unmarked police car, with Keeley behind the wheel. Vincente put on his sunglasses because the early morning sun was so bright, his eyes felt like they were on fire. He still wasn't sleeping; he couldn't stop thinking about the similarities between Greave's murder and Peggy's abduction.

"Rumor has it that Reyes and Walters are on the take. They are also pigs. Female officers do not like to be around them." Keeley announced breaking the silence.

As they arrived at the 3rd precinct, Keeley parked the car in a "no parking" zone. Vincente removed his sunglasses, slipping them into his pocket before stepping out onto the busy sidewalk.

The 3rd precinct was a stark contrast to the professionalism of the SIU. The rundown building was in a rough neighborhood. Inside the 3rd precinct chaos reigned. Loud voices and heated arguments filled the air. Sex workers, pimps, drug dealers and petty criminals under arrest were screaming while being escorted away by uniformed police officers. There was a line of people waiting to talk to the desk sergeant. A drunk man was vomiting in a garbage can.

Keeley exclaimed, "What a shit show!"

Flashing their badges at the busy desk sergeant, Detectives Vincente and Keeley worked their way into the busy squad room where plain clothes detectives sat at desks. Keeley spotted Reyes and Walters right away, and she and Vincente approached them. Reyes, a short, stocky figure with receding hair and a boisterous demeanor, was watching porn on his laptop screen. Walters, on the other hand, looked tired, he was almost falling asleep at his desk.

As Reyes caught sight of Keeley, his voice erupted with sarcasm, "Ah, if it isn't Mulder and Scully!"

Reyes closed his laptop and put his feet up on his desk.

Keeley fired back, "Oh, if it isn't Dumb and Dumber!"

"Watch your mouth, Keeley!" Reyes yelled.

"Shut the Fuck up!" Keeley shouted.

Reyes, furious by the audacity of a woman challenging him, rose from his seat.

Before the tension could escalate, Vincente stepped directly in front of Reyes, towering over the short man Without uttering a single word, Vincente stared at Reyes his gaze conveying a silent warning.

"What the fuck do you want?" Reyes sneered at Keeley.

Vincente stepped closer, closing the distance between him and Reyes, their faces mere inches apart. Walters, not wanting to get involved in any confrontation, quietly remained seated.

Even though Reyes was anxious to confront Samantha Keeley, he was fearful about a confrontation with Vincente. Reyes had heard rumors about Vincente's temper, cops did not want to mess with Detective Anthony Vincente.

"What the fuck do I want? Here's what I fucking want! We're investigating the abduction of Dr. Peggy Scott from the ME's office," Vincente shouted into Reyes' now red face.

Reyes scoffed, failing to grasp the gravity of the situation. "So, what the fuck does that have to do with us?"

Keeley retorted, "We've heard reports that you assaulted her, slapped her on the ass in the morgue."

Reyes laughed. "Oh, please! That chick parades around in her tight little scrubs, purposely bending over and shoving her ass in our faces. She was asking for it. She fucking enjoyed it!"

The squad room erupted with raucous laughter, at Reyes sexist remarks.

Vincente's voice boomed through the squad room "That is sexual assault, asshole! Sexual assault is an act in which one intentionally sexually touches another person without that person's consent."

The weight of Vincente's words hung in the air; the squad room went quiet.

Keeley pressed on. "Tell us, where were you and Walters on Thursday night, June 16, from 11:00 p.m. to 12:00 a.m.?"

Reyes looked at Walters, who appeared bored. Reyes avoided the question, and asked, "What? You two clowns think we had something to do with that missing cunt? We were on duty. Check the log. We responded to a domestic dispute call! We have alibis, geniuses!"

Vincente's rage reached its boiling point, he grabbed Reyes by the lapels of his cheap, ill-fitting suit.

Keeley firmly grasped Vincente's arm and said, "He is not worth a suspension."

Keeley kept hold of Vincente's forearm and guided him away from Reyes. The squad room erupted once again, their laughter and catcalls mocking the SIU detectives. Outside the 3rd precinct, Vincente's frustration and worry weighed heavily on his shoulders. His thoughts were consumed by Dr. Scott, hoping for a breakthrough or lead in the puzzling case.

Chapter 26

Thursday, June 23 (Later that Night)

The sound and feel of zip ties being cut awoke Dr. Peggy Scott, as the man freed her ankles. However, her wrists remained bound and the gag still in place, as he roughly led her to the bathroom.

As Peggy entered the small, dimly lit bathroom, she caught sight of her disheveled appearance in the filthy mirror. Bruises marked her face and body, her hair a tangled mess. She fought back tears, trying to summon strength.

After using the bathroom, Peggy glanced up at the mirror one last time. Before she could react, the man stormed into the bathroom, forcefully dragging her back to the bed. The bathroom door remained open and the faint light cast an eerie glow, revealing the man, now completely naked, standing above her. His face remained a mystery, shrouded in darkness. Peggy was so consumed by fear, she couldn't move.

This time, the man secured zip ties around each of Peggy's ankles, attaching them to the wooden bedposts at the foot of the bed. He then freed Peggy's wrists, only to swiftly bind each of them to the bedposts at the head of the bed. Peggy struggles against her restraints, were met with a harsh slap across her face. Helplessly tied spread-eagle to the bed, she tried to scream, but the gag muffled her cries.

The chilling sound of the man's laughter echoed throughout the small room.

This visit, he did not give her food or water.

Peggy saw the light reflect off something held in the man's hand. A knife. Peggy whimpered. He climbed on the bed and sliced off her bra, so she naked from the waist up.

The man climbed between her spread legs and began squeezing her naked breasts with his rough hands. He painfully marked her breasts and nipples with bite marks, as Peggy thrashed her head from side to side, the only part of her bound body she could move. His heavy breaths and moans morphed into animal grunts. She felt his naked erection brush her stomach as he mauled her breasts. She knew her time was running out and hoped the man would lose patience and just kill her. Peggy tried to block his assault from her mind – she pretended she was at the morgue performing a complex autopsy.

After she felt his hot semen coat her naked breasts, she felt her panties being cut off with the knife. Now she was completely naked. The room seemed darker as she felt the man shift his body between her legs. As she felt his hot breath on her vagina, the man went completely still. She heard a quiet sob escape from him.

"What have you done?" He screamed at her as he slapped her across the face.

Dr. Peggy Scott heard the man's muffled laughter as he kept slapping her face. The sound was sinister. She tried to scream.

"Shut up!" The killer screamed. "How could you do this to yourself, you bitch, you cunt!"

When the man roughly yanked the gag out of her mouth she gasped.

"When will it grow back?" The man cloaked in darkness asked.

"Why are you doing this?" Peggy asked and her voice broke.

"Shut up." He slapped her again and asked, "When is it coming back?"

Peggy begged, "Please stop. I don't know what you're talking about!"

"Your cunt doesn't have any hair! It is bald! When is the hair growing back?"

To her horror, Peggy realized that this man was the serial killer that mutilated and murdered Cassie Greaves. The killer with a pubic hair fetish.

"It won't grow back. I had it lasered off." She whispered.

"Why?" He moaned.

The man shoved the gag back in her mouth.

As his fury escalated his vicious slaps to Peggy's face and breasts became heavy punches. Soon his hands were around her neck, and he was squeezing the breath out of her.

"You stupid bitch! You cunt! You ruined yourself!" He screamed as his hands tightened around her neck.

Peggy passed out as he lost control and tried to strangle her.

He pulled his hands away before he could kill her. He didn't want his muse dead, yet. He grabbed his clothes and walked out the basement door which had been left open. *Good*, he thought, *I want to be alone.*

That stupid bitch! That stupid cunt! How could she disfigure herself like that? How could she main herself like that. She has a bald, naked cunt – not even a landing strip. She lasered her hair all off! He thought.

The killer went to his bedroom to look at the wall of photos he had discreetly taken of Dr. Scott. His uncontrollable rage at the state of her body made him punch a wall until his knuckles were bloody.

The killer recalled what his abusive Father had always said about women, "If you turn them upside down, they all look the same."

The killer's sick father believed all women were whores. His father liked to go for walks late at night and peep in windows of unsuspecting young women. He kept a hidden stack of porn showing women having sex with animals. While the killer was growing up, his drunken father spent nights and weekends beating up his wife and son. The killer finally found relief and happiness when his abusive father and pathetic mother died in an accidental house fire. The killer beamed with pride as he recalled how he made the fire look like an accident.

"She has ruined everything!" The killer screamed.

I should burn the bitch! Dump acid on her. Shove a fiery hot poker up her bald cunt!

The killer hated Dr. Peggy Scott now. He envisioned flaying her skin off. Ripping her blonde hair out or scalping her. He had craved pulling her lovely pubic hairs out one by one and watching her wince. Now, because she had mutilated her body, he didn't know how to satisfy the dark cravings that haunted him.

He paced back and forth through his small house as a ghoulish idea formed in his mind. Now he needed to prepare for a hunt.

Chapter 27

Saturday, June 25

In the dark basement, the killer returned to his captive, Dr. Peggy Scott. With a swift motion, he cut off the zip ties that bound her body spread-eagle to the bed. Weary and weak, Peggy was led to the bathroom by her captor who stood guard at the doorway. The cold tiles chilled her bare feet as she relieved herself under his watchful gaze. Once finished, she was forcefully taken back to the bed, her gag removed. The killer offered her bitter water, forcing her to drink, followed by a few bites of a granola bar.

As the drugs took hold, Peggy felt a chilling coldness seeping into her bones. She tried to voice her discomfort, but the gag was quickly replaced, keeping her silent. Helplessly, she was once again restrained, naked and vulnerable, with her wrists and ankles secured to the bedposts. A thin blanket was thrown over her, providing some protection from the cold.

In the confines of the cold basement, Peggy's thoughts drifted to her life. Memories of her father, the faces of her friends, and the image of Detective Anthony Vincente lingered in her mind. She knew deep down that she would never see any of them again. Overwhelmed by despair, she fell into a restless sleep, tears staining her cheeks.

Chapter 28

Monday, June 27

In the captain's office, Detectives Keeley and Vincente stood before Captain Delacroix, who wore a look of frustration and impatience.

"What is going on with the Scott abduction? Any leads? It has been nearly two weeks!" Delacroix voiced his concern.

Keeley responded, recounting their limited progress with the case, "We've interviewed her ex-boyfriend and coworkers. Everyone seems to have an alibi. We also followed up with the homicide detectives from the 3rd precinct who had shown interest in her. They, too, have alibis."

Delacroix sighed, "Ben Scott is convinced that attorney from the DA's office something to do with his daughter's abduction. He's pushing for an arrest!"

Vincente stated firmly, "It wasn't him. I still suspect that morgue tech on leave – Troy – but he has an alibi.

Hoping that Vincente would forget about Eric Troy, Keeley stated, "He has an ironclad alibi – he didn't do it, Tony."

Vincente, however, was persistent in his hunch. "I'd like to keep an eye on Troy. Something doesn't sit right with me. We sent some uniforms to the pharmacy to pull receipts and videos of his visits. The pharmacy is cooperating."

Delacroix responded, "That's good because no judge would give me a fucking warrant based on your bad feeling about Troy. I am not going to put a tail on him at this point – there just isn't enough Vincente – I mean just because he is a loser who lives with his mom doesn't make him a killer!"

"I am starting to think it was a random stranger." Keeley interjected.

"A stranger wouldn't have known Dr. Scott's work schedule. They wouldn't have abducted her right behind police plaza either." Vincente argued.

Vincente's bloodshot eyes met the captain's gaze as he rubbed his forehead, the weight of the investigation bearing down on him.

The captain instructed, "Well keep digging, maybe something will shake loose. I have to say, detectives, it is not looking good for Dr. Scott. My guess is that she is probably already dead."

Just as the weight of the situation settled upon them, the captain's phone rang. He answered the call, and as he listened, a troubled expression washed over his face. The call was brief, and Delacroix's expression turned grim. The detectives exchanged concerned glances, sensing that the news was not good. The room fell into an uneasy silence.

"They found a body – the next state over -- a young blonde woman that matches the description of Dr. Scott." The captain announced, delivering the news with a heavy heart.

"Oh my God!" whispered Keeley, her eyes locked with Vincente's.

Vincente remained silent, his heart breaking at the possibility that Peggy was dead.

The captain swiftly dialed another number and issued the command, "Go! Take the police chopper!"

Without hesitation, Detectives Keeley and Vincente bypassed the elevator and took the stairs, racing up to the rooftop of the Police Plaza building. The detectives boarded the Police Plaza Helicopter. As they put on their headsets, Keeley couldn't help but express her unease, "I hate helicopters."

The Helicopter soared through the unseasonably cool summer air.

Vincente appeared visibly agitated, his emotions on edge. He silently prayed that the body did not belong to Peggy. The captain's words echoed in his mind, "They found a body – a young blonde woman that matches the description of Dr. Scott." The thought of Peggy being dead was unbearable.

The helicopter touched down on a deserted highway, its busy lanes redirected by police. A uniformed officer greeted them, and together they walked toward a remote wooded area. Crime scene tape cordoned off the surroundings. The body had been abandoned in a shallow ravine beside the highway.

Vincente and Keeley were escorted beyond the crime scene tape, donning white paper coveralls and surgical gloves. The scene was already chaotic with crime scene technicians, who had erected a tent to protect any evidence. The killer had made no effort to conceal the victim's nude body, leaving it exposed, face-down in the dirt. Observing the hasty manner in which the body had been dumped, Vincente guessed it had likely been thrown from a vehicle and rolled down into the ravine.

Approaching the scene, the possibility of the body belonging to Dr. Peggy Scott, missing for nearly two weeks, weighed heavily on the detectives' minds. A man with a jacket that said "Coroner" was kneeling over the body. Vincente froze in his steps when he saw the back of the deceased woman's head.

Her hair looks just like Peggy's. Vincente winced.

Keeley, noticing his unease, asked, "Are you okay?"

Vincente remained silent; his mind overwhelmed by a mix of emotions.

"Can you roll her over?" Vincente asked the county coroner, trying to keep his voice steady.

With utmost care, the elderly male coroner rolled the body over, revealing the lifeless face of the woman. A wave of relief washed over Vincente and Keeley – it was not Dr. Scott, but the hand marks on her neck, bruising, cuts, and bitemarks on her body were eerily similar to Cassie Greaves. Unlike this victim, Cassie Greaves had a clump of pubic hair missing, this victim's vagina had been mutilated. Detectives Vincente and Keeley had never seen a victim with this kind of mutilation, her labia had been cut away, leaving her vagina an open, bloody mess.

"Oh my God!" A nearby policeman exclaimed and then he gagged trying not to vomit.

"No vomiting on my crime scene!" The coroner ordered.

"It's not her. What have you got?" Vincente crouched near the lifeless body; his brow furrowed with deep concern. He tilted his head to the side, absorbing every disturbing detail, while the county coroner began his preliminary examination.

"Young woman, age approximately 18 to 25 years old," the coroner began, his voice somber. "Time of death within the last 24 hours. Asphyxiation by strangulation is the cause of death. No large stab wounds, although I see a small puncture wound the size of a needle on her neck. Her breasts and buttocks bear cuts, bruising and shallow bite marks. Evidence of genital bruising indicates sexual assault, although there are no obvious signs

of semen. As you can see, the outer set of skin folds around the opening of the vagina
– the labia majora, which typically has pubic hair on the outer surface, has been
sliced away. The labia minora, the inner set of hairless skin folds around the opening
of the vagina are still intact. I will have a clearer picture once I examine her at the
morgue."

Keeley pressed for more information. "Did the crime scene techs find the missing
labia?"

"No," the coroner replied with shake of his head. "She was likely killed elsewhere
and dumped here. No identification, no clothing, nothing. I'll know more after I
perform the autopsy. Poor woman was brutalized before she died."

Vincente handed the coroner his card, urging him to keep them updated. "Let's
go, Keeley."

As they peeled off their surgical gloves and discarded their coveralls, the detectives
made their way back to the waiting chopper. Vincente was walking so quickly that
Keeley was having a hard time keeping up with him.

Keeley immediately called the captain. "The body is not Dr. Scott."

The captain's voice crackled through the phone on speaker, "That's good news-"

Vincente interrupted, "This woman was killed by the same killer that killed Cassie
Greaves."

"What?" Yelled Captain Delacroix. "Dr. Scott is missing and now we have a serial
killer? Fuck! Keep me informed."

Keeley's phone went dead.

The call abruptly ended. Vincente's mind racing with a troubling realization.

"Tony, tell me what you're thinking," she implored.

Vincente's words came out in a rush, his emotions driving his thoughts. "I believe
Dr. Scott was right. We're dealing with a serial killer. This woman, just like Cassie
Greaves, fell victim to the same murderer. Both were young, beautiful blondes,
abducted in a similar manner. Dr. Scott, a young, beautiful blonde herself, was also
taken. The three cases are definitely connected. I believe the man responsible for
Cassie Greaves and this woman's death is the one who abducted Dr. Scott."

Keeley's voice trembled with a mix of hope and concern. "Do you think Dr. Scott
could still be alive?"

Vincente remained silent. This was the third blonde woman that had met with foul
play. He didn't want to entertain the possibility that Peggy was dead. He refused to believe

that her naked body lay abandoned in a ditch. His thoughts fueled his determination to find her, and to bring her back alive.

Chapter 29

Tuesday, June 28

D etectives Keeley and Vincente were exhausted as they sat at their desks in the squad room. Vincente's face was unshaven mirroring the inner turmoil he felt. The answer eluded him, just out of reach, yet he knew it was there, taunting him. Dr. Scott's abduction held the key, a puzzle with missing pieces, a connection they had yet to uncover. It had to be someone she knew, someone who knew her. He also knew that the man who abducted Peggy had killed Cassie Greaves and the dead woman from yesterday. The thought of a connection between the three cases gnawed at Vincente, fueling his determination to find Peggy.

Their latest lead came from the coroner's report on the new victim, another life tragically snuffed out by the same deranged killer who had taken Cassie Greaves. The gruesome details painted a haunting picture: strangulation, rape, traces of ketamine, and a thorough cleansing with bleach. The evidence was clear; they were dealing with a sadistic predator who left no trace behind. A killer who could very well be holding Dr. Peggy Scott captive.

Vincente's commitment to finding Peggy consumed. He pushed himself to the limits, working day and night, fueled by the nagging sense that time was slipping through their fingers. His dedication left little room for rest, except for the occasional nap on the breakroom couch or short visits home for a shower and change of clothes. He was obsessed with the case and even had nightmares when he slept. One harrowing nightmare showed her partially eaten body, a sight that left him shaken and unable to go back to sleep. Visions of Peggy's lifeless body haunted him. He was driven by a desperate need to find her alive.

***

Late that Night...

The killer returned to the basement for his sadistic rituals. He released Peggy from the confines of the bedposts, allowing her to relieve herself in the bathroom. But her freedom was short-lived as he brought her back to the filthy bed, tightly securing her wrists and ankles with zip ties.

Lying beside her on the bed, the killer's hands roamed her vulnerable and naked body. Peggy felt a wave of revulsion at the touch of his hands. The feel of his savage strokes twisted her stomach in fear and disgust. Each excited breath he took was loud and filled the room with menace. And then came the sound that frightened her the most—his chilling laughter that pierced the silence. As he threw the blanket over her, he left the basement room, leaving Peggy trapped in darkness.

Chapter 30

Thursday, June 30

The conference room in the SIU is a professional and functional space that supports effective communication, collaboration, and decision-making among detectives and other law enforcement officials. It provides a private space for exchanging information, strategizing, and addressing critical matters pertaining to ongoing criminal cases.

The room is a spacious and well-lit room with a dated, large rectangular wood table positioned in the center. Surrounding the table are twelve mismatched upholstered chairs.

One end of the oblong room has a whiteboard mounted on a wall for presentations and to jot down important information during meetings. At one end of the room, there is a presentation area, with a large smart TV that can be connected to laptops or other devices for displaying slideshows, videos, or data.

Within the confines of the SIU conference room, Detective Vincente, Detective Keeley, and the captain met about the three cases Vincente believed were connected. The air in the conference was heavy with anticipation, as Vincente took the lead. Standing before the whiteboard covered with pictures, he started on a mission to connect the dots, to bridge the gap between Dr. Peggy Scott's abduction and the two unsolved murder cases.

Pointing to the photographs, Vincente touched each woman's face, two lives tragically murdered, and one held captive. His voice filled with determination as he outlined the chilling similarities. "We have two murder victims—Cassie Greaves and the as-yet-unidentified woman—alongside Dr. Peggy Scott, who was taken from us," he began, his finger tapping on each image.

"What have these two murders got to do with Dr. Scott's abduction? Is this another one of your wild theories?" The captain asked his frustration evident.

The captain, silently questioning Vincente's motives, dismissed the possibility of a connection between the three cases. The clock was ticking, and Ben Scott's relentless inquiries were a constant reminder of the urgency they faced to find his daughter. Unbeknownst to Mr. Scott, the captain was positive that Dr. Peggy Scott was lying in a ditch somewhere, dead.

Vincente pressed on with unwavering conviction. "Allow me to present the evidence," He opened a file folder and showed the captain and Keeley more images, close ups of the puncture marks on the two murder victims' necks. "The killer injected both women with ketamine, rendering them unconscious."

"Almost identical to Dr. Scott's abduction." Keeley remarked as she looked at the captain.

Vincente added, "Exactly. There are striking similarities that connect all three crimes – Dr. Scott was abducted at night while she was alone, the same as Cassie Greaves, and probably the same as the killer's latest victim. The video shows that Dr. Scott was injected with a syringe to subdue her, most likely ketamine, that was present in the killer's other two victims. All three women are similar in appearance, young, petite, and have blonde hair. Cassie Greaves and Dr. Scott could be sisters.

"But two of those women are dead!" Delacroix exclaimed.

Vincente pressed on, sharing the gruesome details that tied the two murders together. "Yes, and they were murdered by the same killer. Both victims were found naked, discarded like garbage. Forensics revealed they were killed elsewhere and then unceremoniously dumped in remote areas. The wounds inflicted upon them bear striking similarities—bruises, bite marks and cuts, likely from the same knife. Their wrists and ankles were bound with zip ties, their bodies raped and violated, yet no trace of semen was found. The killer was meticulous, cleaning both bodies with out with bleach, erasing any evidence. Both women died by asphyxiation by strangulation."

Keeley sighed heavily knowing what Vincente would say next.

Vincente continued, "And in a grotesque twist, Greaves had a portion of her pubic hair pulled out. The second victim, on the other hand, endured an even more brutal fate—the killer sliced off her labia majora." Vincente retrieved a close-up of the recent victim's vaginal area.

"What the fuck? The captain winced.

"Around the opening of the vagina, there are two sets of skin folds. The inner set, called the labia minora, are small and hairless. The outer set, the labia majora, are larger, with hair on the outer surface. The killer has an obvious escalating pubic hair fetish. Taking a few strands as trophies no longer satisfies his sick need now, he scalps the vagina, taking all the pubic hair."

"Why?" The captain asked as he hid the obscene image by flipping it over on the table.

"The killer collects these trophies, taking with him what he believes as his twisted prize."

"Holy Fuck!" The captain's voice boomed through the room,

Vincente proceeded to calmly share his findings, as he wrote the term "Trichophilia" on the whiteboard. "Trichophilia is an obsession with hair. The fetish manifests as the pleasure derived from plucking or pulling hair, whether it's from the head, face, chest, or even animal fur. Dr. Scott noticed the absence of pubic hair on Cassie Greaves and suggested trichophilia as a motive. It seems our killer is driven by pubephilia, a sexual arousal linked to the sight or touch of pubic hair. In these two homicide cases, the killer's fetish is driving him to take pubic hair as a trophy."

The captain grasped the gravity of the situation. The presence of a serial killer altered the entire course of the investigation. He asserted, "Since this perp is a serial killer. We need to involve the FBI. Our department can't handle this on our own."

Vincente nodded in agreement. "I've already been in touch with the FBI. They have unsolved cases with similarities—naked bodies of murdered women dumped in the Midwest; their pubic hair taken."

"But what does all of this have to do with Dr. Scott's abduction, Vincente?"

Vincente continued as he connected the dots. "I'm getting there, Captain. Let me explain. The first victim, Cassie Greaves, had close to a hundred shallow cuts or stab wounds, bite marks, bruises, and a vicious rape that left her vaginal opening swollen shut. The state of her body suggests she was held captive, enduring torture for days, possibly even a week, before she was strangled. The second victim, however, experienced a different fate. While her wounds bore similarities, the intensity of the assault was different. Only a dozen bite marks and bruises on her breasts and buttocks, accompanied by a handful of shallow stab wounds. The state of her body indicates that she wasn't subjected to prolonged torture and captivity like Greaves. Instead, she was quickly violated, murdered, and discarded, as if the killer was in a rush, driven by his escalating and insatiable need."

"Maybe he was afraid of getting caught. Maybe somebody saw him," speculated Keeley.

Vincente considered the possibilities, his gaze fixed on the photographs on the whiteboard. "I don't think so. I'm convinced the killer swiftly mutilated and strangled her in his vehicle and then tossed her body out while he was driving on the highway. Escalating and in a hurry to satisfy his cravings, he wasn't satisfied by taking some of the victim's pubic hairs as a trophy, he had to have all of them."

"I'm confused. Why not hold her captive and torture her like Greaves? Keeley asked.

"Perhaps he didn't need to since he is already holding another young, blonde woman captive. A woman he is drawn to. A woman that is his obsession."

The captain's skepticism was palpable as he questioned Vincente's theories. "Are you suggesting that this serial killer has Dr. Scott? What does this mean for her?"

Vincente pointed to the image of Dr. Peggy Scott, "I believe Dr. Scott is still alive. I believe this killer is keeping her in the same location where he held, tortured, and ultimately killed his first victim, Cassie Greaves." Vincente's finger traced across the photograph, lingering on Peggy's beautiful face. "The third victim," he continued, pointing to the picture of the unidentified woman, "was abducted and killed swiftly because the killer was in a hurry to satisfy his need to kill. He is savoring Dr. Scott, keeping her longer than the others, and I suspect there are many others. There is a possibility that he doesn't even want to kill Dr. Scott, maybe he plans on keeping her as his captive indefinitely."

"If this serial killer indeed has Dr. Scott, logic suggests she should already be dead," Keeley reasoned.

Vincente, his gaze fixed on the photograph of Dr. Scott, declared, "Obsessive love is an overwhelming, obsessive desire to possess another person. Obsessive love disorder is a condition in which one person feels an overwhelming obsessive desire to possess another person, sometimes with an inability to accept failure or rejection. Symptoms include an inability to tolerate any time spent without that person, obsessive fantasies surrounding that person, and spending inordinate amounts of time seeking out, making, or looking at images of that person. Look at Peggy Scott. Dr. Scott possesses an allure—a captivating beauty, youthful and radiant. She embodies that perfect blend of innocence and irresistible sensuality that many find alluring. Even in this squad room, men often discuss how attractive she is and what they would like to do to her. I certainly find her attractive. Hell, she has the body of a pin up girl!"

The pieces of the puzzle started to fall into place as Vincente continued, "The killer noticed Dr. Scott at work, and she became his obsession. He thought of her constantly, consumed by his fantasies. He began watching her, tracing her steps, learning about her life. He discovered that she lived in a touristy area, complete with tight security measures and constant surveillance. Dr. Scott's routine included a driver, ensuring she was never alone. The killer, cunning and aware of the risks, understood that he couldn't abduct Dr. Scott directly without attracting attention. So, he found a woman who resembled her—a substitute, a decoy."

"A substitute?" Keeley questioned.

Vincente nodded, his gaze shifting between the photographs of Dr. Scott and Cassie Greaves. "Yes, Cassie Greaves. The killer's obsession with Dr. Scott fueled his anger and desire, leading him to unleash his sadistic acts upon Cassie Greaves. In his frenzied state, he raped, tortured, and ultimately killed her. Greaves became a mere substitute, a vessel for his twisted fixation. It explains the striking resemblance between Greaves and Dr. Scott—they could easily be mistaken for sisters."

The captain's skepticism lingered as he probed further. "So, the killer changes his mind and decides to abduct the 'real thing,' Dr. Scott? It seems like quite a stretch, even for you, Vincente."

Vincente explained with a determined look in his eyes. "While the first victim, Cassie Greaves, temporarily satisfied the killer's desires, his obsession with Dr. Scott persisted. He continued to see her at work, growing increasingly frustrated that he couldn't possess her. Cassie Greaves wasn't enough. Dr. Scott was his intended target all along—the woman he was truly obsessed with. He couldn't resist her allure, and so he took a bold step. He abducted Dr. Scott from her workplace, right outside the morgue, knowing she would be there, captured by the security camera's constant surveillance. He planned it meticulously, wearing a ski mask to conceal his identity."

The captain's question hung in the air. "Do you still think he works here, in the Police Plaza building?"

Vincente nodded. "Yes, he does. This killer is cunning and methodical. He observed Dr. Scott in the morgue, learned her schedule. He watched her closely, learning her habits and routines. He knew precisely when she would be standing behind the morgue, waiting for her driver. He was intimately familiar with the security camera's placement because he took steps to avoid detection."

"So, this killer could potentially be an employee or even a police officer?" The captain hated to ask.

"Yes. This killer possesses intelligence and a disturbing level of self-obsession. He is highly organized, driven by his compulsions. He meticulously plans his actions, acutely aware of forensic techniques and determined to evade capture. He believes he is untouchable, as he has likely been killing for some time, targeting strangers. However, abducting Dr. Scott was a big mistake on his part—a mistake that will ultimately lead to his downfall. Unlike his previous victims, Dr. Scott is not a stranger to him. He knows her."

The captain and Keeley exchanged a solemn glance, their eyes reflecting a shared understanding of the gravity of the situation. The hunt for the elusive killer had intensified, their focus sharpened on uncovering the identity hidden within the walls of the Police Plaza building.

The Captain and Keeley exchanged solemn glances. Keeley voiced the next question. "Okay, Tony, so now he has the object of his desire in his creepy lair—why hasn't he killed her yet?"

Vincente took a moment to answer, "Maybe he wants to prolong her suffering, or perhaps he deludes himself into believing he is in love with her. It's difficult to say. But what we do know is that he has an insatiable compulsion to kill. He's a lust killer driven by his perverse desires. The primary motive for lust killers is sexual gratification, with fantasy playing a central role in their heinous acts. They derive pleasure from inflicting torture, mutilation, and ultimately, death upon their victims. The need for absolute control, dominance, and power drives them, and they use the infliction of pain and suffering to fulfill their sick cravings. They use weapons that require intimate contact with their victims, such as knives or bare hands. As their killings progress, the time between each kill decreases, or the level of stimulation required escalates—sometimes both. Escalation of his pubic hair fetish resulted in the removal of the latest victim's labia. Even if he imagines he has feelings for Dr. Scott, he won't be able to resist his urges. Sooner or later, he will succumb to the irresistible urge to kill Dr. Scott because for him, murder is the ultimate aphrodisiac."

The captain's questioning continued. "If he still has Dr. Scott, why did he need to kill the second woman?"

Vincente offered his perspective, "The second victim could very well have served as yet another substitute for Dr. Scott. Perhaps he needed to fulfill some sexual need that he wasn't ready or willing to satisfy with Dr. Scott just yet."

The captain pressed further, "If he is as intelligent as you believe, why would he risk abducting Dr. Scott from the morgue? Why didn't he kidnap her away from here?"

Vincente put both of his hands on the conference table and leaned forward. "Because he couldn't abduct her anywhere else. Her building has a doorman, 24/7, and the street the entrance is on is constantly flooded with tourists. She is never alone in a car or a parking lot since she uses a car service. From what we've gathered, Dr. Scott's activities are quite limited—she seldom ventures beyond the morgue and her home. The only moment she is truly alone is when she waits outside the morgue for her driver. This killer knew that because he had been watching her closely. He knew her schedule. The only way he knew her comings and goings are because he either works or visits here often."

"If it is someone who knows Dr. Scott, then who could it be? You and Keeley have interviewed everyone who has come into contact with her, and they all have alibis!"

"This individual is a narcissist and a predator, someone who possesses an unsettling level of organization. He meticulously planned every aspect of this abduction, ensuring he wouldn't be caught. He knew he would have an alibi—a watertight cover." Vincente explained.

Keeley chimed in, "But how? How could he be in two places at once?"

"Unless someone lied for him," Vincente muttered, a furrow forming between his brows.

"Okay detectives, time is running out. The police commissioner wants me to assemble a task force to find Dr. Scott."

"A task force? That will take days to put together! Dr. Scott doesn't have that kind of time. We must find her as soon as possible." Vincente remarked as he sat in one of the conference room chairs.

Sinking into the chair, Vincente's weariness became apparent.

"Keep working the case. I believe you're right Vincente, these cases are connected. The killer either works here or frequently visits this building."

"Could be a cop." Keeley interjected.

Vincente's mind raced as he considered the various possibilities. "I still have my suspicions about the morgue technician."

Keeley swiftly countered, "Alibi."

"The uniforms will provide you with a list of individuals who have had contact with Dr. Scott at the morgue, along with their background checks, later today."

"Finally." Keeley muttered.

"Detectives, the clock is ticking. Take another look at everyone you've already interviewed, even those with alibis."

Emotions hung heavy in the room— the weight of Dr. Scott's abduction by a serial predator who reveled in torture and murdering women, settling upon them. The knowledge that their investigation had taken a darker turn brought a renewed sense of purpose. The clock ticked, the tension mounting, as the detectives prepared to delve deeper into the mind of a monster lurking in the shadows.

Vincente stood up, removing the photos from the whiteboard, a mix of determination and frustration etched on his face. The chilling realization gnawed at his mind— *This twisted bastard knew her and wanted her, and now he has her. She has been held captive for two fucking weeks!* Vincente, determined to find Peggy, knew her fate was uncertain, and time was running out.

As they prepared to leave the conference room, Keeley's ringing cellphone pierced through the silence. She quickly answered the call.

"Detective Keeley speaking."

Keeley pulled a police report from her folder as she listened to the caller.

After she ended the call she explained, "I did some digging on our friendly detectives over at the 3rd precinct, Reyes and Walters."

Vincente's eyebrows shot up.

"That Thursday night when Dr. Scott was abducted, Reyes claimed they were responding to a domestic dispute. Here's the report Reyes filed," Keeley handed the report to Vincente. He skimmed its contents, his eyes scanning the details.

"I had two uniforms speak to the wife mentioned in the report. That was them on the phone."

Vincente leaned in, "What did the wife have to say?"

"She claims only one cop showed up—Reyes. According to her, he left alone, and there was no sign of Walters. She stepped outside after Reyes left."

The pieces of the puzzle began to fit together, leaving Vincente with a mix of realization and disbelief. He rubbed his chin thoughtfully, "So, Reyes lied."

"Yes, he was covering for Walters. But the question remains: why?"

Without hesitation, the captain issued a direct order. "Go fucking ask him."

Vincente and Keeley wasted no time, they drove swiftly to the 3rd precinct, with the siren blaring. They arrived at the busy 3rd precinct and held their badges up to the haggard desk sergeant.

"Where is Reyes!" Keeley's voice commanded attention.

"He's at his desk," came the begrudging response from the desk sergeant, his eyes rolling in annoyance.

Vincente and Keeley marched through the precinct, their eyes locked on Reyes, who sat nonchalantly at his desk, engrossed in his cellphone. Walters was conspicuously absent.

Vincente shouted at Reyes, "Where was he?"

With a swift and forceful motion, Vincente pushed Reyes's feet off the desk, his anger at the boiling point.

"What the fuck, Vincente! What the fuck are you talking about?" Reyes retorted.

"The night Dr. Scott was abducted, you claimed that you and Walters responded to a domestic dispute! So, where was Walters?" Vincente's voice rang out.

"He was with me, just like I told you! Check the damn report, asshole!" Reyes shot back.

"We did check the report," Keeley retorted, "But guess what? When we talked to the wife, she said the only cop that showed up was you! Where was Walters?"

"Walters stayed in the car. He wasn't feeling well. He had a migraine."

Keeley's voice rose with indignation. "That's funny! The wife clearly stated that she didn't see anybody else in the car when you got in and drove away."

"Well, that bitch is wrong. He was in the car!"

"She was outside when you got in the car. She watched as you drove away, and there was no one else with you!" Keeley yelled.

"Where the fuck was he?" Vincente's voice boomed.

Vincente pounded his fist on Reyes' desk, the sound echoing through the squad room. All eyes turned towards Reyes, who looked visibly shaken.

"Okay, alright," Reyes stammered, "He went home early. He had a migraine. I covered for him. So what?"

Keeley pressed for more information, "What time did he leave?"

"About 10:00 p.m., right after the call came in," Reyes confessed.

Vincente loomed over Reyes, his presence intimidating. "Where the hell is Walters now?"

"He took the afternoon off for a dentist appointment."

"Tell us about Walters." Keeley demanded.

Reyes's defensiveness began to crumble under the pressure of their relentless questioning. "Tell you what? He didn't have anything to do with that broad's kidnapping. He never even talked to her!"

Keeley's voice rose with authority, "Either you talk to us here and now, or we will haul your ass down to our station. Your choice, Reyes."

Reluctantly, Reyes relented, "Okay, okay. He's a nice guy—single, in his forties. I don't know that much about him. He likes to hunt. Once a year, he goes hunting, deer, I think. Takes a vacation. He's a good cop. Never misses a day of work except when he gets a migraine. Normal guy, quiet, keeps to himself. I think he's dating some court reporter over at the courthouse."

Keeley pressed further, "What's her name?"

"Angela, something."

Vincente and Keeley hurried out of the 3rd precinct, urgency fueling their every step. The truth hung precariously in the air, waiting to be unraveled.

Keeley pulled out her cellphone, her fingers dialing with urgency. "Tony, I'm calling a friend at City Hall to see if she knows Angela's last name. We need to talk to her. I'll have Human Resources email me Walters' file."

"We need to go to Walters' house. We need to find out where he lives." Vincente's urgency and determination palpable.

"We need a warrant, Tony. We don't have enough probable cause. It's after 5:00 p.m., and all the judges are gone for the day. Let's talk to Angela first thing in the morning."

Vincente's mind raced with worry and frustration. The desire to storm Walter's house and uncover the truth burned within him, but he knew Keeley was right—they lacked probable cause. His heart ached for Peggy, praying that she could hold on for just one more day. He couldn't sleep that night. His mind was consumed by concern for Peggy's safety.

Chapter 31

Friday, July 1

Morning arrived, bringing a ray of hope in finding Dr. Peggy Scott.

Detective Keeley had used her contacts at city hall to get Angela's last name. Keeley and Vincente drove over to the county courthouse, where Angela worked as a court reporter. Keeley pulled up Angela's employee ID picture on her cellphone, sharing it with Vincente as they parked their car in a no parking zone outside the courthouse.

The halls outside the courtrooms were vacant, court was in session. Vincente and Keeley entered the employee breakroom, their eyes scanning the room for Angela. And there she was, Angela Slovek, looking confused as the two detectives approached her.

"Angela Slovek? I am Detective Keeley, and this is Detective Vincente."

Angela nodded, an uncertain look on her face as she met their gaze. Dressed in a black skirt and white blouse, she was attractive and slender and stood around 5'5". Long dark brown hair cascaded down her back, giving her an exotic look. Her appearance reminded him of Vanessa.

"We are detectives with the SIU. We need to talk to you about Detective John Walters. Do you have a minute?" Keeley inquired.

"What? What about him? Is he in trouble?"

"No, he's not in trouble. We just have some questions. Is there somewhere we can talk?" Keeley reassured her.

Angela led them down a quiet hallway adjacent to the busy main corridor, its emptiness providing some privacy. The women sat on a bench, Keeley sitting beside Angela, her cellphone ready to record the interview. Vincente stood nearby, one hand clutching his notebook, the other buried in his pocket, restless anxiety radiating from him.

"Are you and Detective Walters still dating? We heard you were his girlfriend," Keeley began the interview with a question.

"Girlfriend? No. We dated over a year ago, for about two months."

Vincente, eager for information, interjected, "Tell us about him."

Angela hesitated, her gaze shifting nervously. Her voice wavered as she recounted their brief relationship. "Not much to tell. We met during a hearing—he testified for a case. I bumped into him afterward, and he had waited for me. He said he thought I was cute and asked me out. I thought he was a nice guy, somewhat sweet. We dated for a couple of months, and then we broke up."

Vincente instincts told him that Angela was holding back. Time was slipping away, and they needed to find Peggy. "Did anything unusual happen between you and Walters? We are investigating the abduction of a woman." He probed.

Angela shifted uncomfortably; her discomfort obvious.

"What about sex? Were you and Walters intimate?" Keeley asked.

"Yes, we had sex. Not much to tell." Her unease grew, her voice trailing off. "He's a nice guy. I'm sure he wouldn't harm any woman. He's a cop!"

Vincente, ever perceptive, sensed that Angela was hiding something. With determination, he crouched down, bringing himself eye to eye with Angela, hoping to coax out the truth. "I get the feeling, Angela, that you don't want to talk about Walters. Did something happen?"

Embarrassed, Angela's cheeks flushed as she whispered, "I don't want to get him into any trouble."

"Angela, why are you protecting him? Do you still have feelings for him?" Keeley pressed.

"No, I just don't feel comfortable discussing this. "We did have sex a few times. He could only get hard if he put his handcuffs on me... which, I don't mind a little kink. The sex was fast and rough, and I was rarely satisfied, if you know what I mean, but he never harmed me."

"What else?" Vincente prodded.

"It was nothing, really. Everything seemed fine. The sex was adequate, I suppose. I've had worse."

"Please, Angela. It might be important." Keeley implored.

Vincente, sensing Angela's reluctance to discuss intimate details in the presence of a man, stood up and sat on the bench on the other side of Keeley.

Angela paused before she began to share what happened. "Well, one day, my girlfriend and I decided to get bikini waxes. Brazilian waxes—you know, we had all the hair down there removed."

Keeley leaned in; her eyes focused on Angela. "We get the picture. How did Walters react?"

"Well, most guys love that, you know. I thought John would love it too. I thought it would add some spice in the bedroom, but he completely freaked out! He started yelling at me—'how could you do that, you ruined yourself, what's wrong with you?' He called me names, crude and demeaning. He was so angry."

Keeley pressed for more. "And then what happened?"

"He just left. I never saw him again. He ghosted me. It was insulting."

"What color was your hair when you were dating him?" Vincente asked, his voice filled with urgency.

Angela responded. "I was a blonde back then."

"Let's go!" Vincente exclaimed, his hand gripping Keeley's arm as they hurriedly exited the courthouse, leaving Angela behind on the bench.

"Tony, I'll call the captain. Maybe he can expedite a search warrant for Walters's house. I'll have a couple of uniforms meet us there."

Without an argument from Keeley, Vincente took the driver's seat of the unmarked police car, his heart pounding with a mix of hope and apprehension. As he turned on the siren, the wailing sound pierced through the air.

***

In a remote unincorporated suburb, outside the city of Chicago, Dr. Peggy Scott lay on a bed, her body naked and bound. As the killer walked into the dark basement room, he flicked on the overhead light. The room flooded with brightness, causing Peggy to close her eyes. The harshness of the light pierced through her pain-ridden body. When she opened her eyes again, she saw her abductor, entirely nude. She finally knew who he was. Her desperate scream was muffled by the gag tightly shoved in her mouth.

With a knife in hand, the killer swiftly cut the zip ties binding Peggy's ankles and ordered her to go to the bathroom. Weakened and disoriented, she stumbled towards the bathroom, her wrists still restrained, her movements unsteady. Dehydration, hunger, and the effects of the drugged water left her woozy, her body aching from the previous beatings.

Disgust filled the killer as he noticed Peggy had wet the bed. He ripped the soiled sheet off the bed and tossed it on the floor.

***

Detective Vincente, Detective Keeley, and four uniformed police officers arrived at John Walters' small ranch home, almost hidden by dense foliage at the end of a desolate block. Dilapidated houses stood abandoned; their windows boarded up.

Turning off their police sirens, the element of surprise was on the detectives' side as they silently rolled up in front of Walters's house. Armed with a search warrant, they knew Walters was home because his car sat in the driveway. Vincente's intuition told him that Dr. Scott was likely being held somewhere in the house. Wearing bulletproof vests, and carrying their Glocks, the detectives and police officers cautiously stepped out of their vehicles, preparing to confront the serial killer.

"Tony, maybe we should wait for the SWAT team." Keeley whispered to Vincent.

"No. Dr. Scott is running out of time."

***

Inside the bathroom, Peggy waited, bracing herself for the horrors to come. She knew Walters was just outside, listening intently.

"Come here!" He screamed.

Peggy couldn't move. Enraged, the killer seized her arms, forcibly throwing her back onto the bed. Removing her gag, he forced her to drink stale, bitter water from a bottle. He shoved the gag back into her mouth. He cut her wrists free from the zip-tie only to quickly bind them and her ankles to the bedposts, leaving her naked and spread-eagled.

***

Vincente quietly kicked open the side door to the garage. They needed to surprise Walters and not risk him harming Peggy if she was still alive. The garage was empty, allowing the two detectives and the uniformed officers to enter the residence in silence. Guns drawn, they moved through the darkened and deserted kitchen. Vincente signaled for the uniformed officers to search the rest of the first floor.

***

Meanwhile, Walters placed his knife, a small cooler and tray of instruments beside Peggy on the bed. Peggy noticed the tray of instruments included a needle already threaded. As he picked up a soaked washcloth and a bar of soap, Walters's voice dripped with sadistic delight as he said, "I have to make you all nice and clean."

Roughly scrubbing her breasts, underarms, and genital area, he was enjoying himself. Smirking, he dried her off with a worn towel before grabbing a pillow. Placing it under her buttocks, he elevated and exposed the smooth, vulnerable flesh of her vagina. He donned a head-mounted magnifier, used by jewelers, for close work. Walters climbed on the bed and sat next to his mysterious collection of items. Peggy struggled futilely against her restraints as Walters prepared the items for his macabre task.

***

Keeley's grip tightened around her Glock as she trailed Vincente into the kitchen, her senses on high alert. Her gaze locked onto an open door, silently signaling Vincente. Without a word, Vincente acknowledged her nod, recognizing that the open door likely led to the basement. Faint sounds of movement reached their ears, urging Vincente to investigate. With his Glock held firmly, he quietly descended the basement stairs. Keeley followed close behind, their determination fueling their steps. The dimly lit basement revealed a partially open door, a glimpse of a small, dimly lit room within. The detectives heard a muffled voice and the sounds of struggling as they inched toward the room.

The four police officers, having cleared the first floor, followed Keeley down the basement stairs. Vincente, in the lead, pressed his finger against his lips, a silent command for everyone to keep quiet. He knelt beside the slightly ajar door, trying to catch a brief glimpse inside. The sound of Walters' voice reached Vincente's ears.

***

Walters retrieved a clear plastic bag from the cooler and proudly showed its gruesome contents to Peggy. Peggy's stomach knotted as she beheld the skin of a female's labia majora with dark brown pubic hair still attached. Tears streamed down her face as she struggled against her restraints, her wrists and ankles now bloody with painful abrasions. Walters sat down on her thighs, immobilizing her.

"Stop moving!" Walters screamed.

He viciously slapped Peggy's face, the force splitting her upper lip. The metallic taste of blood filled her mouth. Sobbing uncontrollably, she felt absolute terror consuming her. Walters leaned in, his voice barely a whisper.

"I killed her for you. I need to fix you."

Peggy screamed through the gag, desperately fighting against the zip ties that held her down. She realized that his pubic hair fetish was fueling his grizzly plan of suturing the preserved labia majora of a dead woman to her hairless vagina.

"Stop that! It won't hurt that much!" Walters sneered, as he pulled one half of his horrific trophy and picked up the threaded needle. "I'm going to sew the skin of her hairy pussy to you, then, we'll have some fun!"

Peggy violently bucked her hips trying to throw Walters off of her.

"Stay still!" Walters commanded.

He delicately arranged half of the preserved labia majora on one of the outer folds of Peggy's vagina.

***

As Vincente silently peered into the small room, the shocking scene before him unfolded. Sitting on an old four-poster bed, Walters was naked, his back turned, wearing a head mount magnifier. He loomed over a woman while sitting on her bare thighs, her body helplessly restrained. Dr. Peggy Scott, gagged and bound, bucked her hips, and fought against the zip ties binding her ankles. Vincente could hear Walters telling her to remain still.

With his gun aimed unwaveringly at Walters, Vincente burst into the room, his voice commanding authority. "Police! Freeze!"

Walters briefly turned his head, grabbed a large hunting knife, and attempted to stab Peggy in the chest. In that critical instant, before Walters's knife even grazed her skin, Vincente fired, his bullet exploding Walters's head. Blood and brain matter sprayed the basement room, as Walters's lifeless body collapsed onto Dr. Scott, who screamed through her gag.

Rushing to the bed, Vincente wasted no time in removing Walters' dead body off the terrified Dr. Scott. His gaze averted, he grabbed a nearby blanket and covered her naked body.

The room was hazy with smoke, the metallic tang of blood lingering in the air. Chaos reigned, and Peggy trembled uncontrollably. Keeley and the other officers rushed into the room, and immediately assessed the scene. With his bare hands, Vincente forcefully tore apart the zip ties that had bound Peggy's wrists and ankles to the bedposts. Gently removing her gag, he ensured she was covered more fully with the blanket, cradling her as he sat her up.

Vincente noticed something unusual on the bed next to Peggy's huddled body. As he looked closer, he realized that is was part of a woman's labia majora. Vincente's skin paled as he realized what Walters's sick intensions were.

Peggy, disoriented and overwhelmed, struggled to comprehend what was happening. Her head throbbed from the sound of the gunshot. Her senses dulled by the drugs Walters had been giving her., She smelled sulfur and saw the swirling smoke, her mind struggling to process the surreal image of Detective Vincente holding a gun. She believed she was either hallucinating or dreaming.

Keeley, checking Walters' pulse and confirming his death, holstered her Glock and retrieved her cell phone. "Walters is dead. I'll call it in. How is she, Tony?"

"She's going into shock. Call the paramedics," Vincente replied, his voice laced with tenderness and concern.

"It's alright. It's over," Vincente whispered. Holding Peggy close, he felt the weight of her sobs, the tremors coursing through her bruised body. She was lost in a sea of shock and pain. He surmised that Walters must have drugged her.

"I've got you," Vincente murmured. In that moment, he hadn't fully realized the extent of Peggy's injuries. But as he held her tightly, he caught glimpses of the bruised and beaten state of her body—the black eye, the split and bloodied lip, the haunting marks of strangulation and bite marks etched upon her shoulders. She sobbed, seeking solace in his arms, her head buried in his chest.

Keeley slipped on a pair of surgical gloves; her eyes fixated on the labia majora that was on the bed. Her gaze shifted to the array of instruments, along with a threaded needle scattered on the bed. "What the Hell was he doing?" Keeley questioned, her voice tinged with disbelief as she retrieved a clear plastic bag from the floor and examined the contents more closely. The implications dawned on Keeley, her face contorting with a mix of horror and disgust. "Oh my God! Was he going to sew the missing labia on her?"

Vincente's nod confirmed their shared realization. "Bag everything. Get a forensics team in here to go through the house," he directed. Aware of Peggy's vulnerable state, Vincente kept one arm around her as he removed his bulletproof vest and handed it to Keeley, along with his gun. Keeley immediately took charge of managing the crime scene.

The wails of approaching sirens filled the room as more police officers and crime scene technicians arrived to meticulously comb through Walters' residence. A pathologist from the medical examiner's office joined them, closely examining Walters' lifeless body. Rumors spread that the FBI was en route, adding to the severity of the situation.

Vincente clung to Peggy, his arms a protective shield, unwilling to let her go until the paramedics arrived. He tenderly held her arm steady, while a paramedic started an IV, causing Peggy to wince in pain. Inserting the needle into her arm was difficult due to her severe dehydration. Once the IV was secured, Vincente gently laid her on the stretcher, carefully covering her with additional blankets. She continued to tremble, her trauma evident. Vincente climbed into the ambulance, never letting go of her hand. He tried to console her by stroking her hair and whispering assurances in her ear.

***

In the emergency room, Vincente remained by Peggy's side, his presence unwavering. His watchful gaze followed the nurse as she took Peggy's vital signs, answering questions for her as she remained silent. Respectful of her privacy, Vincente turned away when the nurse helped Peggy change into a hospital gown. He requested wet cloths, that he gently used to clean up the dried blood that marred her beautiful face.

"You are a very brave young woman. I am so proud of you." Vincente was filled with gratitude that she was found alive.

A young male ER entered the small examination room. After the introductions were made, the doctor asked, his voice filled with concern. "What happened to her?"

"She was sexually assaulted - possibly raped."

Putting on surgical gloves, the doctor began his examination, his touch gentle yet purposeful as he assessed Peggy's neck and arms. "Lot of bruising. I see bite marks, but the skin isn't broken. It must have been very painful." The doctor then made a move to lower Peggy's hospital gown, intending to further inspect her body.

Reacting swiftly, Vincente flashed his detective's badge, his voice firm. "No. She needs a rape kit." Confusion flickered across the doctor's face, prompting Vincente to offer an explanation. "A rape kit consists of microscope slides and plastic bags for collecting and preserving evidence such as clothing fibers, hairs, saliva, blood, semen, or body fluid. It is used by medical personnel for gathering and preserving physical evidence following a sexual assault. The evidence collected from the victim can aid in a criminal rape investigation. Her injuries need to be documented. Photographs of her bruising need to be taken."

The doctor nodded in agreement. "Okay, I can do that."

"No, she needs a woman. Get a nurse or a female doctor," he insisted, concerned about Peggy's comfort.

The doctor agreed to inquire about a rape kit and the availability of a female nurse or doctor. A few minutes later, a nurse arrived, carrying the rape kit. Vincente reluctantly stepped out of the room, his gaze lingering on Peggy's fragile form. He paced anxiously in the hallway, torn between the desire to remain by her side and the necessity of the examination. Recalling the extent of Cassie Greaves' injuries, Vincente knew that Peggy needed a thorough examination.

Inside the room, the nurse carefully unpacked the contents of the rape kit, arranging them on the counter. The items included bags and sheets for evidence collection, swabs for collecting fluids from various areas of the body, sterile containers for urine and samples, blood collection devices, a comb for hair and fiber collection, glass slides, self-sealing envelopes for preserving clothing, hair, and blood samples, a nail pick for debris under the nails, white sheets to collect physical evidence, documentation forms, labels, and sterile water and saline. Once the examination was complete, the rape kit would be sealed and transferred to local law enforcement, a crucial step in the investigation.

Vincente anxiously waited outside the room, worried about the invasive and time-con-suming examination Peggy was enduring. Yet, the examination and rape kit were essential to provide the necessary evidence for the case.

Following the collection of evidence, the rape kit containing Dr. Scott's biological sam-ples would be sent to the forensic science crime lab for analysis. Highly skilled forensic sci-entists would work to develop a DNA profile of the assailant using the samples obtained. Their efforts would involve searching the DNA profile against databases containing DNA profiles of convicted offenders and other crime scenes, such as the three-tiered Combined DNA Index System (CODIS) used in the United States. The goal was to establish a connection and identify the perpetrator.

Outside Peggy's exam room, the nurse conducting Peggy's examination, found Detec-tive Vincente still pacing outside.

"Detective, we managed to have Dr. Scott disrobe and stand on a white sheet. We collected all the trace evidence that fell from her body, securing it in bags. We took photographs of her injuries. Her breasts bear bruises and shallow bite marks, but her skin remains intact. She has strangulation marks and bruising on her neck, face, abdomen, thighs, and buttocks. But, when we attempted to proceed with the examination, she curled up in a fetal position, refusing to cooperate. We don't want to sedate her until her bloodwork comes back. Would you like us to use restraints?"

"No, I will come in and sit with her. Perhaps you can set up a privacy drape during the examination."

Vincente reentered the exam room, where he found Peggy curled up on the exam table, her trembling body covered by a paper blanket.

Gently stroking the top of her head, Vincente tried to reassure her. "Hey, the nurse needs to examine you. They must collect evidence and make sure you aren't injured." Pulling a chair close to the exam table, he sat down and took hold of one of her hands.

"Dr. Scott, we need you to lay flat on your back." The nurse instructed.

Aided by CNA, Vincente helped Peggy roll onto her back, while a privacy curtain was rolled over, shielding the lower half of Peggy's body.

"I've got you," Vincente assured her, his voice filled with compassion. As the nurse guided Peggy's feet into the stirrups, Vincente gently squeezed her hand.

"We're going to collect evidence and perform a pelvic exam now. Just relax." Over-whelmed, Peggy's tears flowed freely.

Vincente clasped Peggy's hand tightly, as he whispered softly, "Everything will be okay."

The nurse, preparing to proceed with the examination, announced, "I am going to insert the speculum now. Just relax."

Vincente understood a speculum was used by Gynecologists to open the walls of the vagina, for cervical exams. His grip on Peggy's hand remained firm. As the nurse inserted the speculum, Peggy flinched in response to the discomfort. The nurse meticulously examined her vagina and cervix, carefully swabbing the area before removing the speculum.

"Now, I'm going to swab other parts of your body," the nurse explained. She meticulously swabbed Peggy's rectum, mouth, and other areas where bodily fluids might be present. When it came time to swab her breasts, the nurse lifted the paper blanket, prompting Vincente to turn away. Additionally, the nurse scraped beneath Peggy's fingernails, ensuring that all potential evidence was collected.

"Next, I'll be taking a photograph of your genitals using a special camera," the nurse informed Peggy, who winced in discomfort as the colposcope was inserted. Vincente stroked Peggy's forehead and continued to squeeze her hand.

Vincente, sensing Peggy's growing exhaustion, asked, "Are you almost finished?" Aware that she had endured enough poking and prodding.

The nurse told Peggy, "You are doing great. Just hang in there it will be over soon."

The buzz of Vincente's phone broke the heavy silence in the exam room. As Vincente checked his phone, he noticed a text from Keeley informing him that Benjamin Scott, Peggy's father, was on his way to the hospital.

When the exam was over, the nurse gathered all the swabs, slides, and other items and carefully placed them evidence in the box. The CNA took Dr. Scott's feet out of the stirrups. She put a blanket over Peggy's waist, so she was covered up when they took down the privacy drape. Vincente put another blanket over Peggy because she was shaking.

"I'll be right back." Vincente told Peggy, he temporarily stepped out of the room to confer with the nurse in the hallway.

"Detective, would you like to see the pictures of the bruises and bite marks?" the nurse asked, holding a digital camera in her hands.

"No," Vincente replied, not wanting to see the extent of the harm inflicted upon Peggy by that monster.

The nurse shared her initial findings, "I did not observe any bruising or signs of sexual assault or forced penetration in her genital area. However, we collected swabs that will need to be tested to confirm. We did find traces of semen on her chest, back, and buttocks. We are waiting for her bloodwork results. I will discuss with the doctor the possibility of prescribing a sedative to help her sleep. Given her dehydration, we will likely keep her overnight, to make she receives fluids and some food. She will be transferred to a regular room."

"Thank you," Vincente breathed a sigh of relief knowing that Peggy hadn't been raped—no forced penetration.

Sensing the detective's concern, the nurse assured him, "She is in shock. She needs time. We see this behavior quite often in sexual assault cases."

Vincente reentered Peggy's exam room, finding her curled up in a fetal position once more.

"Hey, I talked to the nurse, and she doesn't think you were raped. I don't know how much you remember, but that is good news." Yet, Peggy remained unresponsive, trapped within her nightmare.

Vincente leaned closer, "They are going to move you to a room now. I will meet you there. I am going to talk to the Doctor." Stepping out of the room, Vincente found the Doctor in the hallway.

"Detective? Dr. Scott's bloodwork came back. She has traces of ketamine in her system, but otherwise, her blood work is normal," the Doctor revealed. "The nurse informed me that she is still not speaking. She is likely in shock. I will administer a sedative to help her sleep once she settles into her hospital room. She should rest for 8-10 hours. We will keep her overnight to rehydrate her and provide nourishment."

"Thank you. Her father is on his way here."

Returning to Peggy's exam room, Vincente found an orderly waiting with a gurney to transfer her to a hospital room. Vincente gently lifted her and gently put her down on the gurney. The orderly made sure her IV bag was securely attached before pushing the gurney down the hallway. Vincente walked alongside.

Vincente softly spoke, "They are moving you to a regular hospital room. The doctor will prescribe something to help you sleep. Keeley texted me that your father is on his way here. I have to make a call. I will see you in your room." However, Peggy remained unresponsive, Vincente worried about her fragile condition.

Vincente made a call to Keeley, seeking updates on the ongoing investigation at Walters's house. Keeley informed him of the chilling discoveries—a room adorned with pictures of Dr. Scott and a box containing 18 baggies filled with pubic hair samples, likely trophies from his previous victims. With the FBI taking over the crime scene, Vincente promised to meet Keeley back at the station once Dr. Scott was settled in her hospital room.

Finding Peggy's hospital room, Vincente entered without knocking. The small private hospital room was silent except for the soft beeping of the monitors. Peggy lay on the hospital bed, curled up in a fetal position. Vincente longed to pick her up and hold her tightly in his arms.

"Hey, how are you doing?" Vincente greeted her, a gentle smile gracing his lips. Yet, Peggy didn't respond or look at him.

A nurse entered the room, holding a syringe filled with medicine.

"Hi Peggy. I'm your nurse. The doctor ordered some medicine to help you sleep. I am just going to inject it into your IV," the nurse softly spoke, as she administered the medication. With her task complete, she left the room, allowing Peggy to sleep.

Vincente remained by Peggy's side, sitting on the edge of the hospital bed. He leaned down, his gaze meeting her eyes filled with sadness. "I have to leave, but your father should be here any minute," he gently told her. Peggy turned her head away, her pain and vulnerability palpable.

"Listen, I will be back in the morning. I will be here when you wake up. Okay? I promise." Peggy still didn't look at him. Vincente hated leaving her, but duty called him to the station to wrap up the case.

"Look, to make sure that I come back... I want you to hold onto my watch for me," he said, removing his wristwatch with care. Tenderly, he clasped Peggy's arm, not connected to the IV, and buckled the watch around her wrist. A wave of revulsion washed over him as he noticed her torn and bloody fingernails.

"This watch is very special to me. My late Aunt gave it to me when I graduated from college. So, I want it back," Vincente explained, hoping the watch would remind her that he was returning. Peggy's other hand touched the watch, then reached out to touch Vincente's hand. Finally, she looked up at him.

"You saved me," she whispered to Vincente, tears welling in her eyes. Her bruised face and neck told the story of her harrowing ordeal. Then her eyelids grew heavy, and she fell asleep. Vincente kissed the hand he held, gently placing it back on the bed. He quietly left her hospital room, closing the door behind him.

***

Once outside her room, the weight of Peggy's suffering crashed upon Vincente. He was suddenly filled with emotions —sadness, anger, and a burning rage. Helplessness gnawed at him, and tears welled in his eyes. Unable to contain himself, Vincente sought refuge in the nearest men's room.

Inside the restroom, Vincente's mind filled with the unimaginable horrors Peggy had endured at the hands of that sociopath. Thoughts of the other women Walters had brutally violated, tortured, and murdered consumed him. In a rage, Vincente threw a powerful punch at the wall. The drywall caved, leaving a fist-sized dent. Vincente shook his head and ran his hands through his hair trying to calm himself.

As Vincente exited the men's room, he saw Peggy's father, Benjamin Scott, talking to the doctor. The casually dressed billionaire appeared distressed, obviously worried about his daughter. Spotting Vincente approaching, he called out, "Detective Vincente!"

Vincente walked over to Mr. Scott, ready to offer his support and provide any updates on Peggy's condition.

"Thank you, Detective Vincente," Mr. Scott said, his voice filled with appreciation. He extended his hand to Vincente, and they briefly shook hands. Emotion welled within Mr. Scott, and tears streamed down his face. The weight of his daughter's ordeal weighed heavily upon him.

"The Doctor told me what happened! Thank you for saving my daughter."

"It's my job, Sir. Your daughter has had a traumatic experience, and she is in shock. The doctor gave her medication to help her sleep. I will come back in the morning to check on her. Her formal statement can wait for a few days, when she feels better."

"I truly appreciate all that you've done for my daughter. If there's anything you need or anything I can do for you, anything at all, just let me know. You have my number." He placed a reassuring hand on Vincente's arm.

Vincente, touched by the gesture, reassured him, "That's not necessary."

"My daughter holds great admiration for you Detective, and I can see why."

"Thank you," Vincente acknowledged, a slight smile gracing his lips.

With a final nod to Ben Scott, Detective Vincente left the hospital, his mind filled with worry about Peggy's recovery. He saw a squad car and requested a ride to Police Plaza in Chicago. The ride offered a chance to relax and gather his thoughts before he had return to the SIU.

Chapter 32

Saturday, July 2

Detective Vincente returned to the hospital, his heavy footsteps echoing through the corridor. He gently knocked on the door of Peggy's room before entering, finding her no longer in a hospital gown but wearing black a sweatshirt with matching sweatpants. Her hair, freshly washed, was pulled back into a ponytail. The ugly bruises still marred her face and neck, but she radiated strength. She smiled upon seeing Vincente, her eyes lighting up with gratitude. She began unstrapping his watch from her wrist.

"Hey, good morning. How are you feeling?" Vincente asked as he settled down on the edge of her hospital bed.

"Better, thank you."

Handing Vincente his watch, Peggy held back telling Tony the truth, that every time she closed her eyes, she was back in that basement room with that monster on top of her naked body. Walters haunted her every moment. She couldn't bear to confess her fear of falling asleep and having nightmares about her ordeal. A normal life felt like an impossible dream.

Vincente sensed her obvious turmoil but didn't know how to reassure her.

"It looks like they are releasing you."

"Yes. I'm just waiting for the Doctor to sign my release papers. My father is taking me to his house."

"Good. It's probably best that you're not alone right now."

Peggy's voice trembled, a single tear streaming down her cheek. "Thank you for rescuing me. I'm so embarrassed that you saw me like that."

"Don't worry, I didn't see anything. I threw a blanket over you. Look, you're going to get through this. You're a strong young woman."

"My Father has already arranged for me to see a therapist."

"That should help," Vincente acknowledged.

"I just feel bad that he killed all of those other women."

Taking her hand, Vincente consoled her, "None of this was your fault. Walters was a dangerous killer. You were right from the beginning, that Cassie Greaves was a victim of a serial killer." He squeezed her hand gently. "You'll have to come to the station in the next few days to make a formal statement."

"Will you be there?"

"Sure. I can take your statement if you want."

"Yes," Peggy agreed, finding comfort knowing Tony would take her statement.

"Hey, you still owe me a date. So, when you're feeling better, I'd like to take you to dinner," Vincente offered, he smiled warmly.

Their conversation was interrupted by the buzz of Vincente's phone. Vincente quickly glanced at his phone and saw that Keeley had sent a text, urging him to return to the station. Internal Affairs required an interview regarding Walters's shooting.

"I have to go. I'll call you later to see how you're doing."

Peggy smiled and nodded. She silently wished him well.

"Hang in there, Doc," Vincente said, his voice filled with encouragement as he left Peggy's hospital room.

As Tony left, a whirlwind of thoughts and emotions swirled through Peggy's mind. The emotional wounds of her captivity had etched themselves deep within her soul. When Tony reminded her of the date she owed him, Peggy's heart sank, enveloped in a heavy cloud of uncertainty and self-doubt.

While a part of her still held affection for Tony, the thought of pursuing a romantic relationship stirred fears and doubts within her. The trauma she had endured cast a long shadow over the possibility of intimacy.

Being open and vulnerable with Tony seemed like a foreign concept, distant and out of reach. Peggy knew she needed time to heal, to mend the shattered pieces of herself. But a fear gnawed at her—that she needed too much time, that she would lose Tony during her lengthy recovery.

Chapter 33

Tuesday, July 5

Dr. Peggy entered the bustling squad room of the Special Investigations Unit, her presence capturing everybody's attention. Wearing a dark dress that accentuated her figure, its length skimming just above her knees, she wore a silk scarf wrapped around her neck, concealing the fading marks of strangulation. Dark sunglasses shielded her eyes, while carefully applied makeup covered the yellowing bruises on her face. With her hair in a simple updo, she resonated a quiet strength that captivated everyone in the squad room. Vincente stood up from his desk, his smile lighting up the room as their eyes met.

Peggy had requested Vincente to take her statement, and he cordially guided her into an interrogation room. Aware of the watchful eyes of the captain and Keeley behind the two-way mirror, Vincente briefly glanced at himself and nervously straightened his tie.

Stepping into the room, Peggy took a seat at the sturdy metal table, removing her sunglasses to reveal her beautiful royal blue eyes. Vincente sat opposite her.

"You look stunning. How are you doing?" Vincente asked.

"Fine. I didn't want to look like a victim."

"Are you sure you want me to take your statement, and not Detective Keeley?" Vincente inquired, making sure she was comfortable with him listening to the intimate details of her ordeal.

"I'm sure."

Vincente settled into the chair, extending a bottle of water he had brought for her. With a nod toward the mirrored window, he signaled Keeley to begin recording Dr. Scott's statement.

Vincente patiently asked, "Why don't you start at the very beginning? You were at work. Can you tell me what happened? We can stop at any time if you need a break."

Peggy calmly spoke about her ordeal, recounting Walters's early visits, including the times he fondled, bit, and masturbated on her breasts and buttocks. However, as she recounted a later visit, her resolve fractured, and she began to tremble.

"I knew something terrible was going to happen when Walters returned. I was weak from the drugs. My wrists were bound together with zip ties. He released my ankles, letting me use the bathroom. But as soon as I finished, he grabbed me again, and zip-tied my wrists and ankles to the bedposts. I knew he was going to rape me. It was so dark. I couldn't see anything."

Tears streamed down Peggy's face. She started shaking.

Witnessing her pain, Vincente offered, "We can stop if you need a break."

"No. I want to get this over with." Peggy asserted, her voice trembling with vulnerability. "He was naked. He got on top of me, rubbing himself all over me. Then he started touching me. He was rough. He grabbed my breasts and squeezed. When I cried in pain. He laughed as he started to slap and bite me, over and over again. I could feel his heavy breaths on my skin.... hear his moans. Then I saw the reflection of a knife in his hand. He cut off my bra. Then he started biting my nipples. Every time I cried out in pain; he would slap me across the face. When I felt him cut off my panties, I closed my eyes."

Vincente handed Dr. Scott a tissue and suggested. "Why don't we take a break?"

Peggy shook her head no. She wiped her eyes with the tissue.

"Then he began screaming and crying, he sounded like a wounded animal. I opened my eyes, only to see him straddling my thighs and staring at my lower body. He was so furious he was shaking."

"Could you make out who he was at this point?"

"No," Peggy replied, her voice filled with a mix of fear and confusion. "I couldn't really see his face. Then he screamed, 'What have you done!' He called me a Bitch and other awful names. He told me to 'shut up' while he punched my chest and stomach with his fists. I heard him laughing as he beat me – I will never forget the sound of that evil and sadistic laughter. I think I passed out at that point."

Uncapping the water bottle, Peggy took a small sip.

"When I regained consciousness, I heard him whispering in my ear. He had removed the gag. He asked me how long it would take for my pubic hair to grow back. I told him it would never grow back because I had had it permanently removed with a laser. He slapped me across the face, telling me I was a whore, and accusing me of ruining myself. The slaps continued, and he started to strangle me. I blacked out. When I woke up, the gag was back in my mouth. He was gone."

Peggy finished the rest of her statement – including the moment when Walters placed part of a labia majora on her vagina. Listening to the unspeakable horrors that Peggy had endured, Vincente remained stoic, concealing his inner turmoil. He remained the consummate professional, yet inside, his heart burned with fury. He was happy he had killed the bastard.

At long last, the interview was over. Peggy looked relieved. Vincente nodded at the 2-mirror for Keeley to stop recording.

Vincente rose from his seat, dragging his chair close to Peggy's. He sat down and spread his legs, deliberately intruding on her personal space. It was a tactic he used during interviews, a calculated approach to unsettle and intimidate. But in this instance, his closeness was for a different purpose. He wanted to establish a connection, to encourage Peggy to open up to him, and to let her know she wasn't alone.

"Why haven't you returned any of my phone calls?" Vincente inquired; his gaze fixed upon Peggy.

She lowered her eyes and replied softly, "I don't know."

Vincente sighed, "Look, I want to see you."

"I don't think I can see anyone right now. I'm not ready," Peggy admitted, her vulnerability evident. "But I truly appreciate everything you've done for me. Though I don't remember much from hospital, I know you stayed with me. Thank you."

"You were in shock," Vincente reassured her.

"I'm alright now. You don't need to worry about me."

"I know. We had a date, remember?" Vincente smiled.

Vincente's fingers grazed Peggy's face, his hand gently lifting her chin. "I would really like to take you to dinner."

"You don't have to take me to dinner," Peggy whispered with tears in her eyes.

"But I want to."

Overwhelmed by emotions, Peggy confessed, "I feel so broken. I'm so embarrassed that you found me like that. I feel so ugly. It's hard for me to even look at you."

Vincente reached over and held her hand, his voice filled with conviction. "You aren't ugly. My God, you are the most beautiful woman I have ever seen. You aren't broken. Don't feel ashamed—I didn't see anything. I covered you with a blanket. Nobody saw anything."

Peggy sobbed as she pleaded, "Please, the pictures. Please don't look at the pictures of what he did to me. I don't want you to see them."

Peggy buried her face in her hands, feeling raw and exposed.

Vincente leaned closer, encircling her in his arms, and whispered, "Don't worry. I did not look at those pictures. I would never look at those pictures. Peggy, it's okay. I... I won't let anyone hurt you like that again. You are safe now. I just want to be with you. I just want to spend time with you. Please let me see you again." Peggy rested her head on his broad chest and nodded. In his arms, she felt secure, she felt cared for.

Vincente gently caressed Peggy's back as he held her. Touching her ignited something powerful within him, a depth of emotion he had never experienced before. He couldn't bear the thought of letting her go. He was determined to protect her at all costs.

Chapter 34

Saturday, July 30

Tony and Peggy were seated at a secluded table in Vincente's favorite Italian restaurant in the city. Peggy had finally relented and allowed Tony to take her for dinner. The small restaurant was dimly lit, with the soft glow of hurricane lamps and flickering candles casting a warm, intimate atmosphere. The small round tables were covered with red and white checked tablecloths.

Peggy, dressed casually in jeans and a black turtleneck sweater, looked radiant. The bruises that once marred her face had vanished. Vincente thought she looked lovely and was captivated by her.

For almost four weeks, Vincente had waited for this moment. He had enjoyed their daily phone conversations, but he longed to see her in person. Peggy had been hesitant to go out in public, wary of the persistent paparazzi who followed her, always asking about the details of her abduction. The trauma she had endured was unimaginable, and Vincente knew she was undergoing therapy to heal her wounds. Finally, she had moved back into her penthouse and was preparing to return to work on Monday.

"I'm sorry, it feels a bit strange being out in public after being in seclusion for so long," Peggy admitted.

"I can only imagine."

"Thankfully, the press has finally ceased their constant calls and presence. It's a relief."

"How are you really doing?" Vincente asked, concern etched on his face.

Peggy paused for a moment before answering, "Well, honestly, I still have nightmares, but the flashbacks have stopped. I can't count the number of showers I've taken. Therapy is helping -- but I think returning to work will be the best therapy for me."

"It will be great to have you back at work. I've missed seeing you."

Peggy blushed and replied, "I've missed seeing you too."

"In that case," Vincente continued, a playful twinkle in his eyes, "we'll have to make we see more of each other. I especially miss walking down the hall only to hear a sultry female voice calling, 'Detective Vincente,' and witness you stumbling and falling right on your behind!"

The sound of Peggy's laughter filled the air. Peggy liked seeing this relaxed side of Tony. Peggy thought the black jeans and black leather jacket he wore made him look sexy as Hell.

"I know, that was so embarrassing."

"Why were you so nervous around me?"

Peggy smiled as she admitted, "Well, I was attracted to you. Even the sound of your voice was irresistible to me. I wanted to make an impression, to capture your attention."

Vincente chuckled warmly, his eyes twinkling with amusement. "Oh, believe me, I noticed you. I've never had a woman quite literally fall for me before! You see, the only reason I agreed to that coffee date was because I was genuinely concerned you might break your neck!"

A playful smile danced on Peggy's lips. "But let's not forget, you only asked me to that wedding reception because you discovered your ex-girlfriend was bringing a date. I think you wanted to make her jealous."

"That may be true, but when I saw you in that dress, the way you moved on the dance floor, and the look on your face when I slipped that garter on your leg—my heart was captivated. I was a goner, completely smitten by you."

In a tender gesture, Vincente reached across the table and gently clasped Peggy's hands. He expressed his desire earnestly, "I truly want to spend time with you."

Peggy's eyes searched his, "Even after everything that's happened?"

"Yes, truly," Vincente affirmed, squeezing her hands gently. "I want to see you, be with you."

Peggy's voice trembled as she admitted, "I want to see you too. But I'm not ready to be intimate with anyone. I don't want to disappoint you."

"Look, I just want to be with you, to get to know you. I don't expect anything physical from you. I have genuine feelings for you, and I believe you feel the same. Let's take it one step at a time and see where it leads us."

Tears welled in Peggy's eyes as she spoke, "I truly care about you, Tony. I just feel so broken."

Vincente's grip tightened on her hands. "You are not broken. You are the bravest, strongest, most beautiful, and brilliant, woman I have ever met. I see all of that you, and I want to be with you."

Peggy wiped away her tears, her heart swelled with emotions. "Tony, I want to be with you too."

Chapter 35

October 1 (2 Months Later)

At 2:00 a.m., startled and alone in her penthouse, Peggy jolted awake from a sound sleep, senses heightened by a haunting nightmare about Walters. A shiver ran down her spine, as she thought she heard a noise. Tears welled up as fear consumed her. She reached for her cellphone, hesitating before dialing Vincente's number.

Vincente's groggy voice answered, "Vincente," he replied, unaware of who was calling him.

"It's me, Peggy," she whispered, her voice trembling with vulnerability.

Instantly alert, Vincente sat up, fully awake. "Hey, what's going on?" The worry in his voice was palpable.

Through her tears, Peggy confided, "I heard a strange noise, and I'm frightened. I just needed to hear your voice. I'm sorry for waking you."

Without a moment's hesitation, Vincente reassured her, "I'm on my way over."

"You don't have to do that. You have work in the morning."

"I want to come over. I'll go in a little later tomorrow. I'll bring my work clothes with me. See you soon."

Twenty minutes later, Vincente stood outside Peggy's penthouse door. Wearing pajama pants and a t-shirt, he carried an overnight bag and a suit draped over his arm. As Peggy opened the door, their eyes met, Vincente saw how frightened she was.

Abandoning everything he held, Vincente wrapped his big arms around Peggy, in a tender embrace. She wore only a skimpy nightgown on her shapely body. As she pressed against his chest, he could feel the softness of her ample breasts. A surge of desire ignited within him, leaving him almost breathless.

Vincente whispered, "Do you want to talk about it?"

Peggy's tearful response was a soft, "No."

"I'm going to put you to bed," Vincente said, his voice gentle and soothing.

Overwhelmed, Peggy sobbed in his arms, trying to combat the haunting memories of Walters. Vincente sensed the helplessness and pain she was experiencing.

"Anytime you need me, just call, and I will be right here," Vincente assured her, his voice filled with tenderness and support.

Lifting Peggy into his arms, Vincente carried her, bridal style, to the master bedroom. There, he gently laid her on the bed. Slipping in beside her, he held her close, putting her head on his chest. His hand caressed her hair and drew soft circles on her back. He was careful not to her touch breasts or buttocks – he didn't want to invade her boundaries. Though his mind and body yearned for intimacy with Peggy, he held back his desires and focused on comforting and protecting her.

Within moments, Peggy fell asleep, her sobs silenced in slumber. Vincente's arms encircled her, his lips pressing a gentle kiss on her head. As he, too, drifted off to sleep, he felt a profound sense of relief, knowing that she was safe in his arms.

Chapter 36

October 28 (3 Months Later)

Peggy sat beside Tony on his cozy worn leather couch, his arm draped around her shoulders. They watched a movie streaming on Netflix.

Vincente's one-bedroom apartment was tiny compared to Peggy's penthouse. The apartment was sparsely furnished, save for a couch, dated wooden coffee table, oversized flat screen TV, and DVD player in the living room. A small homemade bookcase housed several books and DVDs with unusual titles. The only bedroom had a king-sized bed, one small dresser, and a large desk with a state-of-the-art desktop gaming computer.

Vincente had prepared a simple dinner for them in his galley kitchen. After dinner Peggy watched as he briefly played online video games with his friends. There was a certain charm in observing his intense focus. To Tony's surprise, Peggy had shown him her gaming skills on his vintage Game Cube. She enjoyed spending time with Tony, feeling their connection deepen.

Vincente couldn't help but notice Peggy's beauty. Wearing tight blue jeans and a fitted white t-shirt that accentuated her curves, she looked sexy. Her thick blonde hair cascaded around her shoulders, framing her lovely face. Vincente was captivated by her. He found everything about her irresistible.

As the days passed, Peggy's recovery from the trauma inflicted by the serial killer, John Walters, progressed slowly. The nightmares and flashbacks were almost gone. She had returned to work and seemed contented. Vincente enjoyed spending time with her, cherishing every moment in her company. His feelings for her ran deep, and he could sense that he was falling in love.

Peggy took a deep breath to muster the courage to ask an uncomfortable question, "Tony, I need ask you something, something awkward. I really don't know how to ask this..."

With genuine concern and a gentle caress down her arm, Vincente replied, "You can ask me anything."

"If you were to introduce me to your friends or any group, how would you introduce me?"

"What?"

"For example, would you introduce me by saying this is Peggy, she is my friend or...?" Peggy asked, worried about Tony's answer.

Vincente chuckled, "I would introduce you as my girlfriend," he answered, pressing a tender kiss on her head.

"Really? Because I think of you as my boyfriend. I am not seeing anybody else."

"You, Babe, are my exclusive girlfriend. I will not date anybody else. In fact, I haven't even looked at another woman since I met you because you are so gorgeous!" He playfully kissed her nose.

Peggy asked carefully, "But what about sex? We haven't even had sex yet."

Vincente gently clasped the sides of her face with his large hands. He turned her face towards him and said, "We will make love when you are ready. You lived through a serious trauma."

"But how will I know when I am ready. My therapist said I might never be ready. What if I am never ready?"

Vincente reassured her, "You'll know when you're ready. Just let me know. I want to whisk you away for a romantic weekend. The first time I make love to you I don't want any interruptions or distractions. I want you all to myself." He held her close in his arms.

"Okay, but you haven't even properly kissed me yet."

"Baby, if I kiss you the way I want to kiss you, I will be kissing you all night! And that will lead to other things that you are not ready for."

"What other things?" Peggy asked.

"You will have to wait and see."

"How about a sneak preview?" she playfully asked.

"Nope."

"Spoilers?"

Vincente shook his head, "Nope."

Deep down, Vincente yearned to make love to Peggy. The intensity of his desire was almost unbearable, causing him to constantly fantasize about her body and giving him wet dreams. Never before had he wanted a woman so badly. He hoped she would be ready soon.

Chapter 37

November 9

Detective Vincente sat alone at a bar in his old neighborhood, waiting for his friends to arrive. This traditional monthly gathering allowed him to catch up with the four guys he had grown up with. As he nursed his beer, Vincente's thoughts wandered to Dr. Peggy Scott, the woman who had captured his heart. They had been dating for nearly four months, their connection deepening with each passing day. Despite their emotional intimacy, they had not had sex. Vincente respected Peggy's need to wait until she felt ready.

But the desire within Vincente grew with every passing moment. His mind was consumed by thoughts of undressing Peggy, imagining the sensation of her bare silky skin against his fingertips. The ache within him intensified, the relentless need to fuck her made his cock constantly hard. He wanted to trace the curves of her naked body with his hands. He wanted to kiss the pink pouty lips of her mouth. He wanted to teach her all about her body -- suckle her heavy tits -- slowly run his tongue all over her nude body, until she was wet and ready for his eager cock. He wanted to feast on her pussy until she came. He couldn't wait until his hard cock was deep inside her bare pussy. The mere thought of her naked and willing beneath him drove him crazy.

As Vincente was lost in his sex fueled daydreams, a familiar voice interrupted his thoughts. "Hi Tony," Vanessa greeted him, taking a seat on the barstool next to him.

Startled by her presence, Vincente felt uneasy. "Hi. What brings you here?"

Vanessa smiled, her skintight dress accentuating her figure. Her touch briefly grazed Vincente's arm. "I heard you were meeting the guys tonight, so I thought I'd stop by and say hello."

Vincente crossed his arms, feeling increasingly uncomfortable. "I'm early."

Vanessa chuckled. "Oh, Tony, you're always either too early or too late—never on time! How have you been?"

"Great. And you?"

"I'm good. Congratulations Tony, on solving that big serial killer case."

"Thanks. I had a lot of help. Can I get you a drink?" Vincente offered, trying to be polite.

"No, I'm not staying. That girl he kidnapped—Peggy Scott? She's the same girl you brought to the wedding reception, right?"

"Yes," Vincente confirmed.

"Poor thing. How does one recover from something like that? I hope she's okay."

"I'm sure she will be," Vincente responded, his discomfort growing. He did not want to discuss Peggy with Vanessa.

"Listen, Tony, the real reason I stopped by is to tell you that I miss you. I still care about you. Maybe we could go out sometime?" Vanessa proposed, her hand stroking Vincente's arm.

"No, Vanessa. I'm sorry, but it's over."

Vanessa withdrew her hand, disappointment in her eyes. "I heard you're dating her—Peggy Scott."

"Yes."

"You're in love with her, Tony, aren't you? I can tell."

Vincente didn't answer.

"She's a lucky woman to have someone like you. Well, I should be going. It was nice to see you again, Tony," Vanessa said as she stood to leave.

Vincente nodded, relieved once Vanessa was gone. His thoughts echoed her words, *Vanessa is right, I am in love with her*. The intensity of his emotions left no room for doubt.

Chapter 38

November 14

Tony and Peggy were sitting on the sprawling white couch in Peggy's luxurious penthouse, talking and listening to music. They enjoyed being together. Vincente, pulling Peggy into his arms, marveled at the perfect fit of her body against his. Her always snuggling close to him gave him a feeling of warmth and belonging that he had never experienced before. He never missed an opportunity to touch her, hold her hand, or wrap his arms around her.

Desire and anticipation coursed through Vincente's veins as he eagerly awaited the moment when he and Peggy would make love. He could sense that she was close to being ready for intimacy. He envisioned all the ways he planned to seduce her ultimately fuck her. He had told Peggy to let him know of her readiness ahead of time. A reservation at a lavish downtown hotel, a suite adorned with champagne and flowers—a giant bed for exploring each other's body. He would be patient with her. He wanted to do everything slowly and lovingly. He planned to hold her hand while he gently penetrated her.

To Tony's surprise, Peggy climbed onto his lap, her outfit accentuating every curve of her hour-glass figure. Dressed in tight black leggings and a form-fitting sweater, she was irresistible. Straddling his thighs, she began to kiss and lick neck, the sensation of her delicate tongue ignited his body on fire. His cock became uncomfortably hard. She skillfully began to unbutton his button-down white shirt.

"Umm, hey, what are you doing?" he managed to utter, hoping Peggy didn't notice the huge bulge tenting his pants. "Are you trying to seduce me, Doctor?"

Vincente gripped Peggy's waist, attempting to keep her from sitting on or brushing against his erection.

A glimmer of mischief danced in Peggy's eyes. "I've been thinking," Peggy spoke softly, her words laced with confidence, "Just because I'm not ready for you to make love to me doesn't mean I can't pleasure you."

Vincente's heart skipped as she continued to unbutton his shirt, her lips planting delicate kisses on his exposed chest.

Vincente rubbed his face against her silken hair and whispered, "What do you mean, baby?"

With a hint of hesitation, Peggy revealed, "I've never done this before, but I want to... I want to perform oral sex on your penis."

Vincente burst out laughing, caught off guard by her unexpected request. *That is the most unsexy, clinical thing I have ever heard!* He thought.

Still chuckling, Vincente replied, "Are you trying to sound sexy?"

"That doesn't sound sexy?" She stopped in unbuttoning his shirt, feeling embarrassed by her failed attempt at seduction.

"No, it doesn't sound sexy, too clinical."

"How would you say it?" Peggy asked.

Vincente leaned in, his voice a husky whisper in her ear, "Well, if I wanted to say something sexy to you... I can't wait to trace the curves of your tits with my tongue. I want to bury my face between your long, lovely legs and drive my tongue deep inside of your pussy. I want to eat you out until you come screaming my name. Then I want to fuck you, thrusting my cock deep inside of your tight, wet pussy...umm I kind of got carried away, babe, too much?"

Peggy's eyes widened in astonishment, the sound of Vincente's naughty words coursing through her core. "Oh my! No. I see what you mean."

Vincente, raising an eyebrow, couldn't help but smile at her response. "Would you like that?" he asked, his voice filled with desire.

"Umm, well, yes. No one has ever talked sexy to me before, but I felt tingly all over when you said... all of those...when you said that!" she nervously confessed.

"Peggy? Tingly sounds good." Tony raised one eyebrow and smiled.

Vincente's desire was growing with every passing second. As Peggy continued un-buttoning his shirt, her kisses moving down on his bare chest, his arousal intensified, threatening to consume him.

"Tony? Even though I've never done given someone a blow job before, I just want you to know that I did Google how to do it."

Vincente's laughter filled the room. He gently cupped her face, "No one has ever Googled that for me before. You don't have to do that. I'd rather wait until you're ready. To have your mouth on me would excite me more than anything."

Peggy's lips caressed Tony's neck and he warned, "If you keep kissing me like that, I am going to have to take a cold shower!" He thought his cock was about to explode.

Vincente pulled her tightly against his chest, feeling the rapid thud of their hearts beating together. A mixture of frustration and longing filled Peggy's sigh as she rested her head on his chest. Tony drew soft circles on her back, and thought about work, trying to get his mind off of his painful hard on.

Chapter 39

November 19

Detective Vincente and Detective Keeley were on their way to a crime scene. As Vincente grabbed his notebook from his desk, he spotted Peggy rushing into the squad room. She looked frantic and she was still wearing her coat. Tony was concerned, *What the Hell happened?*

"Can I talk to you?" Peggy asked out of breath.

Vincente nodded, his worry growing by the second. "Sure. Keeley, I'll be right back. Let's step into an interrogation room."

Leading Peggy into one of the small, secluded rooms, Vincente closed the door behind them, for privacy. He almost shuddered as he remembered the last time they were in an interrogation room together, she had given her statement about what that fucking animal, Walters, had done to her. As he turned to face her, he gripped her upper arms, their eyes fixed on each other.

"What's going on?" Vincente asked, his voice filled with genuine concern.

Peggy blushed, her voice barely above a whisper. "I'm ready."

Confusion furrowed Vincente's brow as he tried to understand. "Ready for what?"

"You know." A flicker of anticipation danced in Peggy's blue eyes.

A realization dawned upon Vincente, and he smiled with a mischievous look in his eyes. "Are you coming on to me, Doctor?"

Peggy nodded and rubbed her body against his with an unspoken desire.

"Are you sure?"

He saw the raw desire in Peggy's eyes as she spoke, "I want to feel you moving inside of me."

Vincente's cock got immediately hard. He hugged Peggy, as they pressed their bodies. The intensity of their longing palpable. Tony pressed a kiss upon the crown of her head in silent gratitude.

In a voice filled with passion, Vincente spoke, "I'll make reservations at the City Plaza Hotel for this weekend. It will be just the two of us, no distractions, no cellphones. But before that, we should discuss birth control. Would you like me to wear a condom? I've been tested, and I'm free of STDs. The last time I has sex with someone was almost a year ago."

Peggy reassured him, "I've only had sex three times in my life, and each time my partner wore a condom. I've been tested too, and I'm clean. I have an IUD, so you don't need to wear a condom. In fact, I don't want any barriers between us."

"I'll pick you up Friday night after work, at your place."

"What should I bring?"

Vincente replied, "Just a toothbrush."

As their eyes locked, Vincente leaned in, ready to capture her lips in a passionate kiss. Peggy closed her eyes in anticipation of their first kiss. But instead, Tony pressed a chaste kiss on her forehead.

"See you Friday night," Vincente murmured.

A frustrated groan escaped Peggy's lips, her desire for more palpable. Vincente put his arm around her shoulders and guided her out of the interrogation room.

Chapter 40

November 24 (Thanksgiving)

P eggy's heart felt a tinge of longing as she spent Thanksgiving with her father, knowing that Tony was celebrating the holiday with his brother's family. Peggy's thoughts were consumed by Tony and the upcoming weekend. She was indeed ready to be intimate with him. In fact, the thought of his hands caressing her body caused a delicious throbbing between her legs. A sensation she had never felt before.

***

Vincente enjoyed spending Thanksgiving with his older brother's family. However, he missed Peggy. He wished she had joined him for Thanksgiving but understood her commitment to spending the holiday with her father. The anticipation of their upcoming weekend together consumed him. He could feel the tip of his hard cock leaking with pre-cum anytime he thought about Peggy's naked body writhing with her first orgasm, as he gently fucked her.

Chapter 41

November 25

D r. Peggy Scott couldn't contain her excitement as she got ready for her passionate weekend rendezvous with Tony. Uncertain about what to bring, she bought skimpy lingerie and a delicate silk teddy. She packed the sexy new items, and a few changes of clothes, into her overnight bag. Slipping into a low-cut, clingy, silky blue mini dress that accentuated her curves, she felt sexy. She slipped on thigh high dark stockings and stepped into "fuck-me" high heels. Peggy wore her hair loose and her silky blonde waves cascaded around her shoulders. After a long, relaxing shower, she coated her skin with scented lotion, gently massaging it all over her body. Spritzing the perfume Vincente liked on her neck, wrists, and inner thighs, she felt desirable.

Nervousness shadowed Peggy's excitement about being intimate with Tony. She wanted to please him sexually but couldn't hide her lack of sexual experience. The fear of disappointing him and not knowing the intimate ways to pleasure a man's body haunted her thoughts, reminding her of Clearmont's frustrations during their brief relationship. Yet, she hoped Tony would be patient and understanding with her lack of sexual prowess and her inability to climax.

A knock echoed through Peggy's penthouse, signaling Tony's arrival. She opened the door and was greeted by his radiant smile. He looked dashing in his black dress suit, and Peggy's heart filled with desire.

"Wow! You look amazing!" Vincente exclaimed.

"Hi. I've missed you."

Eager to begin their passionate weekend together, Vincente asked, "Shall we?"

Vincente stepped into the foyer and grabbed Peggy's overnight bag. Ever the consummate gentleman, Tony helped Peggy with her coat. As they stepped out of Peggy's building, Vincente put his hand on her lower back and guided her to a waiting cab.

Arriving at the Hotel, Vincente arranged for a bellboy to take Peggy's bag to their suite. He had checked in earlier to make sure everything was in order.

Hand in hand, Vincente guided Peggy to the Plaza's restaurant for dinner, where an intimate, candlelit table for two was reserved for them.

Vincente ordered a bottle of white wine. Reaching across the table, he gently clasped Peggy's hand, his voice filled with anticipation. "I can't wait to be with you."

Peggy blushed and she shyly glanced down, her hands trembling with a of excitement and nervousness.

Vincente noticed the trembling of her delicate hands. "Look, if you have any doubts or don't feel ready, it's okay. We can simply enjoy our dinner and I will take you home."

"No, no, I am ready. I'm just nervous. I may not be very experienced, but I want to be with you."

"Don't be nervous. I won't do anything you don't want me to. We can take it slow, at your pace. Your comfort is what matters most. If, at any point, you want me to stop, just tell me."

Vincente wanted to show Peggy that sex could be a beautiful experience, devoid of pain or degradation. He longed to awaken her body, to tease and pleasure her, until she came. He wanted her body to burn for him the way his body burned for her.

Vincente wasn't a selfish lover; he wanted her to enjoy every moment, to reach climax, before he took his pleasure and passionately fucked her. Seeking to ease her worries, he asked, "Do you trust me?"

"Of course, I trust you, Tony. I just don't want to disappoint you. I'm not very experienced at this, and I don't want you to get frustrated."

"You could never disappoint me. All I want is for you to relax and let me take care of everything."

"Tony, you know, you didn't have to go to all this trouble. We could have simply ordered a pizza and stayed at your place or mine."

Vincente smiled warmly, his eyes reflecting his sincerity. "I wanted our first time together to be special, a night we will remember forever."

After a romantic dinner, hand in hand, Vincente led Peggy to the elevator, to go up to the suite.

As they stepped into the suite, Vincente placed the "Do Not Disturb" sign ensuring their privacy.

The luxurious hotel suite featured a spacious sitting area, a large bedroom, and an upscale bathroom with a bathtub and shower designed for two. The sitting area had an oversized couch, a loveseat, and a large screen TV. A bottle of champagne chilled in an ice bucket on a nearby table.

Peggy stood in the warm sitting area, as Tony turned on the TV, selecting a soft music station to set the mood. With a graceful pop, he opened the champagne bottle, pouring two glasses and offering one to Peggy.

Vincente discarded his suit coat and tie, placing them casually on a nearby chair. A mischievous glint sparkled in his eyes as he extended his hand to Peggy. "Dance with me."

Setting her champagne glass down, Peggy took his hand, and they started swaying together in a slow dance. She nestled her head against his broad chest, feeling the comforting beat of his heart. As they moved in harmony, Vincente whispered in her ear, "Psychologically, foreplay lowers inhibitions and increases emotional intimacy between partners."

"I love dancing with you." Peggy told him.

"Hmm. We could just dance all night."

She looked up into his eyes, and said, "No. Tony, I want you. I just don't want to dissap-"

"Shh." He whispered in her ear. His gentle caresses traced her back, and she could feel the undeniable presence of his erection as their bodies pressed together.

Vincente cradled Peggy's face in his hands as he looked into her eyes. Their lips met in a tender, exploratory kiss. Slowly, his tongue danced along her parted lips, venturing deeper into her mouth, igniting her desire. Peggy's breath quickened, the sensations overwhelming her. When their lips finally parted, he smiled, and she felt her legs grow weak. His touch was intoxicating.

"Oh, Tony." The way she whispered his name sent shivers down his spine. Vincente couldn't resist the pull of her lips any longer, crashing his lips onto hers and kissing her with a hunger that consumed him. The taste of her mouth, the feel of her lips and tongue, drove him wild with desire. He found himself unable to get enough of her mouth.

Vincente thought, *God she is so damn hot and sexy!* He wanted her like he had never wanted any other woman ever before.

"Relax, baby. I just want to make you feel good. I want to make you come," Vincente whispered in Peggy's ear, his words igniting a fire within her.

Vincente guided Peggy to the plush, oversized couch. He settled her on one end, his eyes filled with hunger and desire. Eagerly, he removed her high heels and delicately placed her long legs on the couch. Seating himself next to her, he pulled her into his arms, their bodies entwined. Their lips collided in another passionate kiss, their tongues probing in an intensity that left Peggy breathless. As his mouth explored her neck, leaving a trail of kisses and licks, Peggy moaned.

"Mmm," Vincente murmured, the erotic sound of her moans made his rock-hard cock throb in pain.

"Ohh!" Peggy gasped.

"What's wrong?"

Flushing with embarrassment, Peggy confessed, "Well, that's never happened to me before."

"What happened?"

"Umm, I just got all wet. This is so embarrassing. It feels kind of icky."

A mischievous grin tugged at Vincente's lips as he whispered, "Mmm, that's not embarrassing—it's a good thing. It means your body is getting ready for me. I can't wait to taste you – fucking devour you." Without delay, he smothered her mouth with another long deep kiss, consuming her with his desire.

"Oh, Tony, my whole body feels tingly all over.

Tony's hungry kisses sent shivers down her spine, making her tingle all over. She could feel her nipples pebble against her lacy bra. Her pussy ached in anticipation.

"I can't wait to fuck you, baby. I want you so much," Tony whispered, his voice laced with raw desire. His filthy words ignited a fiery passion everywhere in Peggy's body.

Rising from the couch, Vincente effortlessly scooped Peggy into his arms, carrying her into the bedroom. Tenderly, he placed her on the bed, removing his shoes and belt before joining her. Leaning against the plush headboard, he wrapped his arms around her, comforting her.

"Just relax, baby," he whispered, placing a loving kiss on the top of her head.

Peggy longed for Tony's touch. She wanted his large, calloused hands to explore every inch of her body. Her heart pounded in her chest as she thought about spreading her legs wide open for his pleasure. She wondered how it would feel to have his hard cock thrusting inside her pussy.

Vincente's lips trailed kisses along her neck, moving down to the exposed part of her chest framed by the revealing neckline of her dress. Peggy ran her fingers through his hair, enjoying the sensation of his mouth on her bare skin.

"I love this dress. You look so fucking hot," Vincente murmured against her skin.

Tracing the top of her low-cut dress with his tongue on her naked skin, Vincente's hands found their way to her legs. He caressed her smooth, slender legs, all the while Peggy was moaning and breathing heavily. The intensity of his Tony's arousal threatened to consume him – all he could think about was ripping off her dress and fucking the Hell of her. But he was determined to seduce her slowly, to tease her until she let go of her inhibitions and enjoyed the intense pleasure of an orgasm.

Vincente moved the hem of Peggy's dress slightly up. He started to massage her thighs with his long fingers. To his surprise, he saw that she was wearing the garter from the wedding reception.

Vincente laughed and exclaimed, "Now that is a sexy surprise!"

"I thought you might want to take it off me!"

"Mmm," Vincente responded, his gaze filled with primal hunger. Moving down the bed and bending over her, he delicately grasped the garter with his teeth, slowly sliding it down her leg, relishing every inch.

When the garter was finally removed, Vincente pulled Peggy into a sitting position. He took her face in his hands and sealed their connection with a deep and dirty kiss. Fueled by desire, Peggy unbuttoned Vincente's shirt, her hands exploring the warmth and hard muscles of his bare chest.

"Ahh," Vincente moaned, his voice dripping with desire. "Can I touch you, baby?"

Peggy nodded, her desire growing with every passing second. Vincente's hand glided down the front of her dress, barely making contact, teasing her covered nipples. With both hands firmly on her tiny waist, his tongue traced a sensual path down her chest, exploring the depths of her cleavage. Through the fabric of her dress, he began to caress and gently fondle her breasts, his fingertips gliding over her sensitive nipples, making them painfully erect. She arched back wanting more.

"God, your tits are so beautiful," Vincente breathed, his voice filled with lust. "So round, so full. I fucking love touching them."

"I think they are too big."

"No way," Vincente replied. "They are perfect. I fucking love your tits. I can't wait to see them."

The movement of his fingers intensified, rubbing, and massaging her nipples, causing Peggy to moan.

Moving downward, Vincente's hands trailed over Peggy's thighs and legs, his touch making her delightfully shiver. Slowly, he lifted her dress, revealing the tops of her toned thighs. He traced the exposed strip of creamy skin between her pink lace panties and the tops of her thigh-high stockings with his tongue, savoring every inch of her. Slowly, he removed her stockings, his kisses and licks exploring the landscape of her naked legs. Pausing at her panties, he made his way back up to her mouth, capturing her lips in a passionate kiss.

The desire to see her naked overwhelmed Vincente, prompting him to ask, "I need to see you. Can I take off your dress?"

Peggy's response was a breathless "Yes."

Guiding Peggy to face away from him, Vincente's lips roamed her naked back, his kisses distracting her from unzipping her dress. With a contented sigh, he pulled the dress down to her waist, leaving her wearing only a skimpy pink lace bra. As she turned to face him, he marveled at her partially concealed breasts, his fingers tracing the delicate lace.

"Wow," Vincente uttered, his voice filled with awe. "You are so gorgeous."

Overwhelmed by desire, Vincente suckled Peggy's erect nipples, pressing his mouth against the thin fabric of her bra. He unclasped the back, discarding the garment, exposing her naked breasts to his ravenous gaze. Kissing his way down to her enticing breasts, Vincente grabbed each full breast with his hands, amazed at how wonderful their creamy softness felt in his hands.

"Oh, God, baby, you are so lovely," Vincente whispered, his voice laced with reverence. "Your tits are incredible."

Peggy's breasts, full and round, adorned with perfectly pink, erect nipples, became the object of Vincente's affection. His lips and tongue caressed every inch of their silky flesh—the tops, the sides, and the sensitive undersides. When his mouth found a nipple,

Peggy gasped, her body arching in response to the pleasurable sensations as he sucked and swirled his tongue over their sensitive tips. The wet sucking sounds his skilled mouth made caused Peggy to clench her thighs. She felt waves of wetness between her legs.

"Oh, Tony!"

Vincente's sensual journey continued as he kissed his way down Peggy's flat stomach, pulling off her dress completely. Wearing only lacy pink bikini panties, she laid on her back before him. The sight of her partially nude body ignited a primal desire within him, his erection ached with intensity. Swiftly pulling off his shirt, pants, and socks, Vincente crawled back on the bed wearing only black briefs. Peggy couldn't help but notice his large erection straining at the front of his underwear. Tony pulled her into his arms as he devoured her mouth in a heated kiss.

"I need to eat your pussy. Would you like that?" Vincente asked, his voice heavy with need.

"Yes." Peggy breathed. The scent of her arousal filled the air.

Positioning himself on the bed, Vincente caressed her sex through the fabric of her panties, his touch sending currents of pleasure coursing through her body.

"One way for a woman to achieve orgasm is by direct sexual stimulation of the clitoris," Vincente whispered, his voice a tender and informative caress.

Vincente's lips caressed Peggy through the thin barrier of her panties, his mouth teasing her sensitive folds. As his tongue brushed against her clitoris, a low, moan escaped lips.

The anticipation was building within Vincente. He needed to see Peggy completely naked. He had always wanted to savor the experience of oral sex with a woman who had removed her pubic hair. He longed to taste her nakedness, to relentlessly drive his tongue into her to bring her to orgasm. Vincente loved giving and receiving oral sex. He hoped Peggy would feel the same way, unlike Vanessa who didn't care for either.

Kissing her inner thighs, Vincente shared his knowledge, "Women are more likely to reach orgasm through oral sex." Peggy could feel Tony's hot breath on her skin, and it made her tremble with need.

Slowly Vincente slid off Peggy's panties, leaving her completely naked. She modestly straightened and closed her legs together, hiding her wetness. The musky scent of her wetness smelled delicious to Tony, and he couldn't wait to taste her.

"Baby, you look like a work of art," Vincente observed. To him, Peggy was a masterpiece, lying naked upon the pristine white sheets, her long blonde hair fanned out like strokes of a brush. The sight of her beauty left him awestruck, his heart brimming with joy.

"Babe, I need to see all of you," he whispered, his voice carrying an urgent plea. He gently grasped Peggy's calves, lifting her knees, and bending her legs. Slowly, he opened her thighs, savoring the sight before him. Her body was so lovely, parting her legs was like opening a delicate flower, her petals tender and pink, glistening with the evidence of her desire. His finger danced lightly across her folds, encountering the slick tightness that awaited him. Peggy gasped, and Vincente's smiled. She was swollen with need, aching for his touch.

My cock is going to explode if I keep looking at her tiny pink pussy. He thought as he swiftly removed his briefs.

"Oh my God, Tony, you are so big. I don't think I'm big enough for you," Peggy exclaimed, her astonishment evident as her gaze fell upon Vincente's long, thick and veiny cock with a dot of pre-com leaking from the mushroom shaped tip.

"Don't worry, baby," Vincente reassured her, his voice filled with tenderness. "I would never hurt you. We don't have to have fuck. I just want to make you come. I can't wait to taste your beautiful wet pussy."

Peggy felt another trickle of wetness run down her inner thighs as he spoke about tasting her.

Vincente's tongue glided over Peggy's stomach, as his deft fingers took their place between her legs, circling her clit with his gentle touch.

"Baby, your pussy is dripping wet for me! Mmm." Tony observed as leaned over and licked the delicious wetness off her inner thighs. The taste of her sweet juices intoxicated him.

Peggy's heart raced; her breaths heavy as Tony worshipped her nude body. She loved the way his naked skin felt against hers. The strokes of tongue were driving her to the edge of ecstasy. She had never been so sexually aroused before.

With a long, slow lick, Vincente savored the taste of Peggy's wetness, his tongue exploring the contours of her sex. The sweet moans that escaped her lips fueled his desire.

Peggy felt the warmth of Vincente's breath on her delicate folds, her core throbbing with anticipation. Vincente's tongue swirled lightly over her clit. A low moan escaped her lips. As the movement of his tongue intensified on her clit, Peggy arched her back, aching for more. With a skillful finger, he teased her, circling her soaked opening and fingering her. Her body responded eagerly, her moans echoing through the air.

"You are such a noisy little thing," he whispered, his voice filled with adoration. "I love that. I also love this delicious pussy. You taste salty and sweet like salted caramel. My new favorite flavor."

"Oh God, Tony," Peggy gasped, her body on fire. The sheets clenched tightly in her fists.

Vincente's whispered against her folds, "The vagina harbors its greatest concentration of nerve endings near the entrance. Stimulating the roof of the vagina can produce intense pleasure and bring forth powerful orgasms." He sucked one of her folds into his mouth.

With both hands, Vincente lifted Peggy's buttocks, positioning himself to delve deeper into the wet opening with his tongue. His tongue plunged deeply into her, moving rapidly in and out of her, consuming her with each stroke. She unconsciously grasped his head and grinded into his mouth, riding his face.

The pleasurable feel of his tongue and sucking sounds of his mouth pushed Peggy over the edge. Her scream filled the room as her orgasm surged through her. She felt like she was shattering all over his face. Never before had she experienced such intense pleasure, her body pulsing and throbbing in ecstasy.

Vincente was amazed at the feel of her pussy convulsing and clenching his tongue. Her pussy swelling and throbbing with need as she squirted her delectable juices on his mouth and face.

Vincente continued thrusting his tongue into her opening wanting to prolong her orgasm as long as possible. The intensity of Peggy's pleasure heightened his own need for release.

"Tony, please," Peggy pleaded, her voice filled with desperation. "I need to feel your cock inside me."

Well, fuck and I need to feel you perfect pussy swallowing my cock. Thought Tony.

Vincente positioned his cock at her Peggy's slick opening, gently easing himself inside of her inch by inch. The feel of her wetness reminded him of warm melted butter. Each inch sent waves of pleasure coursing through Peggy's body. When his cock was fully sheathed, she wrapped her legs around to his waist and clung to him tightly. Her hardened nipples throbbed with desire, aching for his touch, while her sex pulsed and clenched around him, wet and eager.

Wow her pussy is so warm, wet and tight. My cock will never want to leave. Vincente marveled.

"Baby I am going to fuck you now." He whispered as began to thrust inside of her. Her wetness increasing with each thrust. He couldn't hold back his moans of pleasure as in thrusted deeper and harder into her tight wetness. Peggy's hips bucked in rhythm with Vincente's thrusts, her tightness gripping him as he moved faster. Vincente was consumed by pleasure, their connection electrifying. Peggy felt herself let go as his cock hit a sensitive spot inside of her. She started coming, her body feeling like it was shattering with the intensity of her pleasure. The sensation of her tight wetness, pulsing and gripping his cock, pushed Vincente to the edge of his control. He fought against his release, savoring every sensation, and wanting to prolong Peggy's orgasm.

Lost in the intensity of pleasure, Peggy turned her head from side to side, surrendering herself to the repeated orgasms raging through her. Tony held her head in place, capturing her moans with a passionate kiss. The sensations were too much for Vincente, with a final deep thrust, he violently came inside of her.

Overwhelmed with ecstasy, Peggy struggled to muffle her screams. Her body betrayed her with uncontrolled movements, her hips bucking, and body thrashing and writhing in pure bliss.

Whispering softly, Vincente reassured Peggy, "Just relax, baby. You did incredible." Holding her close, he rolled onto his back, so she lay on top of him. He enjoyed the feeling of their combined juices dripping on his stomach. He caressed her naked back and buttocks with a soothing and affectionate touch. Their bodies intertwined; they basked in the afterglow of their orgasms. Peggy, however, couldn't help but feel a little embarrassed by her body's response.

"I'm so embarrassed." Peggy confessed.

Vincente's laughter filled the room as he realized what she was embarrassed about. "I thought you said you couldn't come. I'm pretty sure those were orgasms." As his fingers caressed her heart-shaped bottom, he started to get an erection.

Peggy buried her head in his muscular chest, as she ran a hand over the tightness of his 6-pack abs.

"Don't be embarrassed, baby," Vincente urged. "That was amazing. You're stunning when you come."

"Is that how all women come?"

"I've never encountered a pussy as sensitive and, I can't think of the right word, maybe expressive? You're throbbing and clenching pussy feels extraordinary when you come. Your body is incredible—so hot and sexy. I can't wait to fuck you again."

"I can see that." Peggy smiled as she stroked his cock.

Vincente rolled Peggy over on her back. "You're a mess down there. I'll get a wash-cloth and clean you up," he declared before heading to the bathroom. Returning with a warm, wet washcloth, he gently cleaned her, delicately wiping her folds. Peggy's sensitive response delighted him, further fueling his desire.

As Vincente finished, he settled back onto the bed. He wrapped his arms around Peggy. Tony pulled up the covers and covered their naked bodies. Peggy nestled on top of Vincente and rested her head on his chest. They both felt a sense of contentment they had never experienced before.

Peggy whispered, "I think that was an anomaly."

"I believe those were orgasms—profound, intense, and beautiful orgasms. Your pussy is incredible. I've never felt anything like it before. Did you enjoy coming?"

A mixture of emotions swept through Peggy. "Yes, I did. But I'm afraid it won't happen again. My body's response was likely due to it being my first time."

"Really? Let's test your hypothesis and find out," Vincente said with a mischievous grin, playfully rolling Peggy onto her back.

Vincente's lips and tongue started on another slow, tantalizing journey, tracing a path from her breasts down to her stomach. As he spread her legs, he cupped her wet mound with his hand, his touch gentle arousing. Peggy moaned in response. Vincente nestled his face between her open legs. His tongue explored every delicate fold, savoring the taste of her wetness. When he found her clitoris, she cried out. Her wetness dripped down her inner thighs as he circled, sucked and kneaded her sensitive with his skilled tongue.

As Vincente expertly licked her clitoris in a figure-eight pattern, his middle finger slid inside her. inside He massaged the inner walls of her tight opening, finding that sensitive spot. The intense sensations consumed her, causing her to buck her hips and moan. Her sex pulsated and clenched around his finger, aching for more.

"Mmm, baby, you are so juicy. I love how wet your pussy gets for me," Vincente whispered.

Peggy's need became unbearable. Her hips moved urgently chasing the peak of plea-sure. She screamed as her sex throbbed and clenched around his finger. Vincente, now fully aroused, moaned and slipped his erection into her wetness. Wanting to get deeper he lifted Peggy's legs and placed one on each of his shoulders. He could feel her tightness squeezing his cock. him, the grip of her sex intense.

Fuck I am balls deep in her pussy. He thought.

Thrusting his hips, Vincente buried himself deep inside her. He began thrusting, his cock pistoning inside her. He reveled in the sounds of his cock squelching in and out of her wetness, along with the slapping sounds his balls made when thrusted deep inside of her.

Withdrawing from her, Vincente rolled Peggy onto her stomach, his hands encircling her hips as he thrusted in her from behind. Her sex clung to him eagerly, each thrust met with her responsive movements and moans.

God, I love this ass. I could listen to my balls slapping it for hours. Tony thought.

Her orgasm was deep and powerful and didn't stop. At the feeling of the strong wet clenching on his cock intensified, Vincente thrusted harder and faster.

"Oh, baby, you feel incredible! I could fuck your pussy for hours," Vincente grunted.

Tony cried out as he came deep inside of her. Peggy continued to climax, her breath coming in rapid gasps. Vincente feared she was going to hyperventilate.

"Oh, God Tony!" Peggy cried, trying to catch her breath.

"Baby, relax. I don't want you to pass out on me," he gently reassured, pulling out before he rolled off her.

Vincente couldn't resist the urge to caress her naked back and bottom with his hands.

"Wow. I suppose your first orgasm, or should I say orgasms, weren't an anomaly."

"Ugh!" Peggy scoffed, as she felt their combined juices dripping on her thighs as she enjoyed the aftershocks of her intense orgasm. "Tony, I've never felt this way before. The pleasure you give me is indescribable. I lose complete control of my body."

While Peggy snuggled next to Tony's hard warm body, she couldn't deny her growing feelings for Tony Vincente. As she reached for a pillow and placed it under her head. She thought, *I am in love with him.* She wondered how he felt about her.

Vincente sat up; his gaze fixated on Peggy's exposed backside. In his eyes, she possessed the most alluring and captivating ass he had ever seen.

"Peggy, you have got the sexiest body I have ever seen! I just love your tits, your lovely ass, your sweet and delicious pussy!"

"I've noticed!"

"I'll be right back," Vincente informed her, excusing himself to the bathroom to freshen up and retrieve another wet washcloth. Returning to the room, he found Peggy fast asleep, her naked body serenely sprawled on the bed with the covers entangled at her feet. Vincente couldn't help but ogle her bare bottom and long sleek legs, longing to trace tongue along the curves of her ass. However, he didn't want to disturb her sleep, so he reluctantly covered her up and slipped into bed beside her.

Sleep seemed unlikely with his aching erection. *I am so God damn hard. I could fuck her all night!* He thought. Yet, to his surprise, he felt a warm, naked body snuggle against his back, bringing a smile to his face as he drifted off to sleep.

Chapter 42

November 26 (Saturday Morning)

Tony woke up early in the morning, feeling happy. Peggy remained sound asleep beside him as he quietly rose from the bed and went to take a shower. Wearing a comfortable pair of jeans, a T-shirt and his black leather jacket, Vincente left the hotel suite to pick up bagels and coffee. He didn't want her to wake up and find him gone, so he left her a note on the nightstand.

The vibrant downtown Chicago streets welcomed him, basking in the warm glow of a sunny Winter Day. His thoughts revolved around Peggy, reliving the passionate sex they had last night, hoping for a day and night filled with even more passionate lovemaking.

***

Slowly awakening, Peggy reached out for Tony, finding the king-sized bed empty beside her. She spotted the note on the nightstand which read, "Be back soon, went for coffee and bagels." A smile spread across her face as she stretched, still amazed by the erotic lovemaking from last night. Tony had proven himself an extraordinary lover, igniting a desire within her that ached for more. The anticipation of spending the day and night in bed with him was exciting.

Peggy rose from the bed and indulged in a long, hot shower. She blow-dried her hair and applied a touch of makeup and pulled out the change of clothes from her overnight bag. Unsure whether to dress for the day, she opted for the hotel's long white terry cloth robe, its soft fabric enveloping her. Stepping into the sitting area, she discovered a cup of coffee and toasted bagels with cream cheese waiting on the coffee table. She smiled at Tony's thoughtful gesture.

Vincente stood by the window, a steaming cup of coffee in his hand, his gaze fixed on the world outside. Peggy watched him, her heart filled with hope that he felt as happy about last night as she did. She longed to know how he felt about her but was afraid to spoil their romantic weekend by asking.

As Vincente looked out, he couldn't help but think about the first time he cooked dinner for Peggy. The memory of that dinner made him smile. He had tried to impress her with his culinary skills by preparing his late Aunt's homemade marinara sauce—a recipe passed down through generations of his Italian family. He had playfully remarked that pasta ran in his blood, wanting to share his joy of cooking with her.

Standing side by side in his tiny kitchen, Vincente noticed Peggy's nervousness. Sensing her hesitation, he asked, "Do you know how to cook?"

"Umm. Sure. Everybody knows how to cook." she answered, lowering her eyes.

Her lowered gaze confirmed Tony's suspicion that she was embarrassed to tell him the truth. He suspected that she probably never learned how to cook since she was raised by a billionaire father in a mansion filled with servants. Wanting to spare her any embarrassment, he decided to assign her an easy task.

"Why don't you chop the onion?" he suggested, handing her a wooden chopping board and a large yellow onion, its skin intact.

Peggy took the onion into her hands, studying it with a mix of curiosity and apprehension. Vincente observed her from the corner of his eye, finding her vulnerability sweet. Placing the unpeeled onion on the chopping board, Peggy reached for a meat cleaver, one of the knives in the counter knife holder. Before Vincente could stop her, she grasped the cleaver with both hands, wielding it as if it were a mighty weapon, and struck the onion with force. To her surprise, the onion split in two, its halves flying through the air before landing on the kitchen floor. Vincente stifled a laugh, and swiftly took the meat cleaver out of her hands.

"Leave. Go watch TV," he commanded.

Peggy, undeterred by the flying onion, smiled and asked, "Can I watch one of your porn movies?"

"Nope."

Hearing the sound of Peggy picking up her coffee from the table, Vincente turned his attention to her, a warm smile on his face. As he looked at her, he was overwhelmed by her beauty and naivete; she was unlike anyone he had ever met. He yearned to tell her how he felt about her but feared his feelings would overwhelm her and ruin their romantic weekend.

"Good morning, I had planned to serve you breakfast in bed, but you were in the shower when I got back."

"Umm. Thank you for breakfast."

Peggy settled herself on the couch, eating a bagel, cocooned in her bathroom. Vincente couldn't help but imagine what lay beneath its soft fabric. Setting his coffee aside, he leaned against the closed window and crossed his ankles.

Peggy was envisioning Tony's muscular naked body and 6-pack abs when his voice interrupted her thoughts, "Peggy last night was amazing. I can't seem to get you out of my mind."

Her blush turned her cheeks pink as she spoke, "Yes, you were incredible."

Raising an eyebrow, Vincente met her gaze. "And so were you, babe."

Changing the subject, Peggy asked, "What do you want to do today?"

Standing up from the couch, Peggy walked toward Vincente, enveloping him in her arms. She nuzzled against his middle, seeking warmth and closeness.

Vincente chuckled, as he wrapped his arms around her. "Do I really need to answer that?" Peggy nodded. "Alright, how about going to the movies?"

Peggy shook her head, her desire for something different obvious. "Nooo."

"A walk?" Vincente suggested as he rested his chin on the top of her head.

"No."

"How about playing cards? I can show you some magic tricks."

"I like cards."

"No. I want to do this." Peggy announced as she started unbuttoning Vincente's shirt, her lips caressing his bare chest. Her fingers skillfully undid his pants and pushed his briefs down revealing his growing erection.

"Babe, you don't have to do that."

"I want to make you feel good. I want to suck your cock." She whispered.

"Oh, fuck! Baby if you keep saying dirty words, I am going to come all over you."

On her knees before him, Peggy traced the contours of his cock with her tongue, simultaneously stroking his shaft with both hands. She marveled at how big he was. Exploring every inch of him, she licked his balls and eagerly took him in her mouth and began to suck his salty tip. Surprising Tony, she hollowed her cheeks and took him all the way to the back of her throat, almost swallowing him.

A moan escaped Vincente's lips,"Ohhh! Thank you, Google," he muttered. With a tender grip on her head, he gently guided her actions, thrusting into her mouth to the back of her throat.

"Look at me. I want to see your beautiful eyes as your sucking my cock." Peggy looked up in his face with tears in her eyes from gagging on his length. "I love seeing your lips on my cock."

He held her head firmer as he thrusted harder and faster. The sight of Peggy taking almost all of his cock in her mouth was just as pleasurable as the act itself. He couldn't hold back any longer -- his balls tightened and his cock spasmed as he came down her throat. He had not meant to come in her mouth, but he lost control. He watched Peggy as he withdrew from her mouth. She smiled mischievously as his cum ran down her chin. *She looks even more beautiful with my cum on her face*, he thought.

"You are very naughty, girl." Vincente playfully remarked.

Reaching for a tissue from the box on the coffee table, Vincente wiped her face and himself clean, a contented sigh escaping his lips. Peggy, still on her knees, looked up at him, her voice barely a whisper.

"I am all wet now."

Seduced by her words, Vincente seized her arms and lifted her gently, guiding her to the couch. His hands encircled her waist, pulling her close. With a swift movement, he had her naked on the couch. Straddling her legs, Vincente's gaze fell upon the glistening wetness between her legs, proof of her arousal. Lowering his lips to hers, he kissed her mouth. Trailing kisses and licks along her body, he found her hard rosy nipples and teased them relentlessly with his mouth and tongue.

Whispering against her skin, he confessed his desire, "Oh, baby, my mouth can't get enough of your tits."

Vincente's hands moved beneath Peggy, swiftly flipping her onto her stomach. She assumed his favorite position -- on all fours, ramping up his desire. Eagerly, he knelt behind her, his hands parting her legs, impatient to explore every inch of her with his mouth. His lips descended upon her luscious bottom, planting kisses that trailed between her quivering thighs. His tongue caressed her slit and every fold, before suckling her clit, making Peggy moan.

"Oh, God, Tony!"

The sound of his name on her lips fueled Vincente's desire, "Fuck I love the way you smell...the way you taste. I can't get enough of your pussy!" His tongue found her opening, plunging deep inside, thrusting and grinding against her with urgency.

"Come for me, baby!" Tony demanded, while swirling his tongue, intensifying the sensations in her wet opening. Pushed beyond her limits, Peggy grinded her throbbing center into Tony's face. *Fuck, her pussy is trying to grip my tongue!* Wanting to share her orgasm, Tony Immediately shoved down his pants and entered her in one deliberate thrust. Thrusting and circling his hips, he hit the spot inside of her that made her scream in pleasure as waves of her orgasm surged through her.

"Baby that feels so good – your pussy is milking my cock." He could feel her coming over and over again. The feel of her rhythmic throbbing and clenching orgasm overwhelmed him and he couldn't hold back his powerful orgasm, emptying deep inside of her. Deliciously spent, Vincente picked Peggy up and carried her bridal style to the king-sized bed so they could enjoy the afterglow of their shared ecstasy in comfort.

***

After a short nap, their bodies still entwined, Vincente positioned himself on top of Peggy, ready to claim her again. As he slowly entered her, tightness and wetness enveloped him, their need more intense than earlier today. Peggy's hips began to buck, her panting breaths an indication of her complete surrender to the ecstasy coursing through her. She had lost control, her body becoming an instrument for sexual pleasure. Vincente thrust deeply, enjoying the pulsing, and gripping on his swollen cock. Gripping his neck, Peggy's continuous orgasm overtook her while Vincente's powerful thrusts fueled their connection. Moaning, their mutual release overtook them, and they collapsed on the bed, their bodies entangled.

Reaching for a tissue from the nearby box, Vincente carefully wiped away the fluids from their shared passion. Shifting Peggy's position, he placed her on top of him, their bodies pressed together, his arms wrapped around her tightly. He placed a loving kiss on the crown of her head, loving every moment they spent intertwined.

"I love lying with you on top of me. The sensation of our bare skin touching is heavenly," Vincente whispered, his hands gently exploring her back and bottom, caressing her with tender strokes.

Peggy's breath still labored, her body pulsating with the aftershocks of pleasure.

"Baby, are you all right?" Tony asked.

"I'm just trying to catch my breath. Oh, Tony, I love the way you make me feel." Peggy confessed; her voice filled with gratitude for the pleasurable sensations he awakened within her.

Vincente's tone shifted, betraying his nerves as he prepared to speak. Peggy's heart skipped a beat, apprehension seeping in as she awaited his words.

"I need to tell you something," Vincente began, his voice tinged with vulnerability. "I had planned to tell you at breakfast, but you distracted me. Peggy, I am so deeply in love with you that it hurts."

Tony felt the weight of his words hang in the air, uncertain of Peggy's response.

"Oh, Tony, I am in love with you too," Peggy confessed, her voice filled happiness. Vincente's face lit up, a mixture of joy and relief.

Vincente passionately kissed her before he suggested, "Stay here, I'll be right back." He left the comfort of the bed and made his way to the bathroom. With purpose, he began filling the oversized tub, the warm water cascading into the bathtub. He added a small bottle of lavender-scented bubble bath from the hotel, infusing the air with the fragrance of Spring flowers. Satisfied, Vincente returned to the sitting bedroom, lifting Peggy effortlessly into his arms.

"What are we doing?" Peggy chuckled.

"We are taking a bubble bath," Vincente announced playfully.

Carrying Peggy, Vincente stepped into the bathroom, carefully lowering her into the inviting tub. As Peggy settled into the embrace of the soothing warm water, Vincente joined her, his presence a source of comfort. He positioned himself behind her, their bodies fitting together like two perfect puzzle pieces. The warm water enveloped them, soothing their bodies and creating a steamy intimate atmosphere. With Peggy seated on his lap, her back nestled against his chest, they enjoyed the warmth of the fragrant water.

Bubbles caressed their skin, adding a layer of sensuality to their bath. Vincente's hands glided along Peggy's naked body, his touch gentle. The warmth of the water and the tender strokes of his hands lulled Peggy into a state of relaxation.

"Baby, I just can't get enough of you," Vincente whispered, his words filled with longing the weight of his desire palpable.

Moved by an irresistible urge, Vincente lifted Peggy, shifting her onto her knees. The soapy water cascaded down her back and over her rounded bottom as he gently guided her to lean her body over the side of the tub. Excitement coursed through him; his erection evident. With hands that knew every contour of her body, he parted her legs, his kneeling form finding a place between her open thighs.

In this intimate space, Vincente's tongue delved deep into her moist folds, exploring every inch. As he found her clit with his tongue, he thrust a finger into her opening. Peggy's body responded eagerly, her inner walls engorged and slick with arousal. As her intimate muscles began to tighten, Vincente buried his tongue deep within her and grinded his face against her.

"Oh, God, Tony," Peggy moaned.

Vincente remained unyielding; his tongue relentless. He moved it in circles and from side to side, each motion growing bolder and more urgent. Peggy's climax surged through her, wave after wave of ecstasy crashing against her senses. Her hips bucked, her moans filling the steamy room.

"Oh, babe, your pink pussy drives me wild!"

Peggy's orgasm erupted in a passionate scream, her body trembling with the shocks of pleasure. Vincente gently pulled her back into the tub, cradling her against his chest. Peggy's breath came in rapid pants as she turned to face him, straddling him with a sense of purpose. She dipped her hand into the soapy water, guiding his erect cock inside of her soaked and greedy opening. Vincente moaned, overcome by the tight wetness that enveloped him. Gripping his shoulders, Peggy began a rhythmic motion, rising and descending upon his cock, each movement a dance of pleasure. Her hips swayed in slow, deliberate rolls, her moans filling the air as she took him deeper.

With Vincente's cock buried deep inside, Peggy's bare breasts bounced against his chest while her sex spasmed and gripped him with her every move. As her orgasm pushed her to ride him faster and moan louder, Vincente came deep inside of her.

"Oh, fuck baby. I tried to hold back but watching you bounce on my cock along with those marvelous tits, I had to flood your pussy with my cum." Vincente remarked as he brushed Peggy's hair out of her damp face. Exhausted and with his cock was still nestled inside of her, she rested her head on his chest enjoying the aftershocks of her orgasm.

"Um, you may want to soak in the tub for a while or douche because you are full of my cum."

"Mmm, I love the feel of your little swimmers inside of me."

Vincente laughed and said, "My little swimmers? Well, my little swimmers love being inside of you!"

Time seemed to stand still as they sat entwined in the warm embrace of the bath. As the water cooled, Vincente lovingly lifted Peggy out of the tub and gently dried her off. He carried her into the bedroom and set her naked body on the bed. After he ran the towel over his body, he joined her in bed and pulled her next to him.

Peggy, with a newfound energy crawled on top of Tony, put her chin on his chest, and gazed into his dark brown eyes.

"Tony, how did you get so good at making love? You must have been with a lot of women!"

"No. Not really. You just inspire me." He confessed as he stroked her long hair.

Peggy laughed and said, "I doubt that. What was your first time like?"

"Oh, no, we aren't going to go there, are we?" Vincente grimaced.

"C'mon, I bet the girl fell madly in love with you!"

"No, it was terrible and embarrassing I was just a kid. Babe, I really don't want to talk about this."

"Tell me, please."

He sighed, surrendering to the inevitable discussion. "I was a junior in high school, and it was Prom. I asked a girl that I was friends with – a senior. One of my friend's parents were going away for the weekend so they let us use their house for a sleepover after Prom. So, of course, we all got drunk and smoked some hash. I was high. My date led me to one of the upstairs bedrooms. I certainly wasn't expecting sex. We laid down on the bed and she started kissing me, then, things got kind of hot and heavy. She got on top of me and took off her dress. She asked me if I had a condom. I mean we all had condoms in our wallets in case of emergency sex; even though we couldn't even talk to girls!" Vincente laughed, "I never expected to use it."

"What happened?"

"So, I retrieved my emergency condom from my wallet while she took off the rest of her clothes. I was, of course, pleasantly surprised – I was a horny teenage boy, and I wasn't going to say no. So, as I unwrapped the condom, she unwrapped me. She even put the condom on me. I was a virgin. She guided my cock inside of her. Then she started moving her hips and I immediately came!"

Peggy laughed.

"I know -- laughable. Of course, I apologized profusely. I offered to fuck her again, but she got dressed and went home. I never saw her again. It wasn't a magical moment, nor did it spark a grand romance. I was young and fumbling, yet it was a steppingstone on the path that led me to this very moment with you."

Peggy's smile lit up the room.

"Dr. Scott, now it's your turn. What was your first time like?"

Her body stiffening, Vincente knew something had happened that Peggy did not want to talk about. As he put his arms around her, Tony assured her, "Hey, I can tell you don't want to talk about it, so now you have to tell me."

"I have never told anybody this. It is humiliating."

"Babe, you know you can tell me anything."

Peggy's voice trembled with vulnerability as she opened up about her past, her words laced embarrassment. Vincente listened attentively, "I was fifteen when I started college. I had only attended all girls' schools - I had never dated or kissed a boy. The professor of my freshman, English Lit class was in his thirties, handsome, charming, long hair, horn-rimmed glasses, wore jeans to class, and recited poetry. All the girls in my class had crushes on him, including me. Girls would hang around his desk or office after class. I could barely sleep because I thought about him so much. Do you know what I mean?"

"Sure." *I know exactly what you mean. I think about you all the time.* Vincente thought.

"One day he returned my homework assignment, with a B-, even though I was a straight A student. He wrote 'see me after class' on top of my paper. So, I made an appointment to meet at his office the following morning. I was thrilled, I wanted him to ask me out. I wore a short, sexy dress, did my hair and makeup - I was so excited. After he closed the door, he told me to sit on the couch. He sat down next to me and told me how beautiful I was. I was overjoyed when he started kissing me. He pushed me on my back and started fondling my breasts." Peggy took a deep breath, "Then he pulled up my dress and pulled down my panties and started to penetrate me. I was a virgin. When he thrusted inside of me, I felt a sharp pain and I cried out, but he didn't stop. I was in pain and trying not to cry. When he was finished, he stood up, ripped off the condom and threw it in the trash. As he left his office he said, 'I have to get to class. Pull the door closed on your way out.'"

Vincente, going into detective mode, exclaimed, "Peggy, he raped you!"

"I didn't say no. I didn't fight him off. It was my fault. I felt so stupid and humiliated. I was sore and bleeding when I left and ran to my dorm room. I tried to drop his class, but it was too late. I never went back to his class. I emailed him my final paper. He gave me an 'A' in the course."

"It wasn't your fault. You were a child. You were too young to give consent. That was statutory rape! He was a sexual predator. He knew you wouldn't report him because you were only 15. I'm so sorry that happened to you."

Vincente's embrace provided a sanctuary for Peggy, a refuge where she could finally release the emotions, she had had inside her for so long. With a steady breath, Peggy continued, "For years, I blamed myself. I questioned if I had done something wrong -- if I had somehow invited his actions. But deep down, I knew the truth. It was never my fault. I was just a young girl, innocent and trusting."

Vincente's grip tightened, in silent affirmation. "You were never to blame, Peggy. You were a victim of someone's abuse of power and trust. It takes incredible strength to confront and share your story."

She nodded, her eyes glistening with unshed tears. "I carried the weight of shame and silence of my rape for far too long, letting it undermine me. But being with you, Tony, has shown me that love can heal even the deepest wounds."

Vincente kissed her forehead, his lips a tender caress against her skin. "You are so incredibly brave, Peggy. Opening up about your past takes courage, and I'm honored that you trust me with your story. You deserve love and happiness, and I promise to cherish and protect you."

Peggy looked up at him, her eyes reflecting a mixture of vulnerability and hope. "I believe you, Tony.

Their connection deepened as they held each other, their bodies intertwined. In that moment, Peggy felt the weight of her past begin to lift, replaced by the warmth and love of Tony Vincente.

"My next sexual partner was Clearmont and that was a disaster. I had sex with him twice and both times were awful. That's why I have never liked sex. Of course, now I love sex with you." Peggy confessed.

"Well, you can have sex with me anytime you want to!" Vincente said and kissed her.

For the remainder of the weekend, their lovemaking was filled with tenderness and passion, their bodies moving in perfect harmony. Vincente worshipped every inch of Peggy's skin, his hands tracing the contours of her body, leaving a trail of desire in their wake. With each caress, he whispered words of adoration, affirming her beauty and worth. Peggy surrendered herself to the depths of pleasure, allowing Vincente's love to wash away the lingering shadows. In his loving arms, Peggy discovered a newfound freedom, a liberation from the chains of her past – her past traumas were replaced with happiness.

Chapter 43

November 28 (Monday Morning)

As the SIU hummed with the daily grind, Detective Samantha Keeley sat at her desk, immersed in a police report. Vincente sat down at the desk next to hers, his gaze fixed on his laptop screen, ignoring her. Lost in heavy thoughts that remained consumed by Peggy, there was an air of intensity about him. Peggy had quickly become a beacon of light in his life, a light that both enthralled and frightened him. Their weekend together had been a turning point, that not only left an indelible mark upon his heart but triggered his fear of commitment.

Curious, Keeley couldn't help but ask about Vincente's weekend. She always asked about his personal life, attempting to bridge the gap between their professional and personal lives. Yet, she received only curt responses, as if the happenings in his personal life were a precious secret.

"Hey, Tony, how was your weekend?"

"Fine."

"What did you do? I tried calling you several times and left several voicemails, but you ignored me."

Not looking up, Vincente replied, "I was busy."

Keeley pressed wanting to know how Vincente spent his time, "Busy doing what?

"I spent the weekend with Peggy at the City Plaza Hotel." Vincente answered, revealing that he had been with Peggy at the City Plaza Hotel—spoke volumes. It was clear that their relationship had evolved into something meaningful, a connection that consumed his thoughts.

"Wow, sounds serious!"

Vincente raised an eyebrow and said, "Yes."

"Wow! You are in a serious relationship now! Congratulations, Tony!"

Tony finally looked up at Keeley and said, "Thanks."

"Hey, what are you going to do with your massive porn collection?"

"Um, what? How do you know I have a porn collection?"

"Easy, single guy, never dates and plays video games – has to have a porn collection."

"I will probably give it to one of my friends."

"Why? Oh wait, you probably don't want her to know you watch, 'Hot Nude Cheerleaders on Ice,' on a regular basis." Keeley laughed.

Vincente raised one eyebrow and said, "I think I will keep a few of the movies."

Chapter 44

Tuesday, December 8

Detective Vincente sat at a corner table in an upscale restaurant in the downtown Chicago, anxiously waiting for his lunch meeting with the man in charge of the FBI's Behavioral Analysis Unit, Director Samuel Anders. Nervously, Vincente straightened his tie and ran his hand through his hair. The atmosphere of the expensive restaurant, with soft jazz playing in the background, did little to relax Vincente.

As Vincente sipped his water, the aroma of gourmet cuisine filling the air, he couldn't help but feel a mix of excitement and trepidation. He had admired the work of the FBI Profiling Unit since he left to become a detective in Chicago detective, and the chance to meet the renowned Director Anders was a dream come true. His recent success in solving the Walters's serial killer case had drawn attention, and he knew this lunch could be a turning point in his career.

Finally, an impeccably dressed Agent Anders entered the restaurant, and Vincente stood to greet him. Tall and composed, wearing a three-piece black suit, Anders exuded an aura of authority and experience that demanded respect. A firm handshake confirmed the importance of the meeting. They settled into their seats, and the conversation began.

"Detective Vincente, it's a pleasure to finally meet you," Anders said warmly.

"The pleasure is mine, Sir. Your work has been an inspiration to me throughout my career."

The waiter arrived to take their orders, and as they scanned the menu, Anders continued, "I've been keeping a close eye on your work on the Walters's case. Your skills in profiling and your ability to decipher the serial killer's patterns were nothing short of remarkable."

Vincente felt a sense of pride swell within him, knowing that his dedication and talent had not gone unnoticed. "Thank you, sir. Solving that case was a team effort, and I had some invaluable help from my colleagues."

Anders nodded thoughtfully. "Your captain speaks highly of you. But, Detective, I believe your talents extend beyond the SIU. Your profile abilities have the potential to be of tremendous value to the entire nation."

Vincente's heart skipped a beat. He had a hunch where this conversation was heading, and the thought both thrilled and terrified him. "Are you suggesting what I think you are, Director?"

A knowing smile tugged at Anders' lips. "Yes, I am. We'd like to offer you a position as supervisory special agent in the FBI's Behavioral Analysis Unit at Quantico, Virginia. A job that involves traveling all over the United States, assisting on murder cases, and applying your skills to help solve the most heinous crimes imaginable."

Vincente's mind raced. This was the opportunity he had always dreamed of, the chance to work on high-profile cases and make a significant impact on catching serial predators. But it also meant leaving behind everything he had built in Chicago - his friends, his job, and, most importantly, Peggy.

"I'm honored by the offer, Director. But I need time to think. This is a life-changing decision, and it affects not just my career but my personal life as well."

Anders nodded understandingly. "Of course, Detective. Take all the time you need. But I must emphasize that we believe you have a rare gift, and your contribution to our team would be immeasurable."

The food arrived, but Vincente's appetite had waned as he wrestled with the magnitude of the decision before him. He and Anders delved into a deeper discussion about the work at the BAU, the cases they had tackled, and the impact they had made.

As the lunch progressed, Vincente's mind became a battleground of conflicting emotions. The allure of being a profiler for the FBI was undeniable, but so was the thought of leaving his home, his loved ones, and Peggy, the woman who had captured his heart. The mere thought of parting with her filled him with a profound sense of loss.

Anders sensed Vincente's inner turmoil and spoke gently, "I understand the weight of this decision, Detective. But sometimes, the path to greatness requires stepping out of our comfort zones and making sacrifices."

Vincente knew Anders was right, and yet, the decision weighed heavily on his heart. He excused himself from the table, claiming a need for fresh air, as he stepped outside the restaurant into the bustling streets of the city.

The noise of the city seemed to echo the chaos in his mind, he felt torn between two worlds, his past, and his future.

As he paced back and forth, the memory of Peggy's smile, her laughter, and the love they shared flooded his mind. His heart ached at the thought of leaving her, but he also couldn't ignore the yearning for a greater purpose, the chance to make a difference beyond the confines of the city he called home.

After what felt like an eternity, Vincente returned to the restaurant, his mind more settled, and his decision clearer. He faced Anders with a newfound resolve. "I've made up my mind, Sir. I accept the offer."

A gleam of satisfaction sparkled in Anders' eyes. "Excellent choice, Detective. I have no doubt you'll be an invaluable asset to our team."

Vincente knew the next few days would be challenging, and sacrifices would be made. But he also knew that sometimes, the pursuit of a dream required moving on -- stepping away from what was comfortable. As he prepared to start this new chapter of his life, he couldn't help but feel a bittersweet mix of excitement and sorrow. Starting a new life would be difficult, especially without the woman he loved, but he was prepared to face whatever lay ahead.

Chapter 45

Wednesday, December 9

V incente found himself consumed by conflicting emotions. The decision to leave the SIU for a position as an FBI profiler had ignited a sense of purpose and anticipation, but it also intensified the ache in his heart for Peggy. He thought about her warm embrace, and the intimate moments they shared, his heart was torn. How would he break the news to her? How would he find the strength to say goodbye?

After his shift ended, Vincente stepped out onto the bustling streets of Chicago, his heart pounded with anticipation and fear. He needed to see Peggy, to tell her that he had accepted a job offer from the FBI, and would be leaving Chicago, indefinitely.

He took a cab to Peggy's penthouse, feeling the weight of his decision like an anchor. As he stood outside her door, his heart pounding in his chest. He took a deep breath, trying to steady his nerves. He knew that what he was about to say would break her heart, but it was a decision he had to make for both of their sakes. When she opened the door, dressed in tight black leggings and sports bra, her eyes lit up with joy upon seeing him. "Tony! What a surprise! Come in."

Peggy sensed a shift in Tony, as he followed her to her spacious living room, and they sat on the couch together. Immediately, Vincente took her hands in his, his voice quivering with emotion. "Peggy, there's something important I need to tell you."

Peggy's frowned, sensing the gravity of his words. "What is it, Tony?"

"I have been offered a position -- supervisory special agent in the FBI's Behavioral Analysis Unit at Quantico, Virginia. A job that involves traveling all over the United States as a criminal profiler to assist on heinous crimes." Vincente confessed, searching for the right words. "It's a once-in-a-lifetime opportunity, but it means I'll have to leave Chicago, my job, my friends, and... you."

Peggy's eyes welled with tears, and she held back a sob. "Tony, that's incredible! I'm so proud of you, but...leaving, I don't understand, did you accept the position?"

Vincente pulled her into a tight embrace, his heart aching at the thought of being apart. "Yes. I don't want to leave you, Peggy. You mean everything to me."

Peggy's face lit up with joy when she suggested, "Tony you don't have to leave me. We can have a long-distance relationship, or I can come with you."

Vincente swallowed hard, feeling the weight of his decision pressing on him. " Peggy... I can't ask you to move with me or carry on a long-distance relationship. This job will require me to travel all over the country, sometimes for weeks at a time. I won't be able to give you the time and attention you deserve."

Peggy's smile faded, her heart was breaking in a million pieces. "I see," she whispered, her voice trembling. "So, you're saying... this is the end for us?"

Vincente nodded, his heart breaking at the pain in her eyes. "I don't want it to be, Peggy, but it's the best decision for both of us. We have our own ambitions, and this job will consume all my time and energy. I can't bear the thought of holding you back from your dreams."

Tears welled in Peggy's eyes as she tried to keep her composure. "But Tony, I love you. We could make it work, couldn't we? I don't mind waiting for you, being there for you when you come back."

Vincente gently cupped her cheek. "You deserve more than waiting for me, Peggy. You deserve to have someone who can be there for you, to build a life together. My career has always been my priority, and I can't ask you to put your dreams on hold for me."

Peggy looked away, "I thought... I thought we had something special, you told me you loved me."She whispered, wiping away tears with the back of her hand.

"I do love you and we did have something special. Peggy, you'll always hold a special place in my heart. But this job... it's a once-in-a-lifetime opportunity, and I can't let it pass by. I'm so sorry."

"I just... I wish things were different."

Vincente pulled her into a tight embrace, holding her close as they both cried. "Me too," he whispered, his voice choked with emotion. "But I want you to know that you are an incredible woman, Peggy. You have a brilliant career ahead of you in Chicago, and I know you'll achieve great things."

"When are you leaving? Will we be able to spend some time together before you go?"

"The Director wants me to immediately, so I am leaving on Friday for Quantico."

Peggy clung to him, her heart breaking with the realization that they were saying goodbye. "No that's too soon...I..."

"Peggy it's better this way. Long drawn-out goodbyes aren't healthy for anyone. I love you but I need to move on with my life."

"Can you spend the night? I want to make love to you one last time." Peggy cried as she clung to Tony's chest.

"No, baby. Being intimate would just make things harder for both of us." His heart breaking knowing this would be the last time they saw each other; he held her against his chest while she sobbed.

I'll miss you, Tony," she said, her voice muffled against his chest.

"I'll miss you too, Peggy," Vincente whispered, his own tears falling. "But I believe that this is the right decision for both of us. We need to focus on our own paths and dreams, even if it means doing it apart."

Peggy looked into his eyes, her own shimmering with tears. "I know I am trying not to be selfish. I don't want to hold you back from your dreams. But this is going to be hard."

Vincente kissed her forehead tenderly. "I know, Peggy. I love you."

With a final, passionate kiss, Vincente disentangled himself from Peggy's arms and quietly left her penthouse for the very last time.

Chapter 46

December 10 through December 30

I n the following two days, Vincente prepared to leave Chicago. He shared the news with Keeley, the Captain, friends, and colleagues, who all offered their congratulations and support.

As the day of departure arrived, Vincente stood at the airport, looking back at the city that had been his home and the people who had shaped him. He knew he was leaving behind a piece of his heart with Peggy, but he also knew that he was embarking on a new chapter in his life that held endless possibilities.

As he boarded the FBI's plane to Quantico, he looked out the window one last time at the city he had called home, the city where he had found love. The ache in his heart was painful, but he knew that sometimes the greatest love stories were the ones that didn't have a happy ending. In the weeks to come, Vincente decided to lose himself in work, using his skills and determination to help solve criminal cases. But deep down, he knew, a part of him would always long for the love he had left behind.

***

Peggy threw herself into her work as well, finding comfort in the pursuit of knowledge and the healing power of science. She focused on her career, determined to become one of the leading pathologists in Chicago. But no matter how successful she became; she knew there would always be a void in her heart that could never be filled.

The loneliness consumed her, and she found herself constantly thinking about him - his warm smile, the way he held her in his arms, the sound of his voice. Tony Vincente had filled her life with joy and happiness, and now that he was gone, she felt like a part of her was missing.

The nights were the hardest for Peggy. The silence in her apartment was deafening, and she found herself reaching for her phone to call him, only to remember that he was no longer just a phone call away. She missed their late-night conversations, the way they would talk for hours about everything and nothing, never running out of things to say.

As she walked through the busy streets of Chicago, she couldn't help but compare every couple she saw to the love she had lost. She saw them holding hands, sharing affectionate glances, and she couldn't help but feel a pang of jealousy. She yearned for the simple comfort of Tony's his touch, the reassurance of his love.

The pain of missing him was like a constant ache in her chest, and she couldn't help but wonder if he felt the same way. Did he think about her too? Did he miss her as much as she missed him? The uncertainty of it all gnawed at her, filling her with doubt that he had ever loved her.

And so, Peggy carried on with her life, she chose to believe their love had been real, and he knew he would always hold a special place in her heart.

Chapter 47

New Year's Eve

Chicago Police Plaza was unusually quiet for a typical New Year's Eve. Not having plans for the holiday, Peggy volunteered to work in the Morgue.

As Peggy was carefully examining a cadaver, she heard the familiar sound of heavy footsteps approaching. When she turned around, her heart skipped a beat, and her eyes widened in disbelief.

"Tony?" she whispered, almost unable to believe her eyes.

Vincente walked into the morgue, looking dashing as ever in his suit, his dark eyes filled with a mix of nervousness and determination.

"What are you doing here?" Peggy asked, trying to keep her voice steady.

Putting his hands in his pants pockets he answered, his voice tinged with emotion. "Peggy, I know I fucked up, but I miss you. I need you."

"Does that mean you're staying?" she asked, trying to keep her voice steady.

"Yes, it means I'm staying. I couldn't stay away any longer," he admitted, "I realized that no job, no opportunity, is worth losing you." Tears of joy welled up in Peggy's eyes as dropped the scalpel she was holding and rushed towards him. In an instant, she was in his arms, hugging him tightly, never wanting to let go. "I can't believe you're here," she said, her voice trembling with happiness.

"I couldn't bear the thought of being away from you, not knowing if I would ever see you again. I want to see where this relationship goes, Peggy. I love you. I want to be with you." He whispered in her ear, his hands caressing her back lovingly.

Peggy's heart soared with happiness. "Oh, Tony, I love you so much," she whispered, leaning up to kiss him gently. He returned her kiss with passion, lifting her off her feet.

"C'mon, Doc let's get out of here." Vincente set her down on her feet and they walked hand in hand out of the morgue.

As they walked into Peggy's penthouse, the atmosphere became charged with anticipation. They stood looking at each other, the love between them almost tangible.

"I've missed you so much," Peggy said, her voice barely above a whisper.

Vincente cupped her face in his hands. "I've missed you too, every single day."

And then, without another word, they kissed, the warmth of her body ignited a fire within Tony that had been building for weeks. He couldn't resist pulling her closer, his hands gripping her waist possessively. Their bodies were pressed together, fitting together like two pieces of a puzzle.

Vincente carried Peggy to the bedroom, laying her gently on the bed. Tony's strong hands traced every curve, while Peggy's soft moans filled the room.

"I can't wait to fuck you." Tony murmured in her hair that smelled like sweet, warm honey.

In moments their naked bodies intertwined with a raw and intense desire. Kissing hungrily, they explored each other's bodies with passionate intensity.

Peggy breathed in Tony's familiar scent of citrus and fresh linen, while Tony buried his face in Peggy's hair that smelled like sweet, warm honey. As he licked and suckled her tart and sharp nipples, he could smell her arousal, its aroma sweet and pungent. He couldn't wait to bury his face between her legs.

"Oh Fuck, I missed this pussy." Tony explored her slit with his tongue while he began thrusting two fingers into her wet opening. After one long lick and suck of her clit, Peggy came on Vincente's face with a scream.

"Mmm. You're soaking wet!" Tony greedily lapped up her juices as her opening swallowed his fingers.

As Tony moved up her body and settled his cock between her legs, Peggy wrapped her legs around his hips as he slowly penetrated her - pushing further and further into her depths. As Peggy pulled him close with her arms anchored to his muscular back, she felt the power of an all-consuming orgasm deep within her.

Thrusting deeply inside her with skin slapping skin, Vincente thought, *I love that squelching sound her pussy makes when I fuck her.*

Tony grunted as he felt Peggy coming – her wet walls clenching his cock with sweet need. The power of her orgasm milked his cock, and he came with a shudder and emptied inside of her depths.

In the quiet moments after, they lay together basking in the afterglow of their desire. Vincente gently stroked her hair, and Peggy nestled closer to him, feeling safe and loved.

"I promise you, Baby," Vincente whispered, "I'll never let anything come between us again. You are the most important thing in my life."

Tears of joy filled Peggy's eyes as she looked up at him. "And you are the most important thing in mine. I love you, Detective Anthony Vincente, with all my heart."

The next few weeks were a whirlwind for Vincente and Peggy. They spent every moment they could together, enjoying each other's company and making up for the time they had spent apart. Vincente became a regular fixture at the morgue, often stopping by to have lunch with Peggy or just to steal a quick kiss before heading off to solve another case. Their love grew deeper with each passing day.

As the months passed, Vincente and Peggy's love only grew stronger. They navigated the challenges of their demanding careers together, supporting each other every step of the way.

Their love story was far from over, but as they faced obstacles ahead, they knew they were much stronger together than apart.

The End

TO BE CONTINUED...

"Forgotten" –- The Second Book in the Series - will be released soon on Amazon.

If this book has stirred your soul, if it has painted vivid colors upon the canvas of your imagination, please consider leaving a review. Your words possess the power to breathe life into this story for countless others, guiding them towards an experience akin to the one we've shared.

Whether a line of praise or constructive critique, your feedback fuels the flames of creativity, and it helps this humble author grow. So, take a moment, just a few lines, and let your thoughts dance upon the keyboard or page.

Know that your review is more than mere words; it is an act of solidarity, a testament to the indomitable connection forged between storyteller and reader. Your support fuels the desire to spin more tales, to dive into unexplored universes, and to create magic that transcends the boundaries of mere ink and paper.

Thank you, dear reader, for the gift of your time and attention. And as you bid farewell to these characters and their world, I ask one last favor – leave a review and join me once more in the realms of imagination and wonder. Until we meet again.

Please leave a review at: http://www.amazon.com/review/create-review?&asin=B0C DQWCQNG

Or scan the following QR code:

Obsessed Review QR Code

Thank you.

Laura Peterson

About the Author

V isit my website at mafiaromancebooks.com

I am working on my next book in the Chicago Mafia Vows series – please join my mailing list at mafiaromancebooks.com

Visit my Amazon Author page https://business.amazon.com/abredir/author/laurap eterson

FREE GIFT for reading this book: Download your FREE copy of:

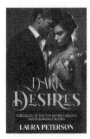

Dark Desires: Checklist of the Top 500 Best-Selling Mafia Romance Books

https://dl.bookfunnel.com/q2bi8vkfvb

Or scan the following QR Code:

Dark
De-
sires

Also By

Laura Peterson

Promised at Birth

Promised at Birth: Chicago Mafia Vows Book One – A Mafia Arranged Marriage

https://www.amazon.com/dp/B0BWVDZV3V

Or scan the following QR code:

A Sizzling Tale of Love of Love, Loyalty, and Deadly Desires

Step into the seductive world of Promised at Birth -- In the heart of Chicago's seedy underworld, a fierce Mafia Boss rules with an iron fist, the ruthless Russian Bratva hungers for power, and a young billionaire's daughter is forced into an arranged marriage.

A Forced Union:

Gwen Fielding, an innocent young woman, finds herself thrust into the dangerous world of mobsters when she forced to marry Chicago Mob Boss Bobby Vincenzio, a man who terrifies her yet ignites a forbidden desire within.

A Seductive Journey:

Discover the intoxicating blend of passion and danger in this tumultuous mafia romance. Promised at Birth will keep you on the edge of your seat, as Bobby and Gwen's arranged marriage ignites an explosive battle between the Chicago Mob and the Russian Bratva for power.

Forbidden Desires:

Discover the depths of forbidden desires that lurk beneath the surface of this intense arranged marriage, captivating the hearts of readers.

A Saga Begins

This is only the beginning of a thrilling series set against the backdrop of Chicago's ruthless underworld, where passion, power, and danger collide, leaving you breathless and yearning for more.

Get Ready to Be Enthralled. Read Now!

If you crave the irresistible allure of mafia romance and the tantalizing dance between darkness and desire, then this is the novel you've been waiting for.

Order your copy of this addictive book now and indulge in the seductive world of the Chicago Mafia.

Available in two formats: Kindle and Paperback

Order Now.

WARNING: This book contains scenes that may be disturbing to some readers.

18+ only.

Author's Note: This book contains subject matter related to abuse and violence that may be triggering to some readers.

Bratva's Captive

Bratva's Captive: A Mafia Romance – Chicago Mafia Vows Book Two

https://www.amazon.com/dp/B0CD7JTL94

Or scan the following QR code:

Step into the dangerous and seductive world of the Russian Mafia, where passion and power collide in an intoxicating tale of love and betrayal.

A forbidden passion that defies the Mafia's rules.

Nikolai, a cold and ruthless Russian Bratva boss, finds himself entangled in a web of forbidden passion when he crosses paths with Adalina, a strong-willed young woman being forced into an arranged marriage with a treacherous Chicago Mafia Boss.

Survival, desire, and the blurred lines between captor and captive.

After Adalina is kidnapped by Nikolai, she must learn to survive her cruel captor while fighting to protect her heart. Nikolai, torn between his duty and his desire, grapples with the consequences of his choices and the deadly price he may pay.

Will love conquer all, or will their world tear them apart?

With each page, Bratva's Captive delves deeper into the depths of their tumultuous relationship, exploring the blurred lines between captor and captive, loyalty, and betrayal. Will they surrender to a passion that defies all rules, or will the dangerous world they live in tear them apart?

Get ready for a dark and addictive Mafia romance.

For fans of dark mafia romance books filled with steamy encounters, suspenseful twists, and unforgettable characters, Bratva's Captive is a must-read. Lose yourself in a world of forbidden desires, twisted loyalties, and high-stakes conflicts, where love is a dangerous game.

Order your copy of "Bratva's Captive: A Mafia Romance" today and immerse yourself in the captivating world of the Russian Mafia.

Available in two formats: Kindle and Paperback

Order Now.

Book Two of Chicago Mafia Vows. Be sure and read the first book in the series: Promised at Birth: Chicago Mafia Vows Book One – A Mafia Arranged Marriage Romance

WARNING: This book contains scenes that may be disturbing to some readers. 18+ only.

Author's Note: This book contains subject matter related to abuse and violence that may be triggering to some readers.

Paul Vincenzio – Alpha Male – An Enemies to Lovers Mafia Romance – Chicago Mafia Vows Book 3

https://www.amazon.com/dp/B0CTJ69V4C

Or scan the following QR code:

Chicago's a powder keg, and I'm sitting right on top, ready to ignite.

But here's the twist—I'm now acting CEO of my brother's company. Me, a CEO?
Please. I'm a mob boss, born and bred.
Then there's this college intern, Aisling Drake, and she's gotten under my skin.
I'm about to show her who the real boss is around here.
I'm going to teach her a lesson about power.
I love being a bully.
This was supposed to be a game, but now...
She's turning into a distraction I can't shake.
I want to dominate her and see just how much she can handle.
Drag her into my world and never let go.

"**Paul Vincenzio: Alpha Male – An Enemies to Lovers Mafia Romance - Chicago Mafia Vows, Book 3**" is an enemies to lovers mafia romance that plunges readers into the heart of Chicago's underworld through the eyes of Paul Vincenzio, the ruthless Boss of the Chicago Outfit.

While Paul's hold on Chicago is jeopardized by a powerful and dangerous secret organization, his life, is further thrown off balance by Aisling, a college intern whose fiery temper matches her striking red hair.

Aisling challenges Paul's authority and convictions. Her sharp wit and undeniable beauty penetrate the armor he's built around his heart. As their worlds collide, the line between duty and desire blurs, making Paul question the very foundations of his life as a mafia boss.

Available in two formats: Kindle and Paperback

Order Now.

Book Three of Chicago Mafia Vows. Be sure and read the first book in the series: Promised at Birth: Chicago Mafia Vows Book One – A Mafia Arranged Marriage Romance. May also be read as a stand-alone book.

Author's Note: This book contains subject matter related to abuse and violence that may be triggering to some readers.

*Obsessed - A Police
Romance*

Obsessed: A Police Romance

Get your FREE copy at: https://www.amazon.com/dp/B0B37JYSWZ

Or scan the following QR code:

A perfect blend of romance, suspense, and police procedural.

A Gripping Tale of Love, Crime, and Unyielding Obsession

Prepare to be captivated by a heart-pounding rollercoaster of emotions in Obsessed, a riveting police romance that will keep you on the edge of your seat till the very end. This book is a perfect fusion of romance, suspense, and police procedural, immersing you in a world where danger and desire entwine.

A Race Against Darkness:

Meet Detectives Anthony Vincente and Samantha Keeley, a dynamic duo determined to stop a sexually sadistic serial killer preying on innocent young women.

The Game-Changing Disappearance:

But when Dr. Peggy Scott, a brilliant and beautiful pathologist, disappears the stakes get even higher. With her life on the line, Vincente and Keeley must race against time to save her.

A Tangled Web of Clues:

As the investigation deepens, a web of secrets and lies unfolds, pushing Vincente and Keeley to their limits. Every passing moment brings them closer to the horrifying truth.

Embrace the Intensity. Feel the Love.

If you crave a pulse-pounding romance with a gripping suspenseful backdrop, then Obsessed is the book for you. Dive into the gripping world of crime, love, and unyielding obsession.

Start Your Thrilling Adventure Today.

Order your copy of this steamy and suspenseful friends-to-lovers police romance. Get your heart racing with the first book in this gripping new series.

Available in two formats: Kindle and Paperback

Order Now.

HEA steamy dark mafia romance for readers who enjoy sensitive content – mature language, violence, and adult situations. No cheating.

Dark Desires

FREE GIFT for reading this book: Download your FREE copy of:

Dark Desires: Checklist of the Top 500 Best-Selling Mafia Romance Books

https://dl.bookfunnel.com/q2bi8vkfvb

Or scan the following QR code:

Feel the Irresistible Heat of Forbidden Love and Powerful Men

Dark Desires is your ultimate checklist to the top 500 best-selling Mafia Romance novels. Step into a world where passion and danger intertwine and where love knows no boundaries.

The Ultimate Resource

This book is a list of the top 500 Mafia Romance Books. Each title is preceded by a box to check books off as you read them – a great way to keep track of the books you've already read.

Perfect for Mafia Romance Fans

Dark Desires is a must-have for fans of mafia romance -- whether you're a seasoned enthusiast or a newcomer to the genre, this checklist includes works from both celebrated New York Times best-sellers and talented new authors.

Your Passport to the World of Mafia Romance

This checklist includes the most compelling dark and dangerous Mafia Romance books that have captivated readers across the globe. Compiled from the most popular titles, this checklist is curated from the top list of mafia romance novels on Goodreads.

A Seductive Genre

Order this checklist now and delve deep into sexy, forbidden love stories about powerful mob bosses, arranged marriages, steamy encounters, and dangerous liaisons that blur the lines between right and wrong.

Available in two formats: Kindle and Paperback

Order Now.

Dark Desires Part Two

Dark Desires: Checklist of the Top 500 Best-Selling Mafia Romance Books Part Two: 501 – 1044

Download your FREE copy now at:

https://dl.bookfunnel.com/ak9dgw7x0k

Or scan the following QR code:

ChatGPT for Romance Writers

ChatGPT for Romance Writers: How to Write Romance Novels with AI Chat-GPT

https://www.amazon.com/dp/B0CH7146FD

Or scan the following QR code:

Change the way you write romance novels forever with "ChatGPT for Romance Writers: How to Write Romance Novels with AI ChatGPT." Enter the new world of romance writing, where the magic of technology meets the art of storytelling.

Whether you're a seasoned author or a new writer, this book will show you how to unleash your creativity with ChatGPT and write love stories that will leave readers spellbound.

In this completely comprehensive guide, you'll learn:

Unlock ChatGPT AI Magic: Learn how to harness its potential to enhance your storytelling.

Master the Romance Beats: Dive into the proven 'Romancing the Beat' story structure.

Conquer Writer's Block: Overcome creative obstacles with the help of ChatGPT plot suggestions.

Craft Sizzling Dialogue: With ChatGPT's help, create sparkling and emotional dialogue that keeps readers hooked.

Write Vivid Settings: Let ChatGPT craft new worlds that will transport readers to other realms.

Create Character Chemistry: Create authentic characters with depth with the help of ChatGPT.

Blending ChatGPT and Your Voice: Learn how to use your story telling voice while using ChatGPT.

And much more...

Includes over 400 Romance Novel Plot Prompts!

If you're ready to start writing your romance novel with limitless story possibilities, "ChatGPT for Romance Writers: How to Write Romance Novels with AI" is your ultimate companion. Get ready to captivate readers, ignite passions, and make your mark in the world of romance.

Available in two formats: Kindle and Paperback

Order Now button and unlock the magic of ChatGPT and your imagination today!

Made in the USA
Las Vegas, NV
13 July 2024

92265300R00118